Morgan Kane.

Bethany had never thought she would hear the man's name on her daughter's lips. The man she'd loved with all her passionate young heart so long ago. The man who'd taken everything she had to give—her heart, her body, her very soul. And then he'd left her, without a backward glance. Left her at the mercy of the plans her mother and his parents made for her life. Left her with no choice but to marry his cousin.

Morgan Kane. The man who had left her pregnant with his child.

Dear Reader,

It's no surprise that Intimate Moments is *the* place to go when you want the best mix of excitement and romance, and it's authors like Sharon Sala who have earned the line that reputation. Now, with *Ryder's Wife,* Sharon begins her first Intimate Moments miniseries, THE JUSTICE WAY. The three Justice brothers are men with a capital M—and they're about to fall in love with a capital L. This month join Ryder as he marries heiress Casey Ruban for reasons of convenience and stays around for love.

Popular Beverly Barton is writing in the miniseries vein, too, with *A Man Like Morgan Kane,* the latest in THE PROTECTORS. Beverly knows how to steam up a romance, that's for sure! In *Wife, Mother...Lover?* Sally Tyler Hayes spins a poignant tale of a father, a family and the woman who gives them all their second chance at happiness—and love. *Reilly's Return* also marks Amelia Autin's return. This is a wonderfully suspenseful tale about a hero who had to fake his own death to protect the woman he loved—and what happens when she suddenly finds out he's really still alive. In *Temporary Marriage,* Leann Harris takes us to the jungles of South America for a tale of a sham marriage that leads to a very real honeymoon. Finally, Dani Criss is back with *For Kaitlyn's Sake,* a reunion story with all the passion you could wish for.

Let all six of these terrific books keep you warm as the winter nights grow colder, and come back next month for even more of the most excitingly romantic reading around, right here in Silhouette Intimate Moments.

Yours,

Leslie J. Wainger
Senior Editor and Editorial Coordinator

BEVERLY BARTON

A MAN LIKE MORGAN KANE

Published by Silhouette Books

America's Publisher of Contemporary Romance

ISBN 0-373-07819-6

A MAN LIKE MORGAN KANE

This edition published by arrangement with Harlequin Books S.A.

Printed in U.S.A.

Books by Beverly Barton

Silhouette Intimate Moments

This Side of Heaven #453
Paladin's Woman #515
Lover and Deceiver #557
The Outcast #614
**Defending His Own* #670
**Guarding Jeannie* #688
**Blackwood's Woman* #707
**Roarke's Wife* #807
**A Man Like Morgan Kane* #819

*The Protectors

Silhouette Desire

Yankee Lover #580
Lucky in Love #628
Out of Danger #662
Sugar Hill #687
Talk of the Town #711
The Wanderer #766
Cameron #796
The Mother of My Child #831
Nothing But Trouble #881
The Tender Trap #1047
A Child of Her Own #1077

BEVERLY BARTON

has been in love with romance since her grandfather gave her an illustrated book of *Beauty and the Beast.* An avid reader since childhood, she began writing at the age of nine and wrote short stories, poetry, plays and novels through high school and college. After marriage to her own "hero" and the births of her daughter and son, she chose to be a full-time homemaker, a.k.a. wife, mother, friend and volunteer.

When she returned to writing, she joined Romance Writers of America and helped found the Heart of Dixie chapter in Alabama. Since the release of her first Silhouette book in 1990, she has won the GRW Maggie Award, the National Readers' Choice Award and has been a RITA Award finalist. Beverly considers writing romance books a real labor of love. Her stories come straight from the heart, and she hopes that all the strong and varied emotions she invests in her books will be felt by everyone who reads them.

To my dear friend, mother-substitute and "big sister," Shirley Sanders, who possesses, in abundance, that rare and precious quality known as human kindness.

A special thank-you for all the Birmingham research work you did for me.

Prologue

"Ask your *friend* to wait outside." Knotting her hands into fists so tight that the oval tips of her nails bit into her palms, Bethany Wyndham glared at her stepfather.

Big, robust, with steel gray hair and sky blue eyes, Jimmy Farraday looked a good ten years younger than his sixty years.

Releasing the curvaceous redhead he held in his arms, Jimmy grinned wickedly at Bethany. He swiped the back of his hand across his mouth, removing the young woman's coral lipstick.

"This isn't what it looks like," he said.

"It never is, is it, Jimmy?"

Gregarious, conservative in his public opinions, and the darling of Birmingham's redneck community, Jimmy could do no wrong in the eyes of his television audience. But privately, the man was a loudmouthed sleaze to whom decency and morality had no meaning.

"I was just...er...interviewing Miss Rone for a job at WHNB." Jimmy patted the girl's behind. "Wasn't I, sugar pie?"

Giggling, the silly girl cuddled closer to Jimmy's side. "I'm going to be singing every Friday on Jimmy's Wake Up Birmingham show."

The girl gazed longingly at him, and for one brief moment, Bethany almost felt sorry for her. Good old boy Jimmy seemed to possess some sort of magnetism for certain women. Unfortunately, Bethany's mother was one of those women. What on earth her wealthy, elegant mother had ever seen in this uncouth womanizer, Bethany would never know. And why she endured the humiliation of staying married to him was just as much of a puzzle.

"There's no need to mention this to your mother." Jimmy glanced at the open door behind Bethany. "You know how upset Eileen gets over the least little thing."

"I'd get upset over *the least little thing,* too, if I was married to a man who couldn't keep his fly zipped."

The redhead gasped.

Jimmy chuckled. Bethany clenched her teeth.

"Go on, Retta." Jimmy beamed his three-hundred-watt smile on Miss Rone. "Enjoy yourself at this little shindig my wife's throwing. Eat, drink and be merry, for tomorrow—"

"Tomorrow I'm going to be on Wake Up Birmingham," Retta Rone said in her chirpy, sing-song voice.

Laughing, Jimmy watched the sway of Retta's slender hips as she slunk out of the study. The moment the young woman disappeared up the hallway, his bright smile softened and dimmed to a smirky grin.

"To what do I owe the honor of this private meeting?" Jimmy glanced around the room. "You usually do your best to avoid being alone with me."

"I'd rather be trapped in a pit of vipers than be alone with you," she told him. "I learned when you first married Mother what a vile, disgusting man you are."

"You're never going to forgive me, are you, Bethy, for that little incident? I've tried to explain that I'd had too much to drink, your mother and I had had our first fight and—"

"Save your explanations for someone who's stupid enough to believe them." Taking a deep, steadying breath, Bethany opened and closed her fists. "I despise you for the ten years of pure hell you've put my mother through, but I'm not here to discuss my mother. She's a grown woman. She can take care of herself. Why she stays with you I'll never know, but that's her decision."

"Then if you don't want to tell me, once again, what a good-for-nothing husband I am, what is so important that you'd corner me in my study during one of your mother's parties?"

Jimmy's grin exposed his big white teeth and deepened the dimples in his cheeks. In three long strides, he closed the distance between them. Immediately wary, Bethany stepped backward. He reached out, grabbed her arm and jerked her up against him.

"You wouldn't be interested in finding out what I've got that keeps your mama married to me, would you?"

"You bastard!"

Using every ounce of her strength, Bethany slapped his face. His head jerked sideways from the force of her blow, and his grasp on her arm loosened. She pulled away from him. Swinging his hand up to his red cheek, he covered the mark of her handprint with his spread fingers.

Jimmy glared at her. "You know what your problem is, Bethy? You ain't getting any. What you need is a real man to put a smile on your face."

If ever Bethany had hated Jimmy Farraday, she hated him at that precise moment. The man had a way of making everything seem sordid and dirty.

"Anne Marie told me what you said to her, how you came on to her," Bethany said.

"Is that what this is all about?" Jimmy shrugged. "Your little girl misunderstood. I was just trying to be grandfatherly. That's all. What's wrong with a man having a little birds and bees talk with his fifteen-year-old granddaughter?"

"I'm giving you a warning that you'd better heed," Bethany said. "If you ever touch my daughter, I'll kill you!"

A loud gasp came from the open doorway. "I'm sorry, Jimmy. I—I—that is we didn't mean to..." the woman stammered.

Recognizing the voice, Bethany turned around slowly. Vivian Crosby, Jimmy's secretary at WHNB, stood just outside the study with Tony Hayes, Jimmy's sidekick on his Wake Up Birmingham show, directly behind her.

"We apologize," Tony said. "We've obviously interrupted a private conversation."

"Just a little family squabble. A minor misunderstanding."

Jimmy laughed, but when he reached out to touch Bethany, she slapped away his hand.

"There is no misunderstanding," Bethany said. "I think I made myself perfectly clear. You can mess around on my mother all you want. I gave up on trying to make her see what kind of man you really are." Baring her teeth in a ferocious growl, Bethany narrowed her eyes. Her gaze skewered Jimmy Farraday to the bone. "But, so help me God, if you ever come near Anne Marie again, I *will* kill you."

Tilting her chin and squaring her shoulders, Bethany walked out of the study, past Tony's and Vivian's shocked glances and down the hallway. Back in the throng of her mother's guests, she sought out a waiter and retrieved a glass of champagne from a silver tray. Her hand trembled.

Glancing across the room, she caught a quick glimpse of her mother, gorgeous in her silver lamé gown. Only in recent years had Bethany appreciated how difficult it must have been for her mother to have been widowed at twenty-three and left with an infant to raise all alone. She understood, now that she was rearing Anne Marie alone, to what lengths a mother would go in order to protect her daughter. And with this new understanding had come forgiveness of her mother's past actions.

Suddenly Jimmy Farraday appeared as if out of nowhere and slipped his arm around his wife's waist. When he leaned down and kissed Eileen on the cheek, Bethany snorted and shook her head sadly. Her poor mother was a fool.

Seth Renfrew placed his hand on Bethany's shoulder. She smiled at her handsome, debonair business partner. They both looked across the room at the host and hostess of the evening's gala affair.

"One of these days someone is going to do the world a favor and slit that sorry son of a bitch's throat," Seth said. "Your mother is far too good for him, you know. She deserves a man who loves her."

Patting Seth's arm, Bethany sighed. "Maybe someday Mother will free herself from Jimmy and discover that the man who truly loves her has been within arm's reach all these years."

"Eileen will never be free as long as Jimmy lives," Seth said, then lifted the champagne flute to his lips and emptied the glass.

Sighing deeply, Bethany leaned her head against Seth's shoulder. "As much as I hate to admit it, I'm afraid you're right, my friend."

Chapter 1

He had been home four days. If you could call this mausoleum home. He felt like a caged animal. But he always had felt confined inside the walls of this Greek Revival mansion in Redmont, trapped by his family's vast wealth and imprisoned by the Kanes' social position in Birmingham.

Even though he'd been away sixteen years, things had changed very little. The house remained spotlessly clean and impeccably decorated, the only alterations superficial ones made by an interior designer. The grounds, now tended by a local lawn service instead of a private gardener, were manicured perfection.

The last time he'd come home, he'd sworn that he would never return. And he hadn't. Not when his cousin Amery had been killed in a car crash, not when his mother had undergone heart surgery and not even when his own father had died five years ago.

So what the hell was he doing here now? It wasn't as if he and his mother had ever been close. As a boy, he'd spent more time with the housekeeper than he had with his parents. But when Ida Mae had called and asked him to come home, to come and see his mama before she died, he had agreed to a brief visit.

Perhaps more for Ida Mae's sake than his mother's. She'd never before asked anything of him.

His father had notified the Navy when Amery had died twelve years ago, and his mother had done the same when Henderson Kane passed away. By the time the messages had reached him, it had been too late to attend the funerals or even send flowers. If he were honest with himself, he'd have to admit that he wouldn't have returned for Amery's funeral—he'd despised his cousin—and he wasn't even sure he'd have come home for his father's.

But he was no longer a SEAL, no longer part of the most physically fit and ferocious warriors in the American military. He'd burned out after one mission too many, and three years ago, at thirty-five, he had hired on with Dundee Private Security in Atlanta. Now, when he was on an assignment, he was easier to reach. And after years of running away from the past, he finally realized that sooner or later every man's life comes full circle. No matter how long and hard you run, eventually every road leads home.

Poor health had aged his mother, leaving the once stern matriarch a faded version of her former regal self. Heart surgery in the past had added years to Claudia Morgan Kane's life, but two recent heart attacks had warned the doctors that, despite their best efforts, the sixty-eight-year-old was dying.

The double French doors leading to the study opened slowly and Ida Mae waddled into the room. Morgan supposed if anyone had ever really loved him just for himself, Ida Mae had. And he loved her, that fat, bossy, caring old woman who'd been more of a mother to him than his own mother had ever been. Ida Mae had been the one who had patched his skinned knees, who'd fed him cookies and milk in the kitchen and helped him with his homework before he'd been shipped off to McCallie Military School in Chattanooga.

Shifting his position on the padded seat in front of the bay windows, Morgan smiled at Ida Mae. But she didn't return his smile. Her round, rosy face was somber. She held out the morning newspaper to him, her age-spotted hand quivering.

"What's wrong?" he asked.

"Take a look for yourself." She spread open the newspaper and lifted it up to him, practically shoving it under his nose.

''When your mama learns about this, she's going to be powerfully upset. She sets great store by that girl. Always has.''

''What are you jabbering about? What girl?'' Morgan grabbed the paper out of Ida Mae's trembling hand.

''That girl is like a daughter to Miss Claudia. And the child...Lord, your mama loves that child better than anybody on earth.''

''Shh...'' Morgan read the front-page headlines of Saturday's the *Birmingham News.* Stepdaughter Arrested for Farraday's Murder. Who the hell was Jimmy Farraday? Morgan wondered. And what was the man's connection to the Kane family?

''You'd better call Dr. Bowers before you tell Miss Claudia about this.'' Ida Mae clutched her ample chest dramatically. ''Lord, this is liable to be the end of your poor mama.''

He couldn't imagine anything being ''the end'' of his mother. Despite her poor health, Claudia remained cool, unemotional and totally in control. She was the same strong, powerful woman he remembered. In spirit, if not in body.

Morgan studied the front page photograph of the attractive woman shown emerging from a police car. For a split second, he stopped breathing, then suddenly his heart pounded fast and loud, drumming in his ears. Was it? Could it be? She was older and more sophisticated than the girl he remembered, but he recognized that fragile, angelic face.

Bethany Dow. No, not Dow. Wyndham. His cousin Amery's widow. The last time he'd seen her had been on her wedding day. He'd returned from basic training in San Diego, with a ring in his pocket and stars in his eyes. But he'd been too late. He'd stood in the shadows outside the church that rainy October evening and watched Amery help his bride into the waiting limousine.

Morgan had carried the image of Bethany wearing her white lace wedding gown in his mind for a long, long time. She had been his for the taking once, and like a fool he'd turned his back on her when he'd turned his back on his life here in Birmingham. And he'd realized too late that even though he wanted no part of the world in which his parents lived, he did want the girl they'd chosen for him.

''I can't believe Bethany killed that man.'' Ida Mae planted her pudgy hands on her broad hips. ''He was no good, that one.

And I suppose he deserved killing. But you remember what a kind, loving little thing Bethany was. She couldn't hurt a fly."

Morgan scanned the article, quickly absorbing the gist of the story. Bethany Wyndham, 36, owner of the Bethany's Boutique chain of ladies' apparel shops, had been arrested late last night on suspicion of murder. The victim, her stepfather, had been shot repeatedly with a .25 caliber pistol at close range. The shots had alerted Farraday's colleagues. The body had been found in his WHNB office. The weapon was registered to Ms. Wyndham, who'd been the last person seen entering Farraday's office before the discovery of his bullet-riddled body.

"There's no way to keep this a secret from your mama," Ida Mae said. "It'll be all over the television and newspapers forever and ever. That Jimmy Farraday was as popular in these parts as any Auburn or Alabama football coach. Everybody I know watches his Wake Up Birmingham show religiously."

Folding the paper, Morgan laid it down on the antique tea table to his right. Grasping Ida Mae by one shoulder, he squeezed gently. "Getting this upset isn't good for your blood pressure." He placed his arm around her shoulders and led her over to the tub-backed beige chair near the fireplace. "Sit right here."

Ida Mae eased her rotund body down into the chair, crossed her arms over her chest and glared up at Morgan. "I'm sitting," she told him. "Now what?"

"Now, answer a few questions for me."

"What do you want to know?"

"I assume by your reaction to this article—" he glanced meaningfully at the newspaper on the table "—that Mother has remained close to Bethany since Amery's death."

"Close? I'd say so." Narrowing her gaze, Ida Mae glared accusingly at Morgan. "Who do you think sat at the hospital day and night when your mama had her surgery? And who do you think stood at her side the day they buried your father? And who do you think comes by once a week and calls nearly every day to check on Miss Claudia?"

"Bethany?"

"She's been like a daughter to your mama," Ida Mae repeated. "Of course, if Miss Claudia had had her way, Bethany would have been your wife and our Anne Marie would have...

Well, it don't matter none, I guess. Not after all these years. Anne Marie is as much a grandchild to your mama as she would have been if...if she'd been yours."

Anne Marie? Bethany and Amery's daughter. Named for his and Amery's grandmother, Anne Marie Morgan. He hadn't known about the child until after Amery's death. Ida Mae had sent him a copy of his cousin's obituary.

Up to that point, Morgan had thought the most difficult thing he'd ever have to face was Bethany's marriage to Amery. He'd been wrong. What had hurt the most—what had haunted him for years—was the knowledge that Bethany had given Amery a child. A child that should have been his.

He'd blamed himself. He had rejected Bethany's love and left her defenseless against the machinations of her mother and his parents, who had desperately wanted a union between the two families. She'd been so young, so sweet and innocent—and so much in love with him. Dammit, how could he have been such a fool? He'd walked away from his one chance at happiness, and when he'd come to his senses, it had been too late. In her vulnerable state, Bethany had turned for comfort to his cold, calculating, status-oriented, money-hungry cousin.

Logically Morgan knew he'd been the one at fault. But in the deepest recesses of his heart—a heart that he'd been told, more than once, was embedded in solid rock—he still questioned how, if Bethany had loved him so completely, she could have married another man so soon?

"What are we going to do about telling Miss Claudia?" Ida Mae asked.

"If you think telling Mother about—" he could barely bring himself to say her name aloud "—Bethany's arrest is going to upset her and endanger her health, perhaps we should keep it from her."

"How are we going to do that? Miss Claudia reads the papers and watches television. And somebody's bound to come by or call to tell her about it."

"Then I'll have to tell her."

"Maybe you ought to call Dr. Bowers and have him here when you tell her." Staring directly at Morgan, Ida Mae widened her eyes in a you-understand-what-I-mean expression. "Just in case."

"Call and find out how soon he can come over," Morgan said. "In the meantime, I'll go upstairs and see if Mother's awake, and if she is, I'll make sure she doesn't watch television."

After walking Ida Mae out into the kitchen, he headed up the back stairs. On his way to his mother's room, he heard the telephone ringing. Damn! He hoped Ida Mae was the one who had answered.

As a child, he'd never been allowed entrance into his parents' bedroom, so even now he hesitated momentarily outside his mother's private domain. Gripping the crystal knob, he opened the door and stepped inside the dimly lit interior. His mother's soft, thick Southern drawl whispered quietly.

With every strand of her chin-length platinum blond hair in place, Claudia sat nestled in the antique canopy bed, her back braced against a mountain of pillows. She clutched a gold and white telephone in her hand.

Dear God, she was on the phone! Why the hell hadn't Ida Mae picked up when she'd heard it ringing? He moved slowly across the Persian rug that covered the hardwood floor and approached the side of the heavily draped bed.

"Don't worry, darling," Claudia said into the telephone. "Maxine Carson is an excellent attorney. She was Papa Henderson's choice to take over his practice. She's as good as they come. Bethany is innocent, and I promise you that she won't be convicted of murdering that horrid man."

Morgan stood by his mother's bed, watching and waiting, amazed not only by Claudia's sweet, almost motherly tone of voice, but by the truly concerned look on her face.

"Now, has Nana ever made any promises to you that she didn't keep?" Claudia paused, smiling weakly. "I love you, too, darling. Please tell Bethany that although I can't come to her, I'm with her in spirit." Another slight pause, then Claudia swallowed hard. "Call me every day...and come to see me soon."

Claudia placed the receiver in the cradle atop the nightstand, then glanced up at Morgan. "Good morning, son."

"Who was on the phone?" he asked.

She patted the wide expanse of unoccupied bed to her right. "Sit down. We need to talk."

Morgan sat; Claudia reached for his hand. Surprised by the

gesture, he almost pulled away, but stilled his involuntary rebuff and allowed her to grasp his hand. "That was Anne Marie, Bethany's daughter."

"She calls you Nana?" How was it that his mother's great-niece called her a diminutive of grandmother? Had Amery taken his place in the family so completely that his own mother had considered her nephew a substitute for the son who had sorely disappointed her?

"Anne Marie *is* my granddaughter." Claudia squeezed Morgan's hand. "In every way that matters to either of us."

"I heard your end of the conversation, so I assume you already know what I came up here to keep you from finding out. I was going to wait for Dr. Bowers to arrive before I told you."

"Ida Mae is no doubt in a tizzy. But there's no need to bother Wes Bowers." Claudia's sharp blue-gray eyes, identical to her son's, glared at him. "I may have a bad heart, but my mind functions quite well, thank you. I'm perfectly capable of dealing with this atrocity. And that's what this is—an atrocity. To think that anyone could believe our Bethany is capable of killing someone, even that vile Jimmy Farraday, is—"

"Stay calm, Mother." Morgan clutched her chin gently. "Don't upset yourself."

Releasing her hold on his hand, she jerked away from him. "You're right. I have to remain calm and in control. I can't help Anne Marie or Bethany if I have another heart attack. And I intend to help them in any way I can. You must help them, too, Morgan."

She looked pleadingly at him. He couldn't remember his mother ever begging, either by word or gesture. She was a proud woman. But for some reason she was willing to put aside her pride for the sake of Amery's widow and child.

"You work for a private security and investigation firm, don't you?" Claudia looked him directly in the eye. "You could investigate Jimmy Farraday's murder and find his real killer."

"No, Mother. I can't." He had no intention of seeing Bethany, for any reason, not even to help prove her innocent of murder. "I won't be in town long enough to be of any help. I'd planned to stay only a few more days. Besides, if you want to hire an investigator, I can call my boss and have him send someone over from Atlanta."

"Why request someone else when you're already here?" Claudia asked.

"I came back home to see you, not to become involved with the family again, not to get embroiled in some mess Amery's wife has gotten herself into. And certainly not to become a part of the life I left behind sixteen years ago."

"You're so bitter, Morgan. Why?" Claudia reached out and touched his cheek. He withdrew instantly. "We didn't leave you. You left us. We didn't stop loving you. You grew to hate us and everything our lives represented."

"And the minute I left town, you threw Bethany into Amery's money-grubbing clutches." Morgan shot up off the bed, rammed his hands into the pockets of his tailored slacks and paced back and forth in front of the floor-to-ceiling windows. "You and Eileen Dow were so damned and determined to see the Dows joined with our family in marriage that you gave Bethany to a man who wanted her only because she'd been mine."

"Morgan, no, we didn't—"

"I came home after basic training," he said, cutting off his mother's explanation mid-sentence. "You didn't know that, did you? When I went to Bethany's house, the maid told me that she was getting married that very day. I stood outside the church, in the rain, and watched Amery and Bethany get into a white limousine."

"Oh, Morgan...son, we never knew. You—you had told us that you never wanted to see us again. You cut off all ties to us. You broke Bethany's heart as well as mine and your father's. When you left Birmingham, we had no idea where you'd gone. Not for several years. Not until you finally called Ida Mae."

"You ask me why I'm bitter, Mother. Well, I'll tell you. I came back to Birmingham after basic training to get the one thing I'd left behind that I found out I truly wanted. And guess what? I was too late. My mother and father had already given her to my cousin."

"I'm sorry," Claudia said in a calm, quiet voice. "I am so very sorry."

"And I'm sorry, too. Sorry that I came back to see you. And sorry I can't be the comfort to you that Ida Mae thinks I should be."

When his mother made no reply, Morgan walked out of her bedroom, down the back stairs and outside to the driveway where he'd parked his car. Ida Mae called after him. He hesitated, his hand clutching the door handle.

"Look after Mother," he said. "I've got to get out of here for a while."

"Are you coming back?" Ida Mae asked.

Was he? He wanted to run now as badly as he had sixteen years ago. Run and never look back. "I don't know."

He slid behind the wheel of his black Ferrari F-40, revved the motor, raced around the circular drive and out onto the road. He had to get out of Redmont, off Red Mountain, away from Birmingham.

He never should have come home. Not even to see his sick, possibly dying mother. It had been a mistake to think he could return home and not run headlong into the past.

The spectators at the graveside crowded around the family like vultures preparing to swoop down and devour. Local and state reporters and photographers were bad enough to deal with at such a time, but national TV networks had sent representatives to Alabama to cover the sensational murder of Jimmy Farraday.

Hordes of Jimmy's Wake Up Birmingham fans called out slurs and threats when they saw Bethany. Prompted by the crowd's actions, the police guard that Chief Baker had arranged circled the tent that provided protection and partial privacy for the family.

Eileen Dow Farraday, tiny, delicate and lovely in her black silk mourning suit sat between her eighteen-year-old stepson, James, and Anne Marie. Tears streamed down Eileen's china-doll perfect face.

How could this nightmare they were embroiled in be real? Bethany wondered. If only she could awaken and discover that the past few days had been nothing more than a bad dream.

Someone had murdered Jimmy. That unknown person had emptied all six rounds of her KBI pistol into him. She hated guns. Everyone knew she despised carrying her small handgun for protection. Seth had bought it for her two years ago, right after she'd been mugged leaving Bethany's Boutique in Huntsville.

If only she hadn't gone to WHNB three days ago. If only she had ignored the message Jimmy had left on her answering machine Friday afternoon. But there was no going back to change the past. She couldn't erase the scratch marks from Jimmy's face—the ones she'd put there. And she couldn't alter the fact that she had returned to his office for her shoulder bag that she'd dropped on the floor during her scuffle with him.

After she'd run out into the parking lot, anyone could have gone into his office, picked up her purse and found her gun. Anyone who hated Jimmy Farraday could have killed him. But the police weren't looking for anyone else. They were certain they had their murderer. She supposed if she saw the facts from their point of view, she would believe what they believed. That Bethany Dow Wyndham had made good on her threats and murdered her stepfather. She was the last person seen entering his office. The murder weapon belonged to her, and only her fingerprints were found on it. And the night before the murder, at a gala party in her mother's home, she had threatened—before two witnesses—to kill Jimmy.

Dear God, Maxine was going to have a difficult time proving her innocence. Considering the evidence, if she didn't know better, *she'd* think she had killed Jimmy.

"Are you all right, Mama?" Anne Marie squeezed Bethany's hand as they rose to their feet after the minister finished his final prayer.

"I'm OK, honey." Bethany slipped her arm around her daughter's shoulder and drew her closer. "I suppose I feel a bit like a hypocrite coming to Jimmy's funeral the very day I was released from jail on a half-million-dollar bond."

"Grandmother wanted you here," Anne Marie whispered. "She knows you didn't kill Jimmy. Besides, Maxine said that it was important for you to be there. To show the world that you don't have a guilty conscience."

Coming up behind her, Seth Renfrew eased his arm around Bethany's waist and hugged her. "I'm going to ride home with Eileen and James. Will you be all right?"

"I'll ride with Mama," Anne Marie told him. "We'll see you at Grandmother's in a little while."

Ignoring the ugly shouts and graphic threats that Jimmy Faraday's loyal fans bellowed at the top of their lungs, Bethany eased inside the second limousine waiting in the line of vehicles. Her daughter slid in beside her.

"You should have ridden in the limo with your grandmother." Bethany glanced out the window as the line of cars began the long, slow drive down the winding roads toward the white iron gates at the entrance of Elmwood Cemetery. Eileen's black limousine led the procession past the old crypts and impressive monuments. "I could have asked Maxine to ride with me."

"Grandmother has all the help she needs. James and Seth have hardly left her side for the past few days." Anne Marie kissed her mother's cheek. "I thought maybe you needed me today. Having to spend the whole weekend in jail must have been just horrible for you."

Tears glazed Bethany's eyes. She gripped her daughter's hand tightly as their limousine circled the small rose garden at the cemetery's entrance and followed Eileen's limo out onto Martin Luther King, Jr. Drive.

Sometimes Anne Marie's maturity amazed Bethany. She had long ago decided that the girl possessed an old soul. From the moment she'd first felt her baby move inside her, the child had become the focus of her life, the center of her world. And after she was born, Anne Marie had become more precious with each passing year.

Bethany had done and would do anything for her daughter. She had married a man she didn't love and endured nearly four years as Amery's wife in order to protect Anne Marie and give her child the heritage she deserved.

She had built a business—a chain of successful boutiques—by combining an investment by her business partner and her mother's friend, Seth Renfrew, with years of hard work. She had wanted not only to give Anne Marie every advantage, but had been determined to make her daughter proud of her and to look to her as a role model. She wanted her daughter to grow up strong and confident and able to meet the world on her own terms. She didn't want Anne Marie to ever be as weak and vulnerable and easily manipulated as she once had been. Bethany intended to make sure nothing and no one ever hurt her child. And that very devotion, that maternal protectiveness was what the prosecuting attorney could and would use against her.

What would happen if the grand jury turned her over for trial and she was found guilty? Who would take care of Anne Marie? Her mother? Eileen was hardly the person Bethany wanted in charge of her daughter's formative teen years. She was far too flighty, too entrenched in her old-fashioned ways to raise a modern-thinking young woman. Besides, her mother already had one teenager to worry about. James adored Eileen. And why not? She had been a loving, doting stepmother for the past ten years, showering him with attention when his own father had had little time for him.

And Claudia, who adored Anne Marie, wasn't physically able to take on the responsibility. Although she knew she could always depend on dear Seth, what did a fifty-year-old bachelor know about raising a teenage girl?

No, what Anne Marie needed was her father.

Even if Amery were alive, Bethany knew they would be divorced now, and she doubted that he would have played a major role in Anne Marie's life. Even before his death, he'd paid little attention to her.

Of course, Bethany didn't think of Amery as Anne Marie's father. She never had.

The ride to her mother's home seemed endless, but Bethany was simply glad to be out of jail and sitting in the back of a limousine, holding her daughter's hand. If the trip had taken hours, she wouldn't have cared.

When they arrived at Eileen's huge, stone Colonial Revival house in Mountain Brook, reporters and spectators alike mobbed the limousines as they pulled into the long, narrow drive leading to the mansion.

"What's wrong with those people?" Anne Marie clutched her mother's hand as they stared outside at the screaming, shouting horde. "Why don't they leave us alone?"

"Jimmy was adored by a lot of people here in Birmingham, and I'm afraid they're determined to see his killer punished."

"But you didn't kill him."

"I know that and you know that, but those people—" Bethany nodded her head backward as the iron gates closed behind them, shutting out the angry crowd and curious reporters "—believe I did."

The moment the limousine came to a stop, Seth opened the door and helped Bethany out, then offered his arms to her and her daughter. Flanking Seth, they allowed him to lead them up the wide rock steps, onto the entrance porch and into the house.

"I'm afraid this whole affair is going to be nothing but a three-ring circus," Seth said. "Everyone from the governor on down will arrive shortly, and I'm afraid Eileen has even agreed to allow WHNB to send a reporter and cameraman."

"My God! How can mother be so stupid!"

"You know Eileen. She hasn't been thinking straight. It never occurred to her that your being here is what they'll focus on instead of all the people who are here to pay homage to Jimmy."

"My car is parked in the garage," Bethany said. "I think I'll slip out the back way and go home. Would you ask Maxine to bring Anne Marie home later?"

Tall, willowy and strikingly attractive for a woman of forty-five, Maxine Carson approached her client. "Did I hear my name mentioned?"

"Yes, would you—" Bethany said.

"I'm going home with you, Mama. I don't want to stay here."

"I've already paid my condolences to Eileen," Maxine said. "Why don't the three of us make a graceful exit together? I'll follow you home. We have a lot to discuss, and I see no reason to delay making some vital decisions."

"All right." Bethany turned to Seth. "Later, when she's had time to miss me, tell Mother why I left."

On the way out the back door, Anne Marie said, "I hope there aren't any reporters or Jimmy Farraday fans waiting at our house."

Two hours later, after the police had dispersed the crowd outside Bethany's home in Forest Park, she and Lisa Songer prepared sandwiches and soup for themselves, Anne Marie and Maxine. Fixing supper was such an insignificant thing, but for Bethany the simple act helped her feel as if she had regained some control over her out-of-control life.

Lisa, the manager of Bethany's Boutique in the Galleria, had stopped by after the funeral to bring Bethany up-to-date on the business. And as a friend, she'd stayed to give comfort.

They ate on trays in the cozy living room. A room, like the others in her house, that Bethany had personally decorated for homey warmth and casual livability. She had wanted Anne Marie to grow up in a home, not a museum, not a look-but-do-not-touch mansion.

When the telephone rang, Anne Marie jumped up off the beige and aqua floral sofa. "I'm taking that darn thing off the hook! If it's an emergency, Grandmother and Nana both know your cellular phone number."

Easing out of her brown suede flats, Bethany slipped one leg under the other and leaned back against the sofa arm. "Just turn the volume down on the ringer and on the answering machine." She looked at Maxine. "Isn't there anything we can do to put an end to the phone calls? I can't believe that ten of Jimmy's devoted fans have called here in the past two hours. And two of them threatened me with bodily harm."

"We'll get you an unlisted number," Maxine said.

"Jimmy Farraday catered to some of the worst elements in our society." Lisa stacked the dinner trays and carried them toward the kitchen. "Let's face it, a lot of Jimmy's fans don't have the brains God gave a billy goat."

Maxine reached across from the chair she'd shoved up against the sofa and put her hand on Bethany's arm. "While you were fixing supper, I called the Dundee Agency in Atlanta and spoke to Dane Carmichael, who's in charge now that Dundee himself has retired. I told him that we wanted him to send someone over here to start a private investigation into Jimmy's death."

"What can a private investigator find out that the police can't?" Bethany asked.

"For one thing, a P.I. is going to look for another suspect, and at this point, the police aren't. Even though Detective Varner has some doubts about your guilt, his hands are tied." Rubbing the back of her neck, Maxine turned her head from side to side. "The D.A. believes he has his murderer, but we know he doesn't."

"Just how expensive is a private investigator?" Bethany was not poor by any means, but she was not a multimillionaire in her own right, as was her mother. She poured a great deal of her boutique profits back into the business, and her largest savings account was earmarked for Anne Marie's future.

"You don't need to concern yourself with the cost." Maxine avoided direct eye contact with her client. "Claudia has given me instructions to do whatever is necessary to get you acquited, and to spare no expense."

"Claudia has offered to finance my defense?" Why should she be surprised that Claudia Kane wanted to pick up the tab? Anne Marie's nana was one of the wealthiest women in the South, having inherited a small fortune when her husband died. And Amery's aunt would do anything for her and Anne Marie. They were all the family Claudia had. Except for—

"Yes, and she's the one who suggested using the Dundee Agency," Maxine said. "Of course, my firm has used their agents before, a few times, when a client needed a bodyguard."

"A bodyguard!"

"If the threats on your life escalate, if they become more than phone calls and letters, then we'll have to do as Claudia suggests and have Dundee's send over a personal bodyguard for you."

"Claudia thinks I need a bodyguard?"

"She phoned me the morning after you were arrested and offered to pay for an investigator and a bodyguard." Maxine looked over her shoulder at Anne Marie and Lisa standing by the round, Regency table in the dining room, an open alcove off the living room. "Claudia is very concerned about you and Anne Marie. You know how she feels about the two of you."

"Yes, I know. And we love her, too."

"Bethany, do you want me to continue taking care of your personal correspondence?" Lisa called from the adjacent room as she lifted the stack of letters off the table. "And what about this package that arrived at the galleria store today? It's addressed to you, in care of the boutique."

"Oh, just leave the personal stuff," Bethany said. "I'll look through it tomorrow. You've done more than enough to help me. But go ahead and open the package. It could be those perfume samples Midge Claybourne was supposed to send me."

"Mama, would you like for me to go ahead and make the cappuccino?" Bethany asked.

"Yes, honey. Thanks. That would be nice." Bethany closed

her eyes momentarily, relaxing, thanking God that she was home. Home with her daughter and two good friends.

"You've done a wonderful job raising that child," Maxine said. "She's pretty and bright and self-confident. A lot like her mother."

"Like her mother is now," Bethany admitted. "I was nothing like Anne Marie when I was her age."

The thunderous boom took Bethany and Maxine by surprise. They gasped, then cried out and nervously looked toward the sound of the explosion. The dining room.

"Anne Marie!" Bethany screamed.

"Oh, my God!" Maxine cupped her hands over her mouth.

Bethany jumped up and ran toward the dining room, Maxine quickly following her.

"Mama," Anne Marie whimpered from where she huddled on the floor just outside the alcove. "Mama, what—what happened?"

A large hole gaped in the side of the dining table. Bits and pieces of wood, fragments from the table and nearest chair lay scattered on the rug. Sprawled in an unconscious heap, Lisa Songer's body rested on the floor. Shards of scrap metal that had pierced her clothing hung in her bleeding flesh along her thigh and shoulder. At the end of her right arm, a bloody, torn hand dangled precariously from her nearly severed wrist.

"What on earth!" Kneeling beside Anne Marie, Bethany wrapped her arms around her child. "Are you all right, honey?"

"I—I think so." Anne Marie glanced down at her arms and legs. "What happened?"

"A bomb." Maxine leaned over Lisa's prone body. "She's still alive. I'll call 911. They'll get an ambulance and the police over here."

"A bomb?" Anne Marie stared at her mother, her eyes wide with shock, tears gathering in the corners.

"In the package that was addressed to me," Bethany said to no one in particular, suddenly realizing that her dear friend had almost been killed by a bomb meant for her. Did Jimmy Faraday have a crazed fan who couldn't wait for a trial? Had this person passed judgment and sentenced her to death?

Bethany helped a shaky Anne Marie to her feet. She cupped

her daughter's pale face in her hands, kissed her forehead and then wiped away her tears. "Go sit down in the living room. You'll be safe there. I have to see to Lisa. Do you understand?"

Anne marie nodded, hugged her mother and then went straight into the living room and sat in a large, overstuffed chair. She stared off into space, her blue-gray eyes dazed.

Maxine gave directions to the 911 operator, hung up the phone and turned to Bethany. "They're on their way."

Bethany took a deep breath. "Toss me a throw pillow off the sofa, then go upstairs and look in the linen closet at the end of the hall. Get a blanket for Lisa."

Maxine nodded agreement. After tossing the pillow to Bethany, she ran out into the foyer and up the stairs. Bethany knelt beside her badly injured friend. Easing the pillow under Lisa's head, Bethany caressed her cheek. She wanted to do something—anything—to help her friend. Checking Lisa's pulse in her left wrist, Bethany found it weak. But Lisa was still breathing. Still alive. She lifted Lisa's dangling right hand and held it firmly in place. She didn't know what else to do.

"Mama?" Anne Marie's voice sounded like a small child's.

"Stay where you are," Bethany said. "Lisa is still alive. The paramedics will be here soon."

"Is she going to die?"

"No. She isn't going to die." She can't die, Bethany prayed. The bomb was meant for me, not sweet, cute, funny little Lisa. Lisa, who had never harmed anyone in her entire life.

"Someone meant to kill you, didn't they, Mama?"

"Don't think about it, Anne Marie. Don't do anything except pray for Lisa." *Please, Dear God, let the paramedics get here soon. Keep Lisa alive.*

"You'll let Maxine hire a bodyguard for you now, won't you, Mama?" Anne Marie pleaded.

"I didn't know you'd overheard our conversation," Maxine said as she hurried through the living room and into the alcove. Unwrapping the soft, cotton blanket, she helped Bethany wrap its warmth around Lisa.

"I didn't hear your conversation," Anne Marie said. "When I called to check on Nana yesterday, she told me that she'd suggested you hire a bodyguard for Mama. Nana knows someone personally who works for the Dundee Agency. Someone she wants to be Mama's bodyguard."

Snapping her head up, Bethany glared across Lisa's deadly still body at Maxine. "Who does Claudia know that works for that agency?"

Maxine's gaze met Bethany's and held. "I told Claudia that it was out of the question," Maxine said. "I told her that you'd never agree—"

"He's Nana's son," Anne Marie said. "Morgan Kane. He came home to visit for the first time in sixteen years, and he's still here in Birmingham."

Morgan Kane. Bethany never thought she'd hear the man's name on her daughter's lips. The man she'd loved with all her passionate, young heart so long ago. The man who'd taken everything she had to give—her heart, her body, her very soul. And then he'd left her, without a backward glance. Left her at the mercy of the plans her mother and his parents made for her life. Left her with no choice but to marry his cousin.

Morgan Kane. The man who had left her pregnant with his child.

Chapter 2

Morgan's cellular phone rang insistently. Hell! Someone had been trying repeatedly to reach him for the past hour. It had to be Dane Carmichael. He'd told his boss to use his cell phone number if he needed to get in touch with him on business. His gut instincts warned him that he already knew what this phone call was about.

Picking up the green garden hose, Morgan sprayed the soap suds off his Ferrari. The telephone stopped ringing. Morgan grunted. He reached down on the paved driveway and grabbed a large, tattered towel, then began slowly, methodically drying off his car. Not once since he bought the sleek, black Ferrari had he allowed anyone else to drive it or wash it. This beauty was his baby, and he treated it with tender, loving care.

The phone rang again. Morgan grinned. Dane wouldn't give up until he reached him. No wonder Sam Dundee had turned the reins of his agency over to the man. Not only was Carmichael intelligent, aggressive and levelheaded, but he possessed a bulldog tenaciousness that didn't allow him to give up—ever.

Opening the car door, Morgan reached down on the seat and picked up the telephone. "Yeah, Kane here."

"What the hell have you been doing? I've been trying for

over an hour to call you.'' Dane's deep voice bellowed, aggravation edging his words.

''I'm washing my car,'' Morgan said, grinning broadly as he pictured Dane's face contorted with anger. Another of his boss's personality traits was impatience.

''I should have known that you were either babying that Ferrari or avoiding my call.''

''Actually, I was doing both.'' Morgan braced the phone between his ear and his shoulder as he continued drying off his car.

''Something tells me that you already know why I'm calling.''

''You're a smart man.''

''So, you're accepting the assignment.''

''What assignment?'' Morgan ran the soft cloth over the shiny hood, taking special care as he moved down and over the headlights.

''Don't be a smart-ass,'' Dane said. ''Maxine Carson, from Kane, Walker and Carson called me at the crack of dawn this morning. She wants to hire you as an investigator and a bodyguard for Bethany Wyndham. You do know Mrs. Wyndham, don't you? According to Ms. Carson, the woman is related to you.''

''Mrs. Wyndham is my cousin Amery's widow.'' *And the only woman who's ever meant a damn thing to me.*

''Well, it sounds as if she's gotten herself into a hell of a mess. And according to Ms. Carson, your mother is quite certain that you will want to handle the case personally.''

''My mother is wrong,'' Morgan said. ''I think it would be better if you send Hawk or Denby. Or do the job yourself.''

''What's the problem?'' Dane asked. ''Do you think you're too close to the situation to be effective?''

''Something like that.''

''All right then. I'll phone Ms. Carson and tell her you've declined and that if she'd like, I can have Hawk on the first plane out of Atlanta tomorrow.''

Hawk was a good man. He'd do a fine job. And that's all the assignment would be to him. A job. Nothing more. Nothing less.

''Fine. Do that,'' Morgan told his boss. ''I'll probably be here another day or so, then I'm heading down to the Gulf for a while. If another assignment comes up, give me a call.''

Morgan punched the End button on his cell phone, then tossed it back onto the car seat. He realized that Dane was probably wondering why he wasn't more concerned about his cousin's widow and the predicament she was in. But Dane wasn't the type to pry into his employees' personal business. Morgan liked that about the man.

What could he have said if Dane had asked him any questions? It wasn't that he didn't care what happened to Bethany; it was that, after all this time, he cared too much. Was he too close to the situation to be effective? No, the problem was that he wasn't close enough. He'd stayed away too long, kept his distance all these years and cut himself off from his family.

He wouldn't be in Birmingham now, if Ida Mae hadn't convinced him that his mother was dying. He'd been a fool to come home and an even bigger fool for staying after he learned about Bethany's arrest for Jimmy Farraday's murder. Four days ago when he'd walked out of his mother's bedroom and driven for hours and hours, trying to get his head on straight, he should have kept going. He should have gotten the hell out of town before this showdown came.

''Morgan,'' Ida Mae called from the screened side porch. ''Your mother's having lunch in the gazebo and she'd like for you to join her.''

He didn't want to have lunch with his mother, but he would. After all, she was the reason he was here, wasn't she? He had come home to spend time with her, hadn't he? Besides, telling her he was leaving tomorrow might be easier over one of Ida Mae's delicious lunches.

''Tell Mother I'll be ready in about half an hour.''

''Lunch will be served in an hour,'' Ida Mae said. ''Take your time. And for goodness sakes, change out of those ragged jeans. You know how Miss Claudia is, about being dressed for meals.''

Smiling warmly, Morgan waved Ida Mae away and returned to the job at hand. The sweltering August sun warmed his naked, tanned back as he leaned over the Ferrari. A hot, moist breeze fluttered through the treetops but did little to alleviate the humid heat of late summer.

An hour later, after a shower, shave and change of clothes, Morgan went downstairs and out into the multilevel garden that covered two sloping acres behind the house. Boxwoods surrounded and centered the circular brick paths. A copper sundial had been placed in the middle of one shrub circle. Steps to the right led to a rose garden and those to the left led to the large white gazebo, from where you could look out over the side of Red Mountain and down on the city below.

As he approached the little summerhouse, which was flanked by two huge, old magnolia trees, he heard a couple of feminine voices. One his mother's. One he didn't recognize, but he thought it sounded familiar. Good God, had his mother invited a guest to join them? Would he be at the mercy of some old biddy for the next hour?

But as he drew nearer, he realized that his mother's guest was not some society matron, but a young woman, perhaps not yet out of her teens. The girl sat perched on the decorative crossbar banisters that surrounded the structure.

Resting in an enormous white wicker chair, Claudia looked like a queen on a throne. Glancing at him, she waved. "Morgan, dear boy, come and join us. We're enjoying some iced tea and chatting while we wait for Ida Mae to serve lunch."

The young girl slid off the railing and turned to face Morgan when he stepped inside the gazebo. She smiled at him, a wide, warm, genuine smile.

"Hello," she said, her voice girlishly soft, but not babyish. "I've been dying to meet you. Ever since Nana told me that her son had come home to visit, I've been so excited. She's told me so much about you that I feel as if I know you."

Nana? The girl had called his mother Nana. So this was Bethany and Amery's daughter. Despite his resolve not to react, not to show any sign of emotion, Morgan found himself inspecting the child from head to toe.

His first thought was that she didn't look the least bit like Amery. But she did look like the Morgans, like his mother and Amery's mother, Aunt Danielle. This girl stood a good five foot nine. And she was how old? Fourteen? Nearly fifteen? She'd certainly inherited her height from the Morgan side of the family.

"You're Amery's daughter." Morgan stared at her, wishing she'd stop smiling at him as if she expected a cousinly hug.

"And Bethany Dow's daughter. You do remember my mother, don't you? Nana says that she was your girlfriend before you went away and joined the Navy."

Snapping his head around, Morgan glared at his mother. What possible reason could she have had to share his past history with this child? And there had to be a reason. Claudia Kane never did anything without an ulterior motive, usually to advance her own causes.

"Telling Anne Marie all about my only child has given me great pleasure," Claudia explained. "When she was a little girl and got in trouble of some sort, I'd tell her about what a naughty little boy you were." With tears glazing her cool, blue-gray eyes, Claudia laughed softly. "I suppose that's how it began, my telling her Morgan stories."

"I've always loved Morgan stories," Anne Marie said, her gaze locked with his. "Nana and Ida Mae spoiled you rotten, didn't they? They spoiled you almost as badly as they have me."

When the girl laughed, every muscle in Morgan's body tensed. The sound brought back memories long forgotten, buried in the past. The laughter belonged to another girl, a shy, quiet girl with huge hazel eyes and a mane of dark, coffee brown hair. Morgan stared into Bethany's daughter's eyes, eyes an identical blue-gray to his own. She'd inherited the Morgan eyes, too.

"You sounded like your mother just then. Your laughter—" The words came out of his mouth before he realized that he'd vocalized his thoughts.

"You think so? I'm told our voices are similar. Most people can't tell us apart on the phone now that I'm older." Anne Marie shrugged. "And I think we look a little alike, except that I'm twice as big. Nana says that I'm built like the Morgans. Tall and rawboned. Good pioneer stock."

"Pioneer stock?" Morgan chuckled. "Is that what you've told her, Mother, that your ancestors were pioneers?"

Claudia frowned at her son, then gazed past him up the brick pathway and sighed. "Ah, here comes Ida Mae with our lunch."

Morgan seated Anne Marie, then sat down directly across

from his mother. Glancing back and forth from one to the other, he wondered if the fact that the child resembled her so much had anything to do with the reason Claudia was so fond of Amery's daughter.

"Have you asked him, Nana?" Anne Marie smiled at Ida Mae when she placed a green salad in front of her.

"Asked me what?" Staring at his mother, Morgan held his fork in midair.

"Not yet. I thought you and I could ask him together," Claudia said. "But let's wait until after we've enjoyed a peaceful lunch."

"What's going on?" Cocking his head backward, he looked up at Ida Mae. "Are you in on this little plot of Mother's?"

"There is no plot," Claudia said indignantly, then lifted her fork and pierced a small tomato slice in her salad. "Anne Marie simply wants to ask a favor of you."

Focusing on his mother, Morgan didn't move his gaze a fraction from her calmly composed face as he laid his fork beside his plate. "What kind of favor?"

Reaching around the edge of the table, Anne Marie grasped Morgan's arm. "Nana and I want you to be Mama's bodyguard."

He glanced down at the hand on his arm, noting the long, slender fingers—elegant Morgan fingers. "I'm sure your Nana knows that I've already turned down the job. Maxine Carson did inform you after Dane called her, didn't she, Mother?"

"Yes, I'm aware that you're reluctant to take the assignment because of the family connection, but I...that is, Anne Marie and I think you're the only man for the job."

The girl squeezed his arm and gazed beseechingly into his eyes. "Please, Morgan. Please. Nana and I know that you're the best, that you'd take care of Mama better than anyone else. And you're so smart and brave and—"

"What the hell have you been telling this child about me?" Morgan glowered at his mother.

Ida Mae cleared her throat. "Your mother's pretty well convinced her that you're some sort of white knight."

Squeezing his arm again, Anne Marie frowned, crinkling her nose in the exact same way Bethany used to do whenever she became upset. "Mama didn't kill Jimmy Farraday, but the police don't believe her. We've got to have some help finding the real killer. And now that one of Jimmy's fans sent that bomb to Mama—''

Morgan grabbed Anne Marie's wrist. ''Someone sent Beth a bomb? What happened? Is she all right?''

''She's fine,'' Anne Marie said. ''Mama didn't open the package. Lisa did, and it blew up. She's in the hospital in critical condition.''

''Who is—'' Morgan asked.

''Lisa Songer is the manager of one of Bethany's boutiques,'' Claudia said. ''The package was delivered to the Galleria boutique, and Lisa took it over to Bethany's house. It was addressed to her, not the shop.''

''Who would want to harm Bethany?'' Morgan's heartbeat roared in his ears. Why should he care? Why did the very thought of someone harming Bethany hit him so hard? She didn't mean anything to him. Not after all this time.

Suddenly realizing that he was still manacling Anne Marie's wrist, Morgan released her.

''I told you, we think it was one of Jimmy's fans,'' Anne Marie said. ''They've been calling the house and sending letters, making threats ever since the police arrested Mama four days ago.''

''It might have been one of Farraday's outraged lunatic fans,'' Morgan said. ''But I think y'all have overlooked another possibility?''

''And what is that?'' Claudia asked.

''Whoever killed Farraday might want Bethany dead and the case closed so that there's no further investigation into the murder.''

''See,'' Anne Marie cried. ''You're already figuring the different angles, considering all the possibilities. You know all kinds of ways to track down a criminal.'' She breathed in deeply, then exhaled. ''I wouldn't trust anyone else to take care of my mother. To make sure no one hurts her. She's the most wonderful mother in the world. You remember what a special person she is, don't you?''

Just the mention of Bethany's name stirred up deep emotions inside him. Feelings he thought long dead. Beth—his Beth—

had been special. He just hadn't had sense enough to realize how special until it was too late. "Yeah, I remember."

"Then you will take the assignment, won't you, Morgan?" Anne Marie smiled weakly, a look of pleading in her eyes.

"You can't go away and let Bethany fight this battle alone," his mother said.

Claudia's words hit a nerve. He'd left Bethany once, left her to fight against the will of his parents and her mother. She'd lost that fight and married Amery. A part of him did and always would feel guilty that his desertion had left her defenseless. Had she turned to Amery not only because his parents and Eileen Dow had encouraged the relationship, but because she'd known how much he hated his cousin? Had marrying Amery been an act of revenge against him?

Did he owe it to Bethany to stay in Birmingham and guard her? Maybe. Was he a fool to even consider taking the assignment? Probably.

Claudia patted Anne Marie's hand. "Would you mind running up to my room and bringing me my address book and the cards beside it? They're on my writing desk. I owe so many thank-you notes for the flowers people keep sending. It's such a lovely day, I think I may stay out here for a while after lunch."

"Of course, Nana." Standing, Anne Marie leaned over and caressed Claudia's shoulder. "I think I'll go through the kitchen and check out what Ida Mae fixed for dessert."

The minute Anne Marie and Ida Mae disappeared inside the house, Claudia turned to her son. "Bethany and Amery did not have a good marriage. She didn't love—"

"I don't want to hear about Bethany and Amery's marriage!" Morgan knocked over his chair in his haste to stand. Tossing down his linen napkin, he glared at his mother.

"No, don't leave. Don't run away. Not now. You left Bethany once when she... Please. Bethany needs you, and I believe you need her."

"I don't need anyone. Get that through your head right now."

"You always were so headstrong and rebellious, but you didn't used to be quite so cold and unfeeling. What sort of life have you led that has turned you into a heartless machine?"

"You don't want to know."

"Perhaps not." Claudia ran her fingertips over the glass top of the wicker table. "We made a mistake, your father, Eileen and I, pushing Bethany into a marriage with Amery. They were both miserable. I've felt guilty for such a long time. And ever since you told me the other day that sixteen years ago you'd actually come home, come back for Bethany... If only we'd known... Things could have been so different."

"All of this is past history." Morgan reached down, grasped the back of his wicker chair and set it upright. "What does any of this have to do with my taking the job as Bethany's bodyguard?"

"Bethany is very dear to me. Over the years she has become a daughter to me," Claudia said. "And Anne Marie... I love that child as much as I ever loved you."

"All right, we've established what Bethany and her daughter mean to you, but that still doesn't—"

"In all the years you've been away, the only thing I ever asked of you was to come home to your father's funeral, but the Navy couldn't reach you in time. You were God knows where, doing God knows what.

"Well, I'm asking something of you again. Just this once. Do this one thing for me and I'll never ask anything of you again. Stay here in Birmingham. Protect Bethany. And find a way to prove her innocence."

"I can't!" Turning his back to Claudia, he gazed out at the vibrant, verdant, manicured garden surrounding the gazebo, then let his vision focus on the wide sweep of the city below them.

"You lost her once, and that was partly my fault and partly your own fault." Claudia eased back her chair, stood and walked around the table. She laid her hand on Morgan's rigid shoulder. "Don't you see? This could be a second chance for you and Bethany. Aren't you the least bit curious to find out if—"

"Don't do this!" Stepping hurriedly away from his mother, Morgan leaned forward, grasped the top of the banister railing and clenched his teeth tightly. Was he curious about Bethany? About what kind of woman she had become? About whether or not that same sizzling chemistry existed between them?

Hell, yes, he was curious. And scared. He hadn't wanted or needed anyone in a long, long time. And he liked it that way. People came and went in his life. But there had been no one and nothing permanent. Not caring about someone made life easier. If you didn't care, then no one could hurt you. If nothing and no one mattered, then no one could disappoint you, no one could let you down.

He did his job at Dundee's with the same controlled, unemotional professionalism that had seen him safely through over a dozen years as a SEAL. Could he become Bethany's personal bodyguard and remain uninvolved? It wasn't that he still loved her. Hell, he wasn't sure he'd ever loved her or anyone else for that matter. He hadn't been taught how to love, only to succeed. And he had succeeded. Not by following family tradition and becoming a lawyer, but by becoming one of America's elite warriors.

But he *had* cared deeply for Bethany. More than he'd ever cared about anyone else. She'd been a sweet innocent, whose passionate nature had surprised and delighted him. He'd never been able to forget her, no matter how hard he'd tried, and God knows he'd tried.

"I'll consider taking the job," Morgan said, damning himself to hell with his own words. "But only if Bethany wants me."

Turning down the volume on the radio, Bethany quieted the soft, soothing sound of Yanni at the piano. She glanced at the digital clock on the control panel in her Mercedes. It was already after noon. Her growling stomach reminded her that she hadn't eaten since dinner last night. But in the hours she'd stayed at the hospital while Lisa hovered between life and death, food had been the last thing on her mind. Her major concern was whether or not Lisa would live, but the nagging thought that wouldn't leave her mind was that she, and not Lisa, had been the intended victim.

Keeping her gaze focused on the road ahead, Bethany scrambled in her purse, grasped her cellular phone and punched her mother's number. When one of the new maids, whose name Bethany couldn't even remember, answered, Bethany identified herself and asked to speak to Eileen.

"Darling, are you still at the hospital?" Eileen asked.

"No, Mother, I'm on my way to your house right now."

"How is poor little Lisa? She didn't die, did she?"

"No, Lisa is still alive. The doctors think she's going to make it. They performed microsurgery on her right hand for vascular reattachment, but there's still a chance she could lose the hand."

"Who would do such a horrible thing? Perhaps the person who killed my Jimmy." Eileen's genteel Southern voice rose slightly in anger, then she immediately lowered it again. "What do you think?"

"I don't know. I'll leave the detective work to the police." Bethany had missed too much sleep, left too many meals uneaten and undergone too many shocks in the past few days to be able to think rationally. She was tired. So very tired. All she wanted was to pick up Anne Marie, go home, take a bath and sleep for at least twelve hours. "Let me speak to Anne Marie for a minute, please."

"I can't let you speak to her."

"Why not? Is something wrong? Is Anne—"

"She's not here, darling," Eileen said. "Claudia called and invited her over for lunch."

"And you let her go?"

"Well, yes, of course. She wanted to go, and I saw no reason not to—

"Dammit, Mother!" Tightening her hold on the phone, Bethany groaned. "How could you have let Anne Marie go over to Claudia's alone when there's some lunatic out there trying to kill me? Did you ever stop to think that she, too, might be in danger?"

"You should know I wouldn't send her over there alone. James drove her over and made sure she got in safe and sound," Eileen said. "My goodness, you act as if whoever sent you that bomb might try to hurt Anne Marie."

"We never know, do we? Jimmy seemed to draw a lot of fans from the fringe element in society."

"I'm sorry, Bethy. Really I am. It's just that Claudia and Anne Marie thought they could persuade Morgan to accept the assignment as your bodyguard. After all, he's highly trained. He was some sort of commando for years before he joined that—"

"My God, Mother, will you stop babbling! Have you and Claudia forgotten just who Morgan Kane is?"

"How dare you speak to me in such a way?" Eileen sighed dramatically. "Everything I did, I did because I thought it was best for you. It wasn't my fault that Morgan deserted you just when you needed him most. Claudia and Henderson and I did our best to take care of the mess that ungrateful boy left behind."

Willing herself not to scream at her mother again, Bethany said calmly, "I'm sorry, Mother. You're right. I'll call later and check on you."

"Are you going over to Claudia's?"

"Yes. I'm going to get my daughter and take her home."

"Perhaps—"

"Goodbye, Mother."

Bethany ended the conversation abruptly, knowing that there was no point in discussing the situation with her airheaded mother. Eileen might be beautiful and rich and charming, but she had little sense of reality. She looked at life through rose-colored glasses. Always had. Probably always would. Even Jimmy's murder hadn't changed that aspect of her mother's personality. Bethany thanked God every day that she had inherited a modicum of common sense from her father.

She had no memory of her father, who had died in a plane crash when she was six months old. Anne Marie had no memory of Amery, who had died in a car crash when she was three. Over the years, when Anne Marie had questioned her about Amery, she had answered her questions as succinctly as possible. She had never referred to him as "your father," only as Amery.

Once Anne Marie had asked, "Did you love my father?"

And she had told her yes, that she had loved her father. And she had. Bethany had loved Morgan Kane with every fiber of her being. He had been as important to her as the air she breathed.

She supposed she should have objected when Claudia began telling Anne Marie her Morgan stories. But somehow it had seemed right, giving Anne Marie a white knight hero to admire when there was no way Bethany could have given her child an idealized account of Amery as a father.

Now only two people on earth, besides her, knew that Amery Wyndham hadn't been Anne Marie's biological father. Eileen and Claudia. Henderson, Morgan's father, had known. And of course, Amery. Her husband, who had promised to cherish her, care for her and protect her. Her husband, who had married her to gain favor with his aunt and uncle. To ensure himself a partnership in his uncle's law firm. And to become the father of Claudia and Henderson's sole heir—their granddaughter Anne Marie.

But in the end, Amery had grown to hate Bethany and resent Morgan's child. The night she'd asked Amery for a divorce, he'd left the house drunk and angry. His car had skidded off a treacherous stretch of highway along Altamont Road and crashed into a tree, killing him instantly. Eaten alive with guilt, she had mourned Amery's death, and sworn that after two ill-fated relationships, she'd never love nor marry again.

She had been both mother and father to Anne Marie for the past twelve years, dedicating herself to the child she loved more than life itself. But what if she was convicted of Jimmy's murder and sent to prison? There would be no one to take care of Anne Marie. No one to stand by her, to love her, to protect her.

She had thought that Anne Marie and Morgan would never meet. But at this very moment they probably were eating lunch together at Claudia's. What did Anne Marie think of him, Nana's son, whom she already considered a white knight? And what did Morgan think of her, the girl he thought was Amery's daughter? Would he notice her striking resemblance to himself? Or would he pass it off as simply an inheritance from the Morgan side of the family? Would he look into their daughter's blue-gray eyes, identical to his own, and know on some instinctive level that Anne Marie was his?

She had never thought the day would come when she would consider the possibility of telling Morgan about the child he had fathered. But if she were convicted of murder and sent away from Anne Marie...

Bethany asked Ida Mae not to announce her, and the Kanes' housekeeper smiled sadly and nodded agreement. Did the old woman know or only suspect the truth?

Following the winding brick pathway, Bethany soon found herself in sight of the gazebo. Slowing her gait as she drew nearer, she stared straight ahead and saw the three people inside the summerhouse. Claudia. Anne Marie. And Morgan. For one brief moment her heart stopped. She'd thought she would never see him again. And she had convinced herself that she didn't care, that she no longer felt anything for him.

She hadn't realized seeing him again would be this hard. Sixteen years. A lifetime ago. She wasn't the same naive, lovesick girl. And he wasn't the same rebellious hell-raiser. They were two different people now. Strangers.

Strangers who just happened to share a child.

She could do this, she told herself. She could. She was a strong woman, wasn't she? She had survived a marriage to a man she didn't love. She had raised Anne Marie without a father. She had built a thriving business. And she had managed to keep her sanity after she'd been arrested for Jimmy Farraday's murder and spent a torturous weekend in the Jefferson County jail.

Meeting Morgan Kane again should be easy, shouldn't it? Squaring her shoulders, tilting her chin and taking a deep breath, Bethany walked toward the gazebo. When she was close enough to hear her daughter's laughter, she halted.

The man who looked at and listened to Anne Marie suddenly turned his head and stared at Bethany. She would have recognized him anywhere, despite the changes in his appearance. The last time she'd seen him, he'd been a twenty-two-year-old boy. Handsome to the point of being beautiful. Tall, lean and muscular. Now he was a thirty-eight-year-old man. Still handsome, but the edge of youthful beauty had been replaced with pure, gloriously rugged masculinity.

He glared at her with cold, intense blue-gray eyes. Eyes that had once, long ago, softened and warmed when he'd made love to her.

When Morgan shoved back his chair and stood, Claudia glanced toward the pathway where Bethany waited.

"Bethany, dear, please come join us," Claudia said. "We're finishing our dessert, but I'll have Ida Mae bring you a plate."

Anne Marie swirled around in her chair. "Mama! Guess what?" She shot up out of the chair, flew out of the gazebo and ran up the walkway. "Morgan has agreed to take the job. He's going to be your bodyguard. And he's going to find out who really murdered Jimmy."

Bethany opened her arms to her daughter, who hugged her

fiercely. Glancing around Anne Marie's shoulder, she stared at Morgan. Their gazes met for an instant, then Bethany inspected him thoroughly. He was bigger, broader than he'd been, his body honed to perfection. His muscular frame appeared confined by the tailored brown slacks and pale yellow cotton pullover he wore.

When he stepped down and out of the summerhouse, his dark blond hair shimmered with natural gold and bronze highlights. He walked toward her, strutting almost, his bearing military trained.

"Hello, Bethany." He held out his hand.

She gazed down at that big hand, then hesitantly accepted it for a brief, cordial shake. Once he touched her, her stomach tightened painfully. He held her hand securely within his. She jerked her hand away and stared up at him. Even with her heels on, she was still a good seven inches shorter than he was at six three.

"Hello, Morgan."

Anne Marie stared adoringly up at Morgan, then slipped her arm around her mother's waist. "Isn't it wonderful? Everything is going to be all right now that Morgan is here. He'll take care of everything. I knew the minute Nana said he'd finally come home, that it was meant to be. He came back just when we needed him." Anne Marie reached out, grabbed Morgan's arm and pulled him toward her. "Well, how does it feel seeing each other again after sixteen years?"

Morgan's jaw tightened. His eyes narrowed as he glanced around Anne Marie and glared at Bethany. She stared back at him, silently screaming for him not to look at her that way. With such cold, unemotional scrutiny.

How did she feel? Numb. That's how she felt. Totally numb.

"I promised your daughter that I would stay in Birmingham, if you wanted me," Morgan said.

"Please, Mama, please tell him that you want him." Anne Marie tugged on her mother's arm.

Hesitantly, her insides quivering uncontrollably, Bethany looked him square in the eye and said, "I want you...to stay in Birmingham."

Chapter 3

"Anne Marie?" Claudia called to her granddaughter. "Come here, dear." Lifting one long, slender arm, she held out her hand. "It's getting a bit too warm out here for me. Help me inside, please."

"I thought you wanted to stay out here and write your thank-you notes," Anne Marie said.

"I'll come back outside later this afternoon, when it's cooler." Claudia's gaze jumped quickly from Bethany to Morgan and then to Anne Marie.

"Oo-oh. Yes, ma'am. Good idea. We'll go inside." Anne Marie glanced from Bethany to Morgan. "You two work out all the details about Morgan taking the job." She gave her mother a hug, then turned to Morgan. "It's going to be so great having you live with us. Just think, you'll actually have to stay in our house. We've never had a man live with us before. Heck, we've never even had a man stay overnight, except for Seth. And he doesn't count."

Morgan's lips twitched, almost forming a smile. "And why doesn't this Seth count?"

"Because he's Mama's business partner, and he's old enough to be my grandfather and—"

"And you've said quite enough young lady," Bethany told her daughter.

"You're right. Sorry, Mama." Anne Marie smiled at Morgan, her strong, square-shaped face softening slightly. "You're the answer to my prayers, you know. Someone who can make everything right again."

Morgan had the strangest urge to put his arms around Anne Marie Wyndham and promise her that he would take care of her and her mother. That he could indeed make everything right again.

A lot of people's lives had depended upon him when he'd been a SEAL, and he'd never let anyone down. He'd been trained to rescue under fire and endure unbearable pain to accomplish a mission. In thirty years the Navy SEALs had never left a fellow SEAL behind in combat.

And after he'd joined Dundee's, he'd put his life on the line more than once in his duty as a bodyguard. But never before had an assignment been personal. And never had anyone believed so much that he could make everything all right.

Bethany's daughter looked at him as if he were a god, capable of righting every wrong in her and her mother's life. Why the hell had Claudia filled the child's head with such nonsense about him, with her stupid Morgan stories?

"Anne Marie, I'm waiting for your assistance." Though Claudia's voice grew louder, her tone remained affectionate.

"I think this is Nana's subtle way of leaving you two alone," Anne Marie whispered. "I'm sure she thinks there are things y'all need to discuss that aren't appropriate for me to hear."

"She's probably right," Bethany said. "Go spend some time with Nana before we leave. Morgan and I won't be long."

"Are you moving in with us today?" Anne Marie asked him.

"Maybe. But I need to talk to your mother before we make any decisions."

Anne Marie nodded agreement, then hurried to her nana's side. Arm in arm, the two walked past Bethany and Morgan on their trek up the pathway to the house.

"Would you like to sit down?" Morgan inclined his head toward the gazebo.

"No, thanks. I sat at the hospital for over twelve hours," she told him. "If you don't mind, let's walk and talk. I always enjoy a stroll around Claudia's garden."

A long-forgotten memory suddenly overwhelmed him. The memory of a warm summer night, a shy young girl and a first kiss. Morgan had known that evening at his mother's party why Eileen Dow and her daughter had been invited. His father had made it perfectly clear that he was supposed to be very nice to Bethany Dow.

He'd taken one look at the slightly plump, little brown wren with wire frame glasses and known it wouldn't take much to frighten her away. Hell, he hadn't been interested in a serious relationship with anyone, least of all some mousy daughter of a friend of his mother's. The women in his life were flashier, sexier and a lot more experienced.

But when he'd taken Bethany into the garden with the intention of scaring her with a hot kiss, he'd gotten the surprise of his life. Sweet, innocent eighteen-year-old Bethany responded passionately.

He'd steered clear of her for months afterward, but finally succumbed to his mother's nagging insistence and invited Bethany to his fraternity's Christmas party. He found he had little in common with the quiet, intellectual girl his parents hoped would be a good influence on him and turn their bad boy into the son they'd always wanted.

Over the next few months, he dated Bethany from time to time, in order to pacify his parents and keep them off his case for a while. But not once did he kiss her again.

Looking back later, he realized that their first kiss in his mother's garden had backfired on him. He'd been the one it had scared, not Bethany.

"Is something wrong?" Bethany asked. "You have an odd look on your face." Was he remembering, she wondered, the evening they'd met, the night he had kissed her the first time, here in this very garden?

"No. Nothing's wrong," he said. "I was trying to figure out why you agreed so readily to my taking the assignment as your bodyguard. I'd have thought I would be the last man on earth you'd put your trust in."

Bethany walked away from him, down the winding brick path. "Are you coming with me?"

Catching up with her in several long strides, Morgan strolled along beside her. She didn't glance his way or make any reply to his comment. Somewhere close by, a variety of birds chirped in a mixed chorus. The warm, humid breeze danced through the rows of iris, peonies and foxgloves that grew along each side of the Victorian wrought-iron gates.

Bethany paused, pivoted slowly and glanced up at Morgan. She had a very good reason for wanting him to stay on in Birmingham, but it wasn't something she could tell him. Not now. Not until she had no other choice. If hiring him to be her bodyguard and to investigate Jimmy's death was the only way she could keep him here, close by, in case Anne Marie needed him, then she would agree to his moving in with them.

Bethany looked at him with her big, gold-flecked, greenish-brown eyes, her full pink mouth parting as she took a deep breath, and sixteen years melted away. Morgan felt as if he'd been punched in the stomach. For a second he couldn't breathe. He closed his eyes momentarily to block out the sight of her, then opened them again just in time to see her glaring at him.

"I think you should know, up front," she said, "that despite our...our past history, I neither want nor expect our association to be personal." Bethany twisted the diamond and emerald ring on her finger back and forth as she held her hands together in front of her. "I trust you to do your job because you come highly recommended by the Dundee Agency. I'm putting my life in your hands, Morgan, not my heart."

The words *not ever again* hung heavily between them, like a thick curtain of regret that would forever keep them apart.

The twenty-year-old girl he'd left behind had been warm and sweet—and madly in love with him. But this woman seemed to be cool, almost aloof, and most certainly not in love with him. The plain, plump little duckling had definitely turned into a beautiful swan, one whose haughty stance reminded him far too much of his socialite mother and her type.

Bethany stepped off the brick walkway, through the open gates and onto the grass pathway designed to invite exploring. Morgan followed, staying at her side.

Bethany was the very epitome of a successful and sophisticated woman in her lavender linen slacks and lavender-and-white-striped silk blouse. A gold watch and diamond tennis bracelet graced one slender wrist, while a heavy gold bangle bracelet draped the other. The plain, plump little debutante who had paled in the glow of her elegant mother's radiant beauty no longer existed. Even with her dark hair falling about her shoulders in loose disarray, her makeup faded and her clothes wrinkled, Bethany was lovely. And every masculine instinct Morgan possessed reacted to her undeniable feminine allure.

"Why did you allow Mother to fill your daughter's head with a bunch of those stupid Morgan stories?" he asked. "Surely you hate the idea that Anne Marie seems to idolize me."

Bethany led him through a wisteria-covered arbor, the cross timbers decorated with classic corbels. "I allowed it for Claudia's sake. She so desperately needed to hold on to you in some way." And she needed to share her love for you with your daughter. "And Anne Marie needed a hero in her life. A male figure she could admire. Amery was killed when she wasn't much more than a baby. She doesn't even remember him. And although your father adored her, she was always aware that she wasn't the grandson he had hoped for."

"My parents didn't have any trouble accepting Amery as a substitute son and accepting his daughter as their grandchild, did they?"

"Amery did everything they wanted him to do, including marrying me," Bethany said. "He went into the firm with your father. We bought a house only a block away. We gave them a grandchild. Yes, Amery was a dutiful son to your parents until the day he died."

She had often wondered if the reason Amery had been so distraught when she'd asked him for a divorce was that he'd been afraid of disappointing Henderson and Claudia. Amery might have wanted her because she had belonged to Morgan, but he had never loved her.

Grasping Bethany's arm, Morgan halted her abruptly. She stared up at him. He wanted to ask her why she had married Amery so quickly after he'd left town? If she'd loved him so damn much, why hadn't she waited? Why had she let his parents force her into marrying his cousin? But instead he said, "My mother loves you and your daughter a great deal. She's shown Anne Marie more maternal affection today than she ever showed me."

"Anne Marie is very easy to love." And you were very easy to love, too, Morgan. I think I loved you from the moment you kissed me the first time.

Morgan released his hold on Bethany's arm. "I can see that she'd be easy to love. She's a charming young girl. Not as quiet and shy as you used to be."

"No, she isn't." Bethany wanted to tell him that their daughter had inherited her charm from him, for she remembered a time when he had been charming. "While you're staying in our home, Anne Marie's adulation might wear a bit thin. If it does, please don't let her know. Don't disappoint her. When this is all over, I want her to still see you as a hero."

"When this is all over," Morgan repeated her words. "How the hell did you get yourself in this situation? You're the last person on earth I'd ever figure to get arrested for murder."

"Even though the police believe otherwise, I didn't kill Jimmy. Yes, he was a total sleaze. A loud-mouthed, uncouth womanizer who made my mother's life a living hell. And I'm not the only person who despised him."

"Then we'll have to find out who despised him enough to kill him," Morgan said. "I'll need to set up a meeting with Maxine Carson, and I'll want to talk to the detective in charge of Farraday's murder investigation. Then maybe I can get some help from the FBI agents who investigated the mail bomb."

"How did you know that the FBI was involved?"

"Mail bombs are a federal crime."

"Oh, yes, of course."

"You and I will need to compile our own list of suspects. Everyone and anyone who had a reason to hate your stepfather and might have had a reason to want him dead." Slipping his hands in his pockets, Morgan relaxed and followed Bethany as she started walking again. "But first, I need to get moved in with you and Anne Marie and set up things there. Can you stick around long enough for me to pack my bag and say goodbye to Mother and Ida Mae?"

Bethany paused beside the pond. Instead of looking at Morgan, she glanced out across the pool's surface at the water lilies. The sunlight reflected off the decorative glass balls floating on the pond. "Are you moving in with us today?"

"The sooner I'm on the job, the quicker we can begin our

investigation. And the safer you'll be. I can't think of any reason to delay, can you?" Morgan gripped her chin, lifting her face. "Unless there's someone who might object to your having one of your old lovers sleeping under your roof."

Bethany's mouth opened on a shocked gasp. "Is that how you see yourself? As *one* of my old lovers?" She snorted, the sound a combination of chuckle and grunt. "Just who do you think might object to my having a bodyguard?"

"Who's this business partner that has spent the night at your house? The one Anne Marie thinks is old enough to be her grandfather?"

"Seth Renfrew. And despite what my daughter thinks, he isn't quite old enough to be her grandfather."

"I see," Morgan said. "Will Seth object to your having a live-in bodyguard?"

She could tell Morgan that Seth was one of her best friends and that the two of them loved each other dearly. She could also tell him that their relationship was strictly platonic. The only woman Seth had ever been in love with was Eileen Dow Farraday.

"Seth loves me and he wants what's best for me." Bethany didn't care how Morgan interpreted her comment. Let him think what he would. She owed him no explanations about her personal life.

"And am I what's best for you?" Morgan lowered his head until his lips almost touched hers.

"Right now, your being in my life is what's best for both me and my daughter."

Before he could kiss her, Bethany pulled away from him and ran up the grass pathway. She could not—would not—allow Morgan Kane to seduce her.

When Morgan departed from his mother's home, he had Anne Marie in tow. She'd pleaded with Bethany to let her ride with him. Following close behind Bethany's white Mercedes, he soon realized that she lived farther than one block away.

"Y'all don't still live in the house your parents bought right after they got married?" he asked.

"Oh, no. After my father died, Mama sold their house in

Redmont and we lived with Nana and Grandfather for a couple of years." Resting her head against the leather seat, Anne Marie looked up at the bright blue summer sky. "Then after Mama made a success of her first boutique, we bought a house of our own in Forest Park."

He hadn't known that Bethany and her child had lived with his parents. But then, he didn't know anything about Bethany's life these past sixteen years. "Who took care of you? Ida Mae?"

"Sometimes, but most of the time I stayed at the boutique with Mama. By the time she opened her second shop, I was already in school."

Morgan stole a glimpse of Bethany's child as she sat beside him, her face turned to worship the sun, her shoulder-length, golden brown hair blowing in the warm wind. She was a pretty girl, with strong, sculptured features and a long, lean, well-proportioned body. Large for her age, but then, that was another Morgan trait. Maturing young. He marveled again at how much Anne Marie resembled his mother. Indeed, she appeared to be a combination of Bethany and Claudia.

"You must miss your father a great deal," Morgan said.

"Not really," Anne Marie admitted. "I was just a little thing when he died. I can't remember Amery at all, and Mama never talks about him. I don't think they were very happy."

"Haven't you ever asked your mother about him?"

"Sure. And she's always answered my questions. I know all the vital stuff. What his name was, what he did for a living, who his family was. Things like that. I just don't know anything about him personally. You know, what kind of man he was. What his favorite color was. Did he like rock music or country." Turning in her seat, Anne Marie leaned toward Morgan as far as the confinement of her seat belt would allow. "You were Amery's cousin. What do you remember about him?"

"Why do you call your father Amery?"

"I don't know. I guess because Mama never referred to him as my daddy, just as Amery. And so did Nana and Grandfather. I don't remember calling him Daddy."

"Well, your father and I were cousins, but we weren't friends." He could hardly tell this wide-eyed innocent that he had despised her father, that Amery Wyndham had been a cold, calculating, highly ambitious man who did anything to succeed.

And that Amery had, from the time they'd been children, envied Morgan, had wanted whatever Morgan had. "Amery was a few years older than I, and where I was a hell-raiser and always in trouble, your father was more serious-minded. He always did what other people expected of him."

"Sounds like he was pretty dull." Anne Marie sighed loudly. "I can't imagine why Mama married him instead of you. If I'd been her, I would have—"

"What do you know about your mother and me?"

"What's there to know?" When Morgan glanced at her, she grinned broadly and winked at him. "Nana told me that you were Mama's boyfriend before Amery."

"Your Nana—"

"Hey, here we are," Anne Marie said. "Turn right. See where Mama's turning in?"

Bethany drove into a circular drive in front of a neat beige Colonial saltbox with a brown roof. A breezeway connected the house to a two-car garage. When the garage doors opened, Bethany drove inside and parked. Morgan eased his Ferrari in beside her Mercedes.

"Let me show Morgan up to his room. Please." Anne Marie grabbed Morgan's arm just as he lifted his suitcase from the car. "You'll like our guest room," she told him. "It's right next to my room and straight across the hall from Mama's. It has two big windows, with plenty of sunshine and it has its own bath and—"

"Anne Marie! Enough. You're talking him to death," Bethany scolded teasingly. "Go ahead and show Morgan to the guest room, then leave him alone for a while so he can get settled in."

"Yeah. Okay. I guess you two have stuff you need to discuss, don't you?" Anne Marie frowned, then suddenly smiled again. "Hey, we could have dinner out by the pool, couldn't we, Mama? You'd like that, wouldn't you? It would make things seem more normal for all of us." She looked to her mother for approval.

"I think that's a marvelous idea," Bethany said. "You're right, I'd like to make things as normal as possible for all of us."

Anne Marie walked beside Morgan. "We could grill steaks.

Do you like grilled steaks? I like mine medium rare. How do you like yours?"

Glancing around her daughter, Bethany caught Morgan's eye. She smiled, then shrugged, as if to say, "What can I do with her? She never shuts up, especially when she's nervous. You understand, don't you?" When Morgan returned her smile, the bottom dropped out of Bethany's stomach. Dear God! How was she going to endure living in the same house with this man if every time he smiled at her, she went weak in the knees?

"We'll have dinner out by the pool," Bethany said. "But first, show Morgan upstairs, while I take a bath and make a few phone calls. Find something to occupy yourself for a while, and then after Morgan and I finish with business, I'll turn him back over to you."

"That's a deal!"

Anne Marie led Morgan up the stairs and straight across the narrow hall. A black-and-white toile paper graced the walls of the guest room, and the design was repeated in the draperies. A dark oak cannonball poster bed, covered with a black-and-white checkered spread, dominated the large room. Morgan dropped his suitcase on the hand-painted sisal rug. Taking in the casually elegant splendor of the area, he realized, once again, how much Bethany and his mother had in common, even their good taste and passion for antiques. But where his mother's house had the feel of a museum, Bethany's had the feel of a home.

"The bath's through there." Anne Marie pointed to the open door through which Morgan could see a black laquered vanity. "Now, I'll leave you alone. But when you and Mama finish talking business, let me know, and we can change into our suits and go for a swim before dinner. Mama loves the pool. Maybe a swim will help her relax."

Before he had a chance to reply, Bethany's whirlwind child flew out of the room and down the stairs. He walked over to the double windows and gazed at the backyard, which was enclosed within the boundaries of a tall, wooden fence. A large deck led to a stone patio, that spread out and circled an olympic-size pool. To the left was a flower garden, a condensed replica of his mother's.

What the hell was he doing here? In Birmingham? In Bethany's home? He had allowed too many old feelings to resurface and affect his decision making. He'd been reared from infancy to be unemotional, and he'd trained himself over the past sixteen years to become unfeeling. So why hadn't he been able to walk away and not look back when his mother had pleaded with him to become Bethany's bodyguard?

Don't you see? This could be a second chance for Bethany and you. His mother's words echoed inside his head. Hell, he didn't want a second chance with Bethany. Or did he? He hadn't exactly been eating his heart out for her all these years. There had been other women. Quite a few other women, though most of them were now nothing more than nameless, faceless blurs.

But even if he wasn't interested in second chances for a happily ever after life with Bethany, he couldn't deny that he wanted her. Even when she'd been a shy, plump little bookworm, he'd wanted her. Wanted her more than he'd ever wanted anyone else. And now that she had matured into a ripe, sensuous woman, he wanted her even more.

But he'd be a fool to mix business with pleasure. To become involved in an affair with Bethany while he was working as her bodyguard. Besides, she hadn't given him any indication that she wanted him. Maybe she was involved with her business partner and neither wanted nor needed another lover.

He had agreed to his mother's pleas because he felt that he owed Bethany something for deserting her sixteen years ago and practically throwing her into Amery's waiting arms.

And then there was the child. Not really a child, but a young woman. Why had he allowed Anne Marie's misplaced adoration to affect his decision to stay and take the job? Was it because he had looked at Amery's daughter and known in his heart that she should have been his?

Morgan and Bethany had little time to discuss the details of Jimmy Farraday's murder case, the mail bomb or instigating a personal investigation. And much to Anne Marie's disappointment, they'd had to cancel their plans to grill steaks by the pool. Lisa Songer's condition worsened and Bethany rushed to the hospital. Anne Marie had insisted on accompanying them, despite Bethany's efforts to persuade her to stay with Claudia.

When Lisa passed the crisis and the doctors assured her family that she would live, Morgan urged a reluctant Bethany to leave the hospital.

"I understand that you feel responsible," he said. "That bomb was meant for you, and if you hadn't asked her to open the package, she wouldn't have been injured."

"Mama, it wasn't your fault," Anne Marie said. "You had no way of knowing that there was a bomb in that package."

"Lisa is only twenty-six. Her whole life is ahead of her." Bethany accepted her daughter's comforting hug. "She came so close to dying. And...she could still lose her hand."

"You can't change what happened," Morgan told her. "All you can do for Lisa is find Jimmy Farraday's murderer."

"How will finding Jimmy's murderer help..." Suddenly Bethany understood what Morgan was implying. "You think whoever killed Jimmy sent me that bomb, don't you?"

"It could have been a crazed fan," he said. "But my money is on the real killer."

"But why would the..." Bethany gasped. "Whoever killed Jimmy knows that I'm innocent, of course. And they probably know that I'm not going to go down without a fight, that I and my family and friends will continue to demand more investigations. And even if I'm convicted, Claudia and Mother and Seth won't give up trying to find proof that I'm innocent."

"With you out of the way, permanently, there's a good chance the case would be closed, and whoever killed Jimmy Farraday would get off scot-free."

After leaving the hospital, they stopped at a fast-food restaurant for hamburgers and fries, then went directly home. The mantel clock in the living room struck eleven times just as Morgan took Bethany's keys and unlocked the front door. As if on cue, Anne Marie yawned.

"You'd better go straight to bed, young lady," Bethany said. "You have school registration tomorrow."

"See y'all in the morning." Anne Marie kissed her mother's cheek, then turned to Morgan and smiled. "I'm so glad you're here to take care of Mama. She takes care of everyone else. Me. Grandmother. Nana. All her employees. Even Seth, when he goes on a bender. But there hasn't been anyone to take care of her. Not until now."

Bethany stood in the foyer, frozen to the spot, not wanting to face Morgan and her own uncertain emotions. She couldn't allow any of those old romantic feelings toward Morgan to get in the way of doing what was best for Anne Marie. If she went to trial and was convicted of murder, she'd tell Morgan that he was Anne Marie's father. But what if she was acquitted? Did she have the right to keep father and daughter apart? Did she dare tell them both the truth and risk losing her daughter's love and respect?

"Hey, Morgan," Anne Marie called to him from the top of the stairs. "Tomorrow evening we'll grill steaks and go for a swim. OK?"

"You have a date," he told her, then when she disappeared around the hallway corner, he turned to Bethany. Putting her hand over her mouth to cover a yawn, she closed her drooping eyelids. "Why don't you go on up, too? You look beat."

"I am beat," she said. "But I thought we needed to talk, to discuss the details of your job and put the wheels of our investigation in motion."

"Everything can wait until tomorrow." He fought the urge to lift her into his arms and carry her upstairs. She looked so fragile standing there in the dim foyer light, her slender shoulders sagging, her eyelids fluttering as she fought her sleepiness. "Go on to bed. I'll check the door and turn your security system back on."

"Aren't you coming up now?"

"Not for a while. I'm a night owl."

"I get up at six every morning, so if you intend to accompany me to work, you might not want to stay up too late."

"I don't need much sleep," he said.

"Oh, I see. Part of your military training, I suppose. Claudia told me that you were a navy SEAL."

"What else did my mother tell you about me?" he asked.

"Not much. But then Claudia didn't know much about your life after you left Birmingham. You never wrote or called your parents." He'd never written or called her, either. He'd left her behind, not caring enough to ever contact her again. She'd been barely twenty, pregnant and not strong enough to stand up against her mother and the Kanes.

"I thought that they were better off without me, and I knew I was a hell of a lot better off without them." But not without you, Beth. I came back for you. But I came back too late. Morgan took a tentative step toward her.

She backed away from him. "They missed you, you know? They would have welcomed you home with open arms if you'd come home." And I would have, too. I would have forgiven you anything, if you'd come back to me.

"They didn't need me. They had Amery. Apparently he became the son they'd always wanted." Morgan came toward her, backing her up against the wall. "It didn't take Amery long, did it, to step in and take over everything that had been mine?" He lowered his head until his lips almost touched hers. "Did you love him, Beth...the way you said you loved me? Did you shatter into a thousand pieces when he gave you pleasure? Did you—"

She shoved against his rock-hard chest, but he didn't budge. "My marriage to Amery is none of your business. And you have no right to question me about it. You left me and never once looked back." And I died a thousand deaths knowing that you didn't love me, that I was carrying your child and another man would be her father.

"And if I had looked back, what would I have seen?" Flanking her shoulders with his outstretched arms, he laid his palms against the wall on either side of her head. "I'd have seen you, the girl who swore she loved me, married to my cousin."

Bethany laughed, the sound edged with mockery. "You say that as if you would have cared. Don't try to play the injured party. You left me, remember? 'I've got to get away and find a life for myself,' you told me. 'If I stay here, they'll smother me. They'll turn me into someone I don't want to be. It's not that I don't care about you, Beth. I do. It's just that you're a part of their world—'"

"You remember word for word what I said to you the night I left." Lifting his hands off the wall, he pulled away from her and stepped back. "You did love me, didn't you, Beth? Then why did you marry Amery?"

She glared at him, her hazel eyes suddenly wide open and glimmering. "Yes, I loved you." She laughed again, then bit down on her bottom lip as she shook her head. "I loved you with all my foolish young heart. But that was sixteen years ago. We're two different people now. We've lived separate lives.

And just because you were my first love and my first lover, doesn't mean you can walk back into my life and think we can pick up where we left off."

"Is that what you think I want to do?" he asked.

"Isn't it?" She moved toward him, bringing her body within inches of his. "Isn't that why you're dredging up the past, why you're pretending that it bothers you that I married Amery? Do you think that if we talk about the good old days when we were young lovers, all that sizzling passion between us will ignite again?"

"I don't know, Beth, what do you think?"

Standing on tiptoe, she draped her arms around his neck and pressed her body intimately against his. Closing her eyes, she clung to him as she covered his lips with hers. His sex hardened instantly. Moaning deep in her throat, Bethany thrust her tongue inside his mouth. She gripped his shoulders when he cupped her buttocks and lifted her up and into his throbbing arousal.

As quickly as she had instigated the kiss, she ended it. Lifting her head, she stared into his smoldering blue-gray eyes. "We both needed to know, didn't we?" she asked breathlessly. "It was best to go ahead and find out, to get it out of the way."

Dammit, he cursed silently. The kiss had been some sort of test, a gauge to check their passion. Well, she'd found out what she wanted to know, hadn't she? He still wanted her as much as he ever had. And she still wanted him.

"So now that we know we still want each other, where do we go from here?" he asked.

"We don't go anywhere," she told him. "When I was a teenager, I confused passion with love. I thought that because you wanted me, because we both exploded like Fourth of July fireworks every time we had sex, it meant that you loved me. I'm not that silly, naive girl. I know that people can desire each other without loving each other.

"I still want you, Morgan." Her chin quivered slightly. The moment her gaze faltered, she forced herself to look up at him again. "But I don't love you. If I feel anything, other than this unwanted desire, it's fear. I'm afraid you'll try to use me again. And I'm afraid in a weak moment, I might let you."

What could he say to her? How could he justify his past treatment of her? He wanted to deny that he had used her, that he'd taken her sweet innocence and then left her as if she'd meant nothing to him. If he told her that he'd come back for her—on her wedding day—would she believe him? And if she did, would it change anything between them?

"The passion we feel now, the passion we've always felt for each other, won't just go away because we want it to," Morgan said.

"No, it won't go away," she admitted. "But I intend to do everything in my power to control it. My life is in a big enough mess as it is. I don't need to complicate it even more. I want you—I need you—in my life right now, but not as my lover."

Before he could reply, she turned and fled up the stairs. "Beth!" he called to her, but she ran into her room and slammed the door.

"Would it matter if I said I'm sorry that I used you, that I hurt you, that I deserted you?" He whispered the question into the quiet stillness as he stood alone in the foyer.

Chapter 4

Kane had slept with his door open to the hallway. The fewer physical barriers between Bethany and him, the better. Although he knew no one could break into the house and get past him to her bedroom, he would have preferred sleeping in her room. He was well aware that she would have strongly objected to the suggestion. She'd made it perfectly clear that although she wanted him, she had no intention of giving in to her desire. He'd treated her badly once, and she'd never forgiven him. In a way, he supposed he'd never really forgiven himself.

But he wasn't that same rebellious, self-centered young man he'd been sixteen years ago. If he had it to do over again, he'd take Beth with him when he left Birmingham. But as the old saying went: Hindsight Is Twenty-Twenty.

And Bethany certainly wasn't the same shy, insecure young woman she'd been when he left her. The girl he'd known back then never would have taken the initiative and led him into a passionate kiss the way she'd done last night. Nor would his sweet, trusting Beth have warned him that she was going to do everything in her power to control the desire she felt for him.

What he couldn't figure out was why, if she feared succumbing to their mutual attraction, she had allowed him to take the job as her bodyguard? If she'd asked for another agent, Dane could have sent Hawk or Denby, who were both between assignments. Seeing what a strong woman Beth had become, he didn't think she had given in to either Claudia's or Anne Marie's pleas to hire him. No, there had to be another reason. But what?

I want you—I need you—in my life right now, but not as my lover.

Why did she want him? Why did she need *him*, and not just any bodyguard? He would ask her, if he thought she'd tell him. But his instincts warned him that she wasn't ready to share any more of herself than she already had. The girl he had once known so well was an enigma to him now—a puzzle with several missing pieces. Sooner or later, though, he'd find those pieces and solve the puzzle. Then he'd have the answer to all his questions.

As long as her stubbornness didn't endanger her life, he'd let Bethany have her way. But the minute circumstances changed—the minute another attempt was made on her life—the rules would change. For the time being, she could run the show; later she'd have to let him be in charge.

He stayed awake long after Beth and Anne Marie had gone to sleep. Once he'd checked the security system, he decided it was adequate enough to hinder any amateurs, but not a professional. Farraday's killer wasn't a professional, nor, he assumed, were any of Farraday's thousands of redneck fans. But Kane didn't intend to rule out anything or anyone in this equation. Beth's life could well depend on his highly trained skills and his almost infallible instincts.

He lay in bed, on top of the spread, and listened to the night sounds. An occasional chirping cricket. The howling of a dog several houses up the street. The slamming of car doors when neighbors returned home late.

And he thought about Bethany. About how close she was. About how easy it would be to cross the hall and go into her room. He ached with the need to possess her, to find again the wild, sweet fulfillment he'd never found with another woman.

He slept off and on after midnight. Over the years, he'd grown accustomed to getting by on a couple hours or less of sleep a night. Then when an assignment ended, he'd crash for days.

He seldom used an alarm. His body possessed an internal clock that woke him early every morning. Part of his training. Part of the man the Navy had made him.

He woke before dawn, showered, shaved and dressed, then using his cellular phone, he made a few calls. When he interrupted Dane Carmichael's breakfast, he apologized.

"So what's so urgent you couldn't wait until I got to the office?" Dane asked.

"Later today, I'm going to fax you some information about the Jimmy Farraday murder case and I want you to look over everything I send you. Look it over with an unbiased, critical eye. I can't be totally objective. I'm personally involved."

"The woman, Bethany Wyndham, was married to a relative of yours," Dane said. "According to Maxine Carson, it was very important to your mother that you take this case. I wondered how you'd handle the situation since Ms. Wyndham is practically family."

"There's more to it than that," Morgan admitted. "Years ago...before I went into the Navy, I was involved with Bethany."

"She was your girlfriend?"

"Yeah. She was mine."

"And there's something still there, between the two of you? If there is, you're a fool to take the assignment. You know the first rule of a good agent is to never become personally involved. When you care too much—hell, when you care at all—you make mistakes."

"I can't walk away and leave her. She needs me." Morgan gripped the phone tightly. "I walked out on her once before. But not this time. I owe her."

"Just be careful that your desire to make amends doesn't wind up getting you in trouble and putting your client's life at risk."

"If things escalate around here, I might need assistance. If I send for another agent, I'd like for you to send Hawk or Denby."

"Denby is going out on a new assignment today, but if Hawk's free when you need someone, I'll send him," Dane said. "But if he's on a job, you'll have to settle for whomever I have available."

The other agents at Dundee's were trained professionals, but Kane had never worked with any of them, didn't know them personally the way he knew Hawk and Denby. He'd trust his life to either of them. They were the best at what they did. He didn't know a damn thing about Denby's past, not her age, her place of birth or the natural color of her hair. But he knew she was a sharpshooter with a black belt in karate. And she could out-think, out-smart and out-drink just about any man.

All he knew about Hawk's past was that the man had been a CIA operative. And something had happened nearly three years ago on his last assignment that ended his career.

Morgan decided to call Hawk and obviously interrupted a romantic moment.

"Damn you, Kane. This had better be important," Hawk said breathlessly.

"If you're busy, I can hold on for a couple of minutes." Morgan chuckled.

"I'll call you back."

Morgan grinned as he turned off his cell phone. Hawk seemed to thrive on a succession of one-night stands. Women were drawn to the big, dark man like flies to manure. Wild women. Wicked women. Married women. Bad girls and ladies alike. Despite or perhaps because of the fact that Hawk projected an image of being bad to the bone, women couldn't resist him.

"Yeah, what's up?" Hawk asked, when he returned Morgan's phone call a few minutes later.

"Obviously not you anymore," Morgan said.

"Cut the cute remarks. Why are you calling?"

"I'm on an assignment that I figure is going to require two agents sooner or later," Morgan told him. "I asked the boss to send you if I need someone."

"Let me guess. He said fine, if I was still available."

"I want you to stay available."

"Level with me," Hawk said.

"The case is personal. I want only the best. And that's you."

"I'll stay available. Might even take a little vacation myself for the next week or so."

"Thanks. I owe you one."

After finishing his conversation with Hawk, he tossed his suitcase on the foot of the bed, unzipped it and removed the remainder of his clothes. He hung his two suits and various slacks and jackets in the closet, then returned to the open suitcase and lifted out his shoulder holster that sheathed his 9mm Sig. The well-made German gun was an expensive piece of equipment, but worth the cost. The Sig Sauer was a very accurate semi-automatic that could pump out fifteen rounds. Accuracy and dependability were important qualities to a man in his line of business.

Morgan strapped on the holster over his blue oxford cloth shirt. Bethany's bedroom door opened. He tensed. Turning his head slowly, he glanced out into the hall. Their gazes met and held for a split second, then she looked down at his shoulder holster, and her mouth parted into a surprised oval.

He quickly lifted his navy blue jacket off the bed and slipped it on, then nodded to Bethany. "Good morning."

"You have to wear it, don't you?" She glared at the slight bulge beneath his jacket. "You know the odd thing about my being accused of Jimmy's murder? I hate guns. The only reason I even own one is because Seth bought it for me after I was mugged several years ago."

"Guns are dangerous weapons," he said. "But a gun is only as good or bad as the person who uses it."

"I know."

Morgan remembered that Bethany had been pretty, but his memories couldn't compare to the beautiful woman she had become. Slender and elegant in her neat mauve suit, she stood just outside his open door and stared at him, not even trying to disguise the hunger in her eyes. Had she spent half the night thinking about him, wanting him the way he wanted her? Had she fought the temptation to cross the hall and seek him out?

The minute he took a few tentative steps in her direction, the look of longing disappeared from her eyes and she glanced away.

"I hope you don't mind toast, cereal and coffee," she said. "Anne Marie and I aren't big breakfast eaters."

"Coffee and toast are fine." Rushing out into the hall, he caught up with her before she reached the stairs. He grabbed her arm. She stopped, but didn't turn to face him. "We need to talk about what happened last night."

"There isn't anything to talk about. Nothing happened last night." She pulled out of his grasp and hurried down the stairs.

Morgan hesitated on the landing, watching while she scurried toward the kitchen. His initial reaction had been to chase after her, confront her and force her to tell him why, if she was so afraid of him, she had hired him as her bodyguard.

"Hey, there." A barefoot Anne Marie, wearing a short, blue denim jumper and red T-shirt, eased open her bedroom door and stuck out her head. Thin strands of her long, golden brown hair spiked out from the large electric rollers covering her head. "What did happen last night?"

"Last night?" Turning around, Morgan shrugged. "What are you talking about?"

"That's what I want to know," she said. "I heard you tell Mama that you needed to talk to her about what happened last night, and she brushed you off. So, what gives? What happened? Did you kiss her?"

Morgan crossed his arms over his chest, cocked his head to one side and gave the girl a speculative stare. "Are you in the habit of putting your cute little nose into your mother's affairs?"

"Mama doesn't have affairs." Anne Marie stepped out into the hall.

"Not even with Seth, who is the only man to ever spend the night here?" Morgan asked.

Anne Marie's smile turned into a giggle, which quickly erupted into laughter. "You're jealous, aren't you? You don't like the idea that Mama might have a boyfriend."

"Young lady, you have an overactive imagination."

"Nana told me that you and Mama were a hot item once. I can't think of anyone I'd rather my mother become involved with than you. After all, you were her first love and—"

"Don't go inventing any fairy tales casting your mother and me as the main characters," Morgan said. "I'm in your mother's life temporarily, to keep her safe. Just until we find Jimmy Farraday's real murderer."

"You don't already have a steady girlfriend, do you? You're not engaged or anything?"

"I'm not the kind of man who becomes involved in long-term relationships. Now, I've said all I'm going to on the subject. You'd better get ready and go downstairs for breakfast." He glanced at his wristwatch. "It's nearly seven o'clock."

Wearing a defeated look, Anne Marie went back into her bedroom and closed the door. Then suddenly she swung the door open and called out to Morgan just as he started down the stairs.

"Morgan?"

"What now?"

"If you promise not to break Mama's heart, I won't mind if you and she have an affair."

Before he could even think of a reply, she slammed shut her bedroom door. Hell! Of all the things for a kid her age to say. Tall and big for her age, she looked seventeen, but he figured she couldn't be more than fourteen, possibly fifteen soon. Kids these days were exposed to too much garbage. They grew up too fast and knew too much too soon.

The smell of fresh-brewed coffee lured him toward the kitchen. He found Bethany sitting at the square pine table in the sunny, yellow breakfast nook, a cup of coffee in one hand and the morning paper in the other.

He spied the coffee machine sitting on the black-and-white-flecked granite countertop beneath the white cabinets.

"Mugs and cups are in the cabinet on the right," Bethany said, without glancing up from the paper.

"Thanks." He retrieved a mug, poured a cup of hot, black coffee, then walked over and pulled out one of the Louis XVI-style chairs covered in red white and black plaid. His mother was the only other woman he knew who would use such fancy chairs in a kitchen. But he had to admit that despite the elegance of the style, the chairs seemed to blend into the casual atmosphere of the room.

Sitting across from Bethany, he put his mug down in front of him. "Your daughter has given me permission to have an affair with you."

Bethany strangled on her coffee. Her face flushed. She crumpled the edge of the newspaper in her hand. Coughing several times, she cleared her throat, then glared at Morgan as she placed her cup in its saucer. "She did what?"

"For some reason, Anne Marie thinks you need a man in

your life. Someone besides Seth. And she's chosen me to be that someone.''

''What did you tell her?'' Bethany threw the paper down on the table and balled her hand into a fist. ''Did you lead her to believe that you and I have any kind of future together? So help me, Morgan, if you've given her any ideas about—''

Lightning quick, he reached across the table and grabbed Bethany's wrist. ''Don't blame me for your daughter's romantic notions. Before I ever met her, she'd formed an opinion of me as some kind of knight in shining armor. Now I think she sees me as her mother's Prince Charming.''

''And we both know that you're certainly no Prince Charming, don't we, Morgan?'' She tried to pull her wrist out of his tenacious grasp, but he held fast. They glared at each other across the table. ''I allowed Claudia to fill Anne Marie's head with nonsense about you because I knew what those idiotic Morgan stories meant to Claudia. Since I assumed that my daughter would never meet you, I didn't think the stories could hurt her. And they won't, if you don't encourage her. If you don't give her any false hopes or make promises you can't keep. If you—''

''Who are we talking about, Beth, you or your daughter?'' Morgan slid his thumb across her wrist, then down inside the palm of her hand.

Bethany shuddered, the very touch of his skin against her skin igniting quivers of arousal in the depths of her femininity. ''Don't try to use Anne Marie to get to me. I won't allow it. Don't encourage her romantic fantasies about the two of us.''

''What about my romantic fantasies?'' He caressed the center of her palm in a slow, circular motion. ''After the way you kissed me last night, I had a difficult time going to sleep. All I could think about was crossing the hall to your bedroom. Tell me, did you lie awake wanting to come to me?''

The kitchen door swung open and Anne Marie flew in, quickly assessing the situation as she glanced from her mother's flushed face to Morgan's somber face and then to Bethany's manacled wrist.

''Good morning.'' Anne Marie smiled at Morgan while she bent over and kissed Bethany's cheek. ''So, what are you two going to be doing today while I'm registering for school?''

Morgan instantly released his hold on Bethany, who drew her hand against her chest and rubbed her wrist.

"I'm going to the Galleria boutique today," Bethany said. "With Lisa in the hospital, I'll have to take over some of her workload temporarily."

"If you're going to be doing more work than ever, how are you and Morgan going to do any investigating?" Anne Marie opened a cabinet and removed a small glass. "I thought the two of you'd be running around all over Birmingham together, gathering information and questioning people and...well, you know, all that private eye stuff."

"I'll be conducting a private investigation," Morgan assured her. "But at the same time, I'll be with your mother twenty-four hours a day to protect her. Dundee's, the agency I work for, can do a lot of the leg work using the computer. Our main objective, after keeping Bethany safe, is to compile a list of other possible suspects and then dig deep enough to discover which one actually murdered Farraday."

"Well, that list of suspects is going to be a mile long." Anne Marie opened the refrigerator door, pulled out a carton of orange juice and poured the juice into her glass. "There had to be dozens of people who hated Jimmy and wished him dead. The only people who liked him were the people who didn't really know him."

Loud, repetitive knocking came from the back door. Anne Marie jumped. Bethany gasped. Morgan tensed. All three heads turned.

"Oh, it's probably just James," Anne Marie said, then downed half her orange juice while she walked over and grasped the doorknob.

"Don't!" Morgan shouted.

Anne Marie's hand froze on the knob. "What's wrong?"

"From now on, don't assume you know who's on the other side of the door," he said. "Ask first. And be sure you know and trust the person. Understand?"

Anne Marie shook her head affirmatively, her nose crinkling as she frowned. The insistent knocking continued.

"Hey, what's going on?" a young male voice demanded. "Open the door, will you?"

"It's James," Anne Marie said. "Is it all right if I let him in now?"

"Who is James?" Morgan asked.

"He's mother's stepson, James Farraday, Jr.," Bethany said. "He and Anne Marie are good friends. He's come by to drive her to school today."

"He's a senior at Mountain Brook High," Anne Marie told Morgan. "Dropping me by Redmont Academy is a bit out of his way, so I don't want to keep him waiting too long."

"Let him in." Morgan watched while Anne Marie opened the door and stepped back to allow Farraday's son to enter the kitchen.

"What took you so long?" James asked. "I could hear y'all talking, so I knew you were in the kitchen."

"Morgan wanted to make sure you were who I thought you were," Anne Marie said. "Come on in. I haven't eaten yet. Do I have time for some toast?"

"Yeah, sure." James glanced past Anne Marie, his piercing blue eyes focusing on Morgan. "Who's this guy?"

"He's Nana's son, Morgan Kane." Anne Marie grabbed a loaf of bread off the counter. "Morgan is mother's bodyguard, and he's also an investigator. He's going to find out who really killed your father."

James pulled out a chair and sat down at the table. "You're really a bodyguard, huh? And an investigator? Do you work for yourself or for some big outfit?"

"I work for Dundee Private Security, out of Atlanta," Morgan said, as he sized up young Farraday. Tall and lean, with sharply chiseled features and short black hair, the boy sat there inspecting Morgan with the same thoroughness. The kid possessed a cocky self-confidence that reminded Morgan of his own youthful recklessness.

Anne Marie dropped two slices of bread into the toaster. "Anyone else want toast? How about you, James?" When she smiled at the boy, her cheeks flushed slightly and her cool gray eyes softened to a deep, warm blue.

Morgan remembered a time when Bethany had looked at him exactly the way Anne Marie was looking at James Farraday, Jr. An irrational urge to grab the boy by the collar of his cotton knit shirt overwhelmed Morgan. He wanted to issue a warning:

no matter how much she adores you, this girl isn't yours for the taking. If you touch her, you'll answer to me.

Where had such paternal thoughts come from? Morgan wondered. From his own guilt? Or from some totally irrational need to protect Bethany's child?

"None for me," James said, his gaze still riveted to Morgan. "Are you living here now?" he asked, then answered his own question. "Yeah, I guess you'd have to if you're Bethany's bodyguard. She needs somebody to protect her from the great Jimmy Farraday's idiot fans. Those crazy people. Calling her. Sending her nutty letters. Then trying to kill her with that bomb."

"Come on, James." Anne Marie laid her toast on a napkin. "I can eat on the way." Holding the napkin-wrapped toast in one hand, she lifted her small bag with the other and draped the straps over her shoulder. "After registration, I'll go to Grandmother's with James and y'all can pick me up this evening."

"Have a good day, sweetheart," Bethany said.

James shot up out of his chair, held out his hand to Morgan and said, "Nice to meet you."

Morgan shook the boy's hand. "Drive carefully."

James laughed. "Yeah, sure thing." He walked over, slipped his arm around Anne Marie's shoulders and opened the back door, then paused and glanced back at Morgan. "Hey, I hope you find the person who killed my father. When you do, let me know before you turn them over to the police. I'd like to give them a medal for taking the old man out."

"James!" Anne Marie nudged him in the ribs. "That was an awful thing to say about your father."

"Yeah, well, I just said what everybody's been thinking." James ushered Anne Marie out the back door.

Morgan turned to Bethany. "Any chance Junior might have been the one to empty your gun into Farraday?"

"You don't honestly think that boy could have killed his own father, do you? James didn't get along with Jimmy, but that was Jimmy's fault. The man was a lousy husband and an even worse father. He ignored James all his life. My mother has given that child the only real parental love and attention he's ever known."

"It's apparent that Junior hated his father. Maybe he hated

him enough to kill him. He sounded like he's glad his old man's dead."

"You hated your father, too. Remember?" Bethany looked directly at Morgan. "But you never would have killed him."

"Yeah, I remember." Morgan shifted uncomfortably in his seat. "Even if Junior didn't kill Farraday, I think he bears watching. Just how much do you trust that boy?"

"What do you mean?"

"I mean your daughter's got a thing for that cocky, young SOB, and if he decides he wants her, then he'll take her and to hell with the consequences. He could wind up hurting Anne Marie, breaking her heart and—"

"Now, who are *you* talking about?" Bethany asked. "James and Anne Marie or you and me?"

Late that afternoon, Bethany left the Galleria boutique in the capable hands of assistant manager, Shelly Harris, and went with Morgan to Maxine's office. Although she'd tried to go about her business as usual all day and forget about her bodyguard's presence, she had been constantly aware that Morgan was never more than a few yards away from her. While she had rearranged schedules and discussed with Shelly applicants for a new part-time sales clerk to fill in for her during Lisa's absence, Morgan made numerous phone calls, sent and received several faxes and "borrowed" her computer. Whenever she left her office, he followed her, but remained at a discreet distance while she dealt with delivery men, salesmen and customers.

Business had been brisk for a mid-week day, the shop often filled to overflowing. Bethany had quickly become aware of the fact that more than one customer had stopped by the boutique to get a good look at the woman accused of Jimmy Farraday's murder. Ignoring the rude stares and unpleasant whispers, she'd concentrated on her loyal, supportive clientele.

When Morgan and she arrived at Kane, Walker and Carson, Attorneys-at-Law, Maxine's secretary showed them into her office immediately.

Maxine shook hands with Bethany, then turned to Morgan. "Good to see you again. How long has it been, fifteen or sixteen years? You've grown into quite a man. Your father would be proud of you.''

Why the hell, after all these years, did his father's opinion matter? He'd quit trying to please the old man when he was about fifteen. He'd realized then that no matter what he accomplished, it would never be enough to suit his father. Henderson Kane had expected nothing less from his only son than perfection and complete acquiescence to his wishes. So instead of striving to gain his father's acceptance and approval, he'd done everything and anything to achieve the exact opposite. Smoking. Drinking. Dating little tramps from the wrong side of town. Getting himself expelled from school. And eventually getting himself arrested for attacking a policeman after he'd been stopped for reckless driving. What Morgan had gained over the years of rebellious behavior had been his father's rage and contempt.

''My father was proud of his nephew, Amery, and his protégée, you.'' Morgan assisted Bethany into a chair in front of the massive mahogany desk that had once belonged to Henderson Kane. ''Let's cut to the chase, Max. We don't need to waste a lot of your time, or mine and Bethany's time, either.''

''Not as charming as you used to be, are you?'' Maxine's lips curved into a mocking smile. She nodded toward the chair beside Bethany's. ''Have a seat and let's get started. What do you need from me?''

''Other than the obvious—for you to give Bethany the best legal representation you can—not a great deal,'' Morgan said. ''Since we spoke earlier today and I got most of the information I needed from you then, what I'd like for us to do now is compile a list of possible suspects. As soon as we have a list, I can get to work on narrowing down the possibilities. I've already talked to Hal Varner, the detective in charge of the Farraday murder case. Are you aware that he has some doubts about Bethany's guilt?''

''Yes, of course,'' Maxine said. ''Hal has done everything he can to keep the investigation going, but the district attorney has blocked him at every turn.''

''I think we may have an ally in Varner.'' Morgan unbuttoned his jacket, sat down and crossed one leg over the other as he relaxed in the leather chair. "We can count on him to work with us. Unofficially, of course.

"And I spoke to Pat Griswold, the FBI agent assigned to investigate the mail bombing. They don't have any leads in the case. They're assuming a crazed Jimmy Farraday fan sent the bomb, since its construction was so simple that a twelve-year-old could have put it together. But after I spoke to Agent Griswold, she agreed to check into the possibility that, if Bethany didn't murder Farraday, the real killer might have sent the bomb."

"My, my, my. You have been a busy boy, haven't you?" Maxine braced her hip on the edge of her desk. "With Dane Carmichael's connections within the bureau, I'm sure you'll get all the cooperation you need from Agent Griswold."

"We're hoping that, since the FBI knows the package was mailed from the downtown post office, one of the employees might remember something suspicious. It's a long shot," Morgan said. "But it's all we've got right now."

"The person who made the bomb might not have been the person who mailed it." Maxine grunted. "Well, what do you need from me, Morgan?"

"What I need, before I proceed any further, are the names of everyone either of you think might have had a reason for wanting Jimmy Farraday dead." Morgan glanced from Maxine to Bethany. "Who's going to start this little accusation game?"

"I believe most people who really knew Jimmy either disliked him intensely or hated him," Maxine said. "I didn't know him well enough to hate him. Personally, I just despised him."

"Who knew him well enough to hate him?" Morgan asked. "His wife, his son, his stepdaughter, his stepgranddaughter and..."

"You're including Anne Marie and James on your suspects list?" Bethany glared at Morgan. "And Mother?"

"I'm not saying that I think one of them killed Farraday, I'm—"

"Anne Marie wasn't even in town," Bethany said. "She'd been away at camp all week. She didn't get back to Birmingham until hours after Jimmy was murdered."

"That still leaves James and Eileen." Morgan could tell that this discussion was bothering Bethany more than it should. Did she know something she wasn't telling him? Something she hadn't even told her lawyer? "Do either Eileen or James have an alibi for the time Farraday was killed?"

"It just so happens," Maxine said, "that both of them were at the television station when Jimmy's body was found. Eileen was meeting him for dinner and James had stopped by to ask his father to pull some strings and get him a couple of Vince Gill concert tickets." Maxine slid off the edge of her desk and stared directly at Bethany. "If he's going to help us, then you're going to have to tell him everything."

Bethany folded her hands together in her lap. Sighing deeply, she closed her eyes. "All right." Opening her eyes, she turned in her chair and faced Morgan. "I had lunch with Mother the day Jimmy was murdered. I'd never seen her so upset. She told me that he had disgraced her for the last time, that some young starlet Jimmy had let sing on his television show a few times came to her and told her that she was pregnant with Jimmy's baby. Mother said...she said she wanted to kill Jimmy. And at that precise moment, I believe she meant it."

"So you think Eileen killed her husband?" Morgan asked.

"I honestly don't know," Bethany admitted. "But I can't believe she would let me take the blame for something she did, unless..."

"Unless what?" Morgan uncrossed his legs and eased to the edge of his seat.

"Unless something snapped inside her and she simply doesn't remember shooting Jimmy," Maxine said. "I've seen that sort of thing happen before."

"What about this girl, the one who's supposedly pregnant with Farraday's baby?" Morgan asked.

"She has an airtight alibi," Maxine told him. "She was at an afternoon baby shower her friends gave her where she worked."

"OK, so we put Eileen at the top of our list. Then James Farraday, Jr. Who else?" Morgan dropped his folded hands between his spread knees. "What about co-workers at the television station?"

"Jimmy was so difficult to work with that there was usually a pretty big turnover on his show every so often," Bethany said. "The only permanent fixtures associated with Jimmy's Wake

Up Birmingham were his secretary, Vivian Crosby, and his announcer and sidekick, Tony Hayes."

"Crosby and Hayes?" Lifting one hand, Morgan rubbed his chin. "Aren't they the eyewitnesses who not only heard you threaten to kill your stepfather the night before he was killed, but also saw you right outside Jimmy's office the afternoon he was murdered?"

"That's right." Bethany nodded her head.

"We'll add them to the list," Morgan said.

"But they adored Jimmy," Bethany said. "Vivian has been with him for over ten years. She worshipped him. And Tony...well, Tony was the heir apparent. Jimmy had made it perfectly clear that when he retired, he would turn over Wake Up Birmingham to Tony."

"We'll add them to the list. If Vivian's been around that long, there's a good chance there was more than friendship between her and Jimmy. And who knows, maybe Tony didn't want to wait for his boss to retire before taking over. That gives me four names to work with," Morgan said. "Four possibilities."

"Five," Maxine said.

Bethany shook her head. "No. Don't."

"Don't what?" Morgan asked. "Who is this fifth person?"

"Seth Renfrew." Maxine glanced apologetically at her client. "Sorry, Bethany, but we did agree to be totally honest with Morgan. It's the only way he can do his job effectively."

"Seth Renfrew? Bethany's business partner. What's the guy's motive?"

"Seth loves...he loves the whole family," Maxine said. "His and Eileen's friendship predates her marriage to Farraday. He would do anything for her. And he adores Bethany and Anne Marie. He was outraged that Jimmy Farraday actually made a pass at Anne Marie."

"Farraday did what?" Morgan sprung out of his chair.

"That's the reason I slapped Jimmy and threatened to kill him," Bethany said. "That night at Mother's party, just as Tony and Vivian walked into the study. You see I knew exactly what Jimmy was capable of. He—he tried to rape me not long after he and mother married. I warned him that if he ever touched Anne Marie, I'd kill him."

Morgan closed his eyes as pure rage coursed through his

body. He slammed his fists into the back of the chair in which he'd been sitting, knocking it over.

"Hell, it's a good thing someone's already killed that sorry bastard or I'd kill him myself!" Morgan paced the floor, his big feet thundering against the wooden surface. "Now, I understand why his own son said that whoever killed Farraday deserved a medal." And he would understand if Bethany had killed the SOB. A mother intent on protecting her child would do just about anything, even kill.

"You see why I said that we had to include Seth Renfrew as a suspect." Maxine calmly leaned over, grasped the back of the overturned chair and set it upright again. "Anyone who cares deeply for Bethany, her daughter or her mother had a motive."

Halting directly behind Bethany's chair, Morgan mentally listed the suspects. James Farraday, Jr. Eileen Dow Farraday. Vivian Crosby. Tony Hayes. And Seth Renfrew. Five suspects. And one of them was a man who cared deeply for Bethany. Her friend. Her business partner. A man who had spent the night in her home. Was Seth Renfrew Bethany's lover? Anne Marie didn't seem to think so.

"Anyone who loved Bethany wouldn't allow her to go through the nightmare of being falsely accused of Farraday's murder, would they?" Leaning over the back of Bethany's chair, Morgan laid his hands on top of her shoulders.

Bethany closed her eyes the moment he touched her, savoring the feel of his strong hands on her body.

"Perhaps if the person who killed Jimmy is someone who cares for Bethany, he or she is waiting to see if this case goes to trial," Maxine said.

Bethany opened her eyes and took a deep breath, then laid her left hand on top of Morgan's right hand that tenderly caressed her shoulder. "Has a date been set yet for the grand jury hearing?" she asked.

"Not yet, but I don't think it'll be much longer." Maxine stared at Bethany's hand lying on top of Morgan's. "Our D.A. is in a hurry to make a name for himself."

Bethany patted Morgan's hand. "If you're finished here, we really need to go. I want to stop by the hospital and see Lisa for a few minutes. Then we need to pick up Anne Marie from

Mother's. We promised her that we'd grill steaks and go swimming this evening."

Maxine shook hands with Morgan, then hugged Bethany when they started to leave. "I'll call you as soon as I know anything."

Once alone in Bethany's Mercedes, Morgan knew he had to ask her two questions. He didn't doubt for a minute that she would answer both questions truthfully.

"Beth?"

She wished he wouldn't use the nickname he'd called her after they'd become intimate all those years ago. When he called her Beth, old feelings resurfaced and threatened to consume her.

"Yes?"

"Did you kill Jimmy Farraday?"

She took her eyes off the highway in front of her for a split second, just long enough to glance quickly at Morgan and see the fear in his eyes. He hadn't believed her capable of murder until he'd realized the reason she'd threatened Jimmy's life. A parent would do anything to protect a child.

"No, Morgan, I didn't kill Jimmy."

Relief washed over him, erasing his doubts, like an ocean tide removing footprints from a sandy beach. He wouldn't have blamed her if she *had* killed the sorry SOB, but he was damned glad she hadn't.

He wasn't sure exactly how she'd take his other question, but hell, if she hadn't been offended by his asking if she'd murdered a man, surely she wouldn't get angry over a little personal inquiry.

"Is Seth Renfrew your lover?"

The absurdity of the question burst a damn of pent-up emotions within Bethany. Once she started laughing, she couldn't stop. Sweet, soul-cleansing laughter eased the tension that had been building inside her for endless days.

"I'm sorry..." She giggled. "It's just that..." More giggles. Clasping the steering wheel in one hand, Bethany lifted the other and covered her mouth in an effort to stem her laughter.

"Dammit, what's so funny?"

Gripping the steering wheel with both hands, Bethany stole another glance at Morgan. He glared at her.

"What's so funny? You are," she said. "And I am. The question you asked me is."

"What's so funny about my asking you if Renfrew is your lover?"

"Seth Renfrew is not now nor has he ever been my lover," Bethany said, suddenly sobering, the smile vanishing from her face. "I've had one husband, with whom I had sex. But I've had only one lover."

Chapter 5

Stunned by what Bethany told him, Morgan didn't react immediately. Perhaps he had misunderstood her. Surely she didn't mean that she hadn't been with a man since Amery died.

But no, he hadn't misunderstood. That's exactly what she'd meant by her profound statement: "I've had one husband, with whom I had sex. But I've had only one lover." His heartbeat accelerated. The deafening roar of blood pumping through his body throbbed in his ears.

How was it possible that a woman as beautiful and desirable as Bethany had been celibate for the past twelve years? It didn't make any sense.

And why had she told him that she'd had only one lover? She'd had sex with Amery, but he hadn't been her lover?

Only one lover. He suddenly felt as if he'd been poleaxed. For a couple of seconds he couldn't get his breath, then his lungs began functioning again and he gulped in a deep swallow of air.

Turning toward her, his gaze focused on her face, he watched her as she looked straight ahead, not taking her eyes off the highway. She clenched her jaw tightly. One lone tear trickled from her eye, slid down the side of her face and onto her neck.

"Beth?" He reached out, intending to touch her. Her body

tensed. She bit down on her bottom lip. He dropped his hand, spreading his open palm over his thigh. He realized that she didn't want him to touch her.

They drove in utter silence for a while, north on I-65 and through the interconnecting interstates looping around downtown Birmingham. Watching her intently, Morgan controlled an almost irresistible urge to take her into his arms and comfort her. The idea was laughable. Morgan Kane wasn't the kind of guy who comforted women. Hell, he wasn't the kind of guy who comforted anyone. He'd spent his whole life doing what he wanted, fulfilling his own needs and not giving much thought to anyone else.

"Beth, honey, we need to talk," he finally said.

She gripped the steering wheel with white-knuckled ferocity. "I can't talk to you now, Morgan. Not while I'm trying to drive in this traffic."

He didn't press her to say anything else.

But when they arrived at Carraway Methodist Medical Center and she maneuvered her Mercedes into the parking space, he grabbed her arm as she undid her seat belt.

"Let's talk now," he said. "I think you owe me an explanation."

She glanced down at his hand gripping her arm, then lifted her gaze to his face. "I don't owe you anything."

He released her arm. "You're right. You don't. But I need to know, honey. You can't say something like that to a man and not—"

"You want an explanation?" She whipped around in the seat and faced him, her hazel eyes narrowing as she glared at him. "You want to know why I haven't been with a man since Amery died. You want to know why I said I'd had only one lover."

"You had sex with Amery, but he wasn't your lover? Yeah, I'd say that needs explaining."

"When I was eighteen I fell in love with you that first night, when you kissed me in the garden." Bethany took a deep, calming breath. "And when I was nineteen I gave myself to you. Body. Heart. Soul. I gave you everything I had to give. I trusted you. I thought you loved me as much as I loved you."

"Ah, Beth, honey..." What could he say after all these years?

If he told her that he had discovered, too late, how much she meant to him, would she believe him? Would she think he was lying if he told her that he had come back for her—on her wedding day?

"I was so sure we'd eventually get married. My mother and your parents had everything planned for us."

"But you and I didn't plan anything," he said. "We never discussed marriage. Never made plans for the future."

"You didn't," she told him. "But I did. In my mind." She laid her clenched hand on her chest. "In my heart."

"I was a selfish bastard. I admit it. I gladly took what you offered and I didn't think about you."

She glared at him, her mind accepting his admission for what it was—Morgan's confession of guilt. But her heart would not accept his apology. It was too little, too late. Her heart wanted more. Perhaps more than Morgan Kane had to give.

"When you left...just went away and didn't let anyone know where you'd gone...I was devastated," she told him. "I couldn't believe that you'd cared so little for me, that what we'd shared meant nothing to you."

He reached for her; she eased away from him, until her back pressed against the car door. "What we shared did mean something to me. I did care, Beth. I swear I did."

"Maybe you did, but not enough to stay. Not enough to marry me and build a life with me."

"Hell!" He forked his fingers through his thick hair. "I tried to explain to you then that I had to get away, that I couldn't stay here in Birmingham and live the life my parents had planned for me.

"When I first left town, I thought that you belonged to that life. A life I wanted no part of. You'd been bred to be the kind of woman my mother was, and no matter how much I cared for you, how much I wanted you, I couldn't see myself married to a woman who would one day become a replica of Claudia Morgan Kane."

"Is that what you think I am now? A replica of your mother?"

"There are similarities," he said. "But no, you are not a replica of my mother."

"Claudia might not have been the perfect mother, but she did love you, you know. She's been a wonderful grandmother to Anne Marie. The two of them are very close."

"Yeah, well, sometimes people make better grandparents than they do parents," Morgan said.

"After you left, your mother and father were as devastated as I was. They'd had so many hopes and dreams for you. For us."

"How convenient that Amery was able to step into my shoes and fulfill those hopes and dreams."

Bethany heard the anger behind Morgan's words. She wondered why he seemed hurt and resentful that Amery had wanted what he hadn't. That Amery had gladly taken what Morgan had thrown away.

"Once we realized that you weren't coming back and that you had no intention of letting any of us know where you were, your parents and my mother encouraged me to marry Amery. And to be honest, at the time, I wasn't thinking rationally. I wasn't feeling anything at all. I was numb and in shock and—"

"And so you let Eileen and my parents persuade you to marry Amery. They didn't waste any time, did they? How long had I been gone when you walked down the aisle with my cousin? Two months? Three months?"

"Amery tried to be a good husband. He did everything possible to make our marriage work. He wanted me to love him, even though he didn't really love me. I believe he thought that if he tried hard enough, he could make me forget you. He hated you. Did you know that?" Bethany asked Morgan. "It gave him great pleasure to know that he possessed everything that had once been yours. But after Anne Marie was born and...and he realized that I would never love him, he started drinking. Drinking heavily. And he started seeing other women."

"Then why did you stay with him, if you didn't love him?" And why did you allow my parents to persuade you to marry him in the first place? Why, dammit, why?

For the same reason I married him, she wanted to say. I did it all for Anne Marie. For *your* daughter! "I stayed with him for several years, because your parents convinced me that it was what was best for Anne Marie. But eventually, I couldn't bear it any longer. I told Amery that I was going to leave him, that I wanted a divorce."

"What happened to change your mind?" Morgan asked. "I know you were still married to Amery when he died."

"I asked Amery for a divorce the night he was killed." Bethany's eyes filled with tears. "He pleaded with me not to leave him. He said that he didn't want a divorce. He promised to stop drinking, to stop seeing other women. But I refused to listen to his promises. He—he kept pouring himself drink after drink, until he was so drunk he could barely stand up." She swallowed her tears. "I begged him not to leave the house in his condition, but when I tried to stop him, he threw me on the floor and left. Less than two hours later, the police were at my door, telling me that Amery was dead. He'd run his car off Altamont Road and hit a tree, head-on."

"I never knew the details of how he died."

"I killed him." Covering her face with her hands, Bethany wept. Her shoulders trembled from the force of her sobs. "It was all my fault. I never should have married him. I drove him to drink. My rejection forced him into the arms of other women. And then—" she sucked in air as she tried to stop crying "—I destroyed him when I asked him for a divorce."

"My God! You've been blaming yourself all these years for what happened to Amery. Even knowing that he didn't love you, that he wanted you only because you'd been mine, and married you to please my parents, you still think it's your fault that he drank too much and smashed his car into a tree?"

"I shouldn't have asked him for a divorce." Bethany drew in quick, gasping little breaths in an effort to gain control of her emotions. "We'd made a deal, Amery and I. And I didn't keep my part of the bargain. If I had, he would still be alive."

Morgan hated Amery more at that precise moment than he'd ever hated the man. Somehow, even in death, he had managed to wreak havoc on other people's lives. His selfishness reached out from the grave and kept a stranglehold on Bethany.

Beth. His sweet, loving Beth had made two major errors in judgment. She'd trusted him. And she'd trusted Amery. They had both used her for their own purposes, and in the end they'd both nearly destroyed her. The hatred he felt for his cousin burned deep into his soul, consuming him almost as completely as the self-hatred he felt. If he hadn't deserted Bethany, left her alone to stand against their families, she never would have married Amery.

"Amery's death was an accident," Morgan said. "But if anyone was at fault, Amery was. Nobody drives someone else to drink, honey. There was a weakness in Amery that made him an alcoholic."

"I know," she said. "Rationally, I know that what you're saying is true, but—"

"No buts!"

Morgan reached out and tenderly caressed Bethany's cheek. Closing her eyes, she pressed her face against his hand and sighed. Cradling her jaw, he traced the outline of her upper lip. When she kissed his thumb, the sensation of her moist, warm lips against his flesh sent shock waves of sexual awareness through his body.

"Beth...honey?" He inserted his thumb between her parted teeth and thought he'd die when she closed her lips around him. Leaning over, their bodies not touching, he cupped her chin, lifted her face and kissed her. A kiss edged with passion, but passion held in check by the instinctive knowledge that Bethany needed to be cherished, not ravished.

Sweetly, gently, he possessed her mouth, and she returned the kiss, seeking, pleading and then accepting the tender passion he offered.

Lifting his lips from hers and gazing into her moist eyes, Morgan ended the kiss. As he held her chin in the cradle between his thumb and forefinger, she looked at him and smiled.

"You were my only lover," she whispered. "Amery and I had sex, but we never made love. When I was with you, it was always lovemaking. Even if you didn't love me, you made me feel loved."

"For us, it was always more than sex. With other girls, that's all it had ever been. Scratching an itch. But the first time we had sex, it was different. You loved me so much, you never held anything back." Releasing her chin, he eased his body away from hers. He shook his head. He'd been such an arrogant young fool, so sure of himself and so sure, when he had come back to Birmingham sixteen years ago, that Bethany would be waiting for him.

"No, I never held anything back with you. I gave you everything. But it didn't matter. I wasn't enough for you, was I? You went away and left me all alone."

"You'll never know how sorry I am that I hurt you and that I allowed Amery to hurt you."

"I'm sorry, too," she said. "But perhaps you understand why, after Amery died, I didn't want another man in my life. I was twenty-three years old and had already had two disastrous relationships. I let you almost destroy me, and then I turned around and destroyed Amery.

"But I had Anne Marie. She has always been the most important thing in my life. I've devoted myself to her, to loving her, protecting her, preparing her for life. And I've built my business from nothing. I worked long and hard to make the boutiques a success. I wanted my daughter to be proud of me, to know that I'd made it on my own and she could, too."

"You've done a wonderful job raising Anne Marie all alone. She's a great kid," he said. "At least one good thing came out of your marriage to Amery."

She wanted to beat Morgan's chest and scream at him. *She isn't Amery's child. She's yours. Dear God, can't you look at her and see that she's yours?*

Bethany nudged the monogram-engraved gold case of her Jaeger-LeCoultre Reverso watch, revealing the face of the Art Deco-style timepiece. "It's late. We need to go on in and see Lisa, then hurry over to Mother's and pick up Anne Marie. I'm sure she's counting the minutes until we get there. She probably can't wait for our cookout tonight."

Morgan got out of the Mercedes and rounded the hood. Bethany waited for him beside the car. When he paused in front of her, she looked up at him as if she were silently pleading with him for something. What did she want from him? he wondered. But even more important, what did he have to give her? He could and would protect her, and he'd do everything possible to discover Jimmy Farraday's real murderer. But she already knew that, didn't she? No, she was asking for something more personal, something that only he could give her.

"I still want you, Beth," he said. "But if you're afraid I'll hurt you again, that I'll use you and then leave, I promise that—"

She laid her index finger across his lips, silencing him.

"Don't make me any promises." Not now. Not yet. Wait. Someday soon I may have to ask you for the most important promise of your life. I may have to ask you to take care of our daughter. "And I'm not worried about your hurting me again. I won't let you or anyone else break my heart. No one uses me. Not anymore."

She turned and walked away, her heels clattering loudly on the concrete floor. Quickly catching up with her, Morgan stayed at her side as they made their way out of the parking deck. When they reached the stairs, they met two loudly grumbling women and a sullen man walking up the steps. Bethany paused, waiting for the strangers to pass. As the threesome drew nearer, the air reeked with the stench of strong body odor and stale cigarette smoke. Covering her mouth and nose with her hand, Bethany turned her head.

The older woman, a flat-chested, barrel-shaped bleached-blonde, pointed her finger at Bethany. "Hey, ain't you the woman who killed Jimmy Farraday?"

Bethany tensed immediately, her whole body going stiff. With her hand still covering her mouth and nose, she turned her head slightly and stared at the woman. Morgan slipped his arm around Bethany's waist.

"Yeah, Mama, that's her." The younger woman, who had a tattooed snake crawling up her bare arm, took a draw on her cigarette, then stepped up right in Bethany's face and blew smoke in her eyes. "How could you have killed a man like Jimmy? He was one of us. A real human being. A man who knew what it was like to be poor and have all the rich folks looking down their noses at him."

Easing Bethany behind him, Morgan glared at the pimple-faced teenager. "I suggest y'all go on to your car and leave Ms. Wyndham alone."

The bearded man pulled the girl aside and stood up to Morgan. His beer belly hung over his belt, a strip of hairy flesh exposed by his too-short T-shirt. "Last time I heard, this here was a free country. So that means you can't tell us what to do and what to say. If we want to tell Jimmy's murderer what we think of her, then we will."

Morgan narrowed his gaze, glowering at the sour-breathed

bozo, then turned around, grasped Bethany's elbow and led her down the first step.

"Murderer. Snobby rich bitch," the woman hollered.

Bethany shivered. She took another step downward, her knees trembling.

"Look at 'em run, Joe Bob." The teenage girl laughed.

The man followed Morgan, reached out and grabbed his arm. "Hey, buddy, if I was you, I'd be scared to go to sleep next to that 'un. I'd be afraid she'd kill me if I hadn't pleasured her enough."

Like a flash of lightning, Morgan shoved the man up the steps and straight into the concrete wall. Gripping Joe Bob's neck, Morgan pressed against his windpipe. Bethany stood frozen to the spot on the second step. The cigarette slipped through the girl's fingers as she stared wide-eyed at her chalk-faced mother.

"Get the hell out of here." Morgan issued the warning in a calm, deadly voice. "And keep your opinions to yourself. Do you understand?"

Joe Bob's eyes bulged from their sockets like blue orbs sprouting from his round, red face. He nodded his head affirmatively. Morgan lessened the pressure on his windpipe. Grabbing the man by the back of the neck, Morgan jerked him away from the wall.

"We ought to call the police," the teenaged girl said. "You can't go around beating up on—"

"Shut your trap, sister," Joe Bob warned. "You want to get me killed?" He inclined his head toward the man who hadn't released him.

Morgan shoved Joe Bob toward his sister and mother, then waited while the three scurried away. He glanced toward Bethany, who hadn't moved from her frozen stance on the second step. She stood there, her face pale, her shoulders slumped. When she realized the Jimmy Farraday fan club had disappeared, she let out a long, gasping sigh.

"It's all right, honey. They're gone." Morgan glanced around in time to see the threesome crawling into a rusty, dented, older model car.

Bethany tried to take a step up, toward Morgan, but her knees weakened. Grabbing the handrail along the side of the stairs, she swayed slightly, but didn't crumple. She would not allow those vile people to get the best of her. They were poor, ignorant sheep who'd been led by a master shepherd. The city and surrounding counties were filled with loyal Jimmy Farraday worshippers. She was just lucky that more of them hadn't sought her out and personally attacked her. Letters and phone calls could be ignored, but not a face-to-face confrontation.

Morgan hurried to Bethany and drew her into his arms. Stroking her back, he whispered softly, "Ah, honey, you're shaking like a leaf. They were harmless. All mouth. No action. And now they're gone."

Bethany clung to him for a moment, savoring the powerful protection of his big body, drawing from his strength, then she pulled away and lifted her face. "I'm all right. They just took me by surprise, that's all. I wasn't expecting what happened."

"Do you still want to visit Lisa?" he asked. "If you're too upset, I can drive you straight over to Eileen's."

"No, I'm not leaving without seeing Lisa. I can't let people like that get to me. Even if they'd intended to harm me, you would have protected me. That's why I have a bodyguard, isn't it? To protect me." Squaring her shoulders, she readjusted the narrow straps of her leather bag, straightened the shawl collar on her jacket and took a tentative step downward. Pausing momentarily, she glanced over her shoulder at Morgan. "You're quite good at this, aren't you? You reacted so quickly I hardly knew what was happening before you had good old Joe Bob under control and scared half out of his mind."

What he'd done today was child's play compared to what he was capable of doing. He knew a hundred and one ways to subdue and eliminate the enemy. "I'll keep you safe. No one's going to get to you, except through me. I won't let anyone hurt you."

She believed he meant what he said, and instinctively she knew that his declaration meant more than a professional promise. Keeping her safe had become a personal obligation to him. Perhaps too personal. If she allowed him to get too close, he could hurt her. Again. She couldn't let that happen. Morgan might be able to protect her from every external force in her life, but only she could protect herself from the most dangerous element—Morgan himself.

* * *

Eileen Farraday held her hand over her pink lips that were the exact shade as the polish on her sculptured nails. Rings adorned every finger; gold and gemstones shined and sparkled. Sighing loudly as she swooned melodramatically and sat down on the antique wood-framed sofa by the window, Eileen gazed forlornly at her daughter.

"I simply do not know how much more we can bear." Eileen tilted her head to the left, allowing her sleek chin-length black hair to touch her shoulder. "Isn't it enough that my poor husband was murdered and that my only child was accused of the ghastly crime? Why now must my granddaughter be ridiculed by her classmates?"

"Mother, where is Anne Marie?" Planting one hand on her hip, Bethany glared at Eileen and forced herself not to point her finger in her mother's face and scold her for her theatrical performance.

"I knew something was wrong the minute she and James came home," Eileen said. "I could tell that she'd been crying and that James was furious. At first I thought they might have had a little disagreement, but...but..." Huge tears welled up in Eileen's eyes. She lifted her hand to Seth Renfrew, who sat down beside her and took her hand.

"Your mother phoned and asked me to come over immediately," Seth said. "It seems that Anne Marie locked herself in the powder room and wouldn't come out. Eileen was hysterical by the time she called me."

Bethany didn't doubt for a minute that her mother had been hysterical. Eileen didn't handle crises well. She usually came apart at the seams over the least little thing. And it amazed Bethany that her mother had held up so well since Jimmy's murder. She might be milking the situation for all it was worth in front of the news media and her society acquaintances, crying and bemoaning her great loss, but in private, she'd barely shed a tear.

"Why didn't you call me?" Bethany asked.

"I didn't want to upset you, dear." Eileen smiled weakly. "You've been through so much lately and I had hoped Seth and I could handle the situation and you'd never need to know."

"Is she still in the powder room?" Morgan asked.

"I'm afraid so." Seth shook his head. One thick, shiny curl

of silver-streaked auburn hair fell across his forehead. "I've tried talking to her. Eileen has cried and pleaded. And even James has done what he could. He's still sitting on the floor outside the powder room, talking to her."

Bethany could not believe how drastically her life had changed in the five days since someone killed Jimmy Farraday. Her world had gone from calm, peaceful, orderly and contented to totally crazy, uncertain, disorderly and miserable. And what hurt her the most was the effect it was having on Anne Marie. She couldn't believe that the teachers at The Redmont Academy would have allowed anyone to harass a fellow student. After all, one of the reasons she was paying the astronomical yearly tuition to the private school was to protect Anne Marie from the seamier side of life and the undisciplined, often dangerous, teen-agers who infested many of the public schools.

"Do either of you know exactly what happened?" Bethany looked at her mother first, but when Eileen gasped and clutched her chest, Bethany glanced at Seth.

"James told us that when he picked her up at school, she was in tears," Seth explained. "All she'd said to him was that some of her classmates had made comments about her mother being a murderer."

"Oh, hell!" Bethany swung around quickly and ran out of the living room, into the massive entrance hall and past the marble fireplace that graced the back wall.

Eileen looked pointedly at Morgan. "Bethany has built her whole life around that child. She's raised her all alone, as I did her, without a father."

Morgan didn't know what Eileen expected him to say. He sensed that she blamed him for Anne Marie's fatherless state. But he had no answer for her, no explanation for why both she and Bethany had been widowed in their twenties and left with a child to rear alone. He nodded to her, then gave Seth a quick appraisal, noting that the man was elegant, handsome and closer to Eileen's age than her daughter's.

Following Bethany, he found her with James, who sat on the glistening hardwood floor outside the powder room, his arms draping his drawn-up knees.

"I can't get her to come out," James said. "She's been in

there for the past hour and a half. She said that she's never coming out."

"Anne Marie?" Bethany grasped the brass doorknob. "Sweetheart, please come out and talk to me."

"Oh, Mama, I—I hate them," Anne Marie cried. "I hate all of them!"

"Come out of the powder room and tell me what happened." Twisting the doorknob, Bethany found the door locked.

"How can I ever face anybody again?" Anne Marie asked. "I got so angry that I cried and I said some terrible things. Things I shouldn't have said."

"It doesn't matter what you said," Bethany told her daughter. "Whatever happened, we can talk about it and work through it together."

"Tell James to go away," Anne Marie said. "I don't want him to see me looking like this. My eyes are all swollen and red and...and I—"

"Hey, I'm leaving." James jumped to his feet. "But I'm not going far. So when you need me, I'll be around. OK?" He looked at Bethany and shrugged, then walked off down the hall.

"James is gone," Bethany said.

The door opened a fraction. Anne Marie peeked outside, then continued opening the door very slowly. The moment Anne Marie emerged from her hideaway, Bethany held out her arms. The child dashed into her mother's embrace. Stroking her back comfortingly, Bethany hugged her daughter close, while they both cried.

"It's all right, sweetheart," Bethany said. "Go ahead and get it all out. Cry all you want to."

"Tiffany Lang said that you'd probably been having an affair with Jimmy and...oh, Mama, I wanted to strangle her." Anne Marie lifted her head from her mother's shoulder.

Bethany reached out and wiped the girl's tear-streaked face. "Tiffany is a silly, jealous-hearted child. She's never been your friend. She's always disliked you because you're prettier and smarter. You shouldn't have paid any attention to her."

"It wasn't just Tiffany. It was Kaitlyn and Allison, too. They were just hateful! They said that you were going to prison for the rest of your life and that their parents were going to make sure I wouldn't be allowed to attend the Redmont Academy anymore."

"I'm sorry that this happened." Bethany grasped her daughter's shoulders, encouraging her to stand straight and tall. "But it's at moments like this that we learn who our true friends are. It's a bitter lesson, but one that will make you a better person in the long run. You're strong. Remember that. You're not going to let what some silly, spiteful little girls say make you run and hide, are you?"

Anne Marie straightened to her full five feet nine inches, squared her broad shoulders and tilted her chin. Swallowing the residue of her tears, she smiled triumphantly at Bethany.

"I most certainly am not!"

"Good! I'll give Judy Cordell a call and let her know what's happened. As the Redmont Academy's principal, it will be her job to handle the situation. But she won't be able to prevent whispers and snide remarks behind your back. You'll have to deal with that yourself. But you can do it, can't you?"

"Yes, ma'am. I can, and I will. And when school starts Monday morning, I'm going to be there. And I'm going to look everybody straight in the eye and let them know just what I'm made of."

"That's my girl." Bethany wrapped her arm around her daughter's waist. "Are you ready to go home now? We're grilling steaks and—"

"May I invite James to come over for dinner? He's been just wonderful to me today, and I wasn't very nice to him when he tried to talk me into coming out of the powder room."

"Of course," Bethany said. "Why don't you go back into the powder room, wash your face and then go invite James to dinner? We'll eat in a couple of hours. And tell him to bring his swim trunks."

"Thanks, Mama. You're the best."

Morgan stood several feet away watching the loving exchange between mother and daughter. Comfort and caring. Genuine concern and unconditional support. Where had Bethany learned the art of motherhood? How, with a flighty socialite like Eileen as a role model, had she become such a strong, wise and caring parent?

Anne Marie gasped when she saw Morgan, then smiled and

even giggled a little. "Boy, you must think I'm a real whine baby, huh?"

"Not at all," Morgan said. "I think you had a bad day, that's all. And you're lucky enough to have a mother who helped you sort through your feelings and realize that you're tough enough to deal with your problems."

"Yeah, I am lucky to have a mother like mine, aren't I?" Glancing at Bethany, Anne Marie smiled broadly and winked. "See, Morgan thinks you're special, too." She raced off down the hallway in search of James.

"She's right, you know," Morgan said. "I do think you're pretty special. I always did." He cleared his throat. "You *have* done an amazing job raising that one. You knew exactly what she needed. You knew what to say, how to handle the situation. I can't imagine what I would have done, if it had been my kid. I suppose it's a good thing I never had any children. I'd have probably made a lousy father."

But you are a parent, Bethany wanted to shout. You're Anne Marie's father. And the time may come when you'll have to step in and take over for me. Just as I've been both mother and father to her for fifteen years, you may have to take on the dual role. If I'm convicted of murder. If I spend the rest of my life in prison.

"We don't all start out being great parents, you know," she said. "We learn as we go. I've made my share of mistakes, but two things have always helped me. My love for Anne Marie, and my ability to remember what it was like to be her age."

"Yeah, I remember being fourteen. I was a holy terror. But something tells me that if I'd had a mother like you, she'd have been able to handle me."

Bethany's stomach knotted painfully. Morgan thought Bethany was fourteen. But she wasn't. She was fifteen. Dear God, was that the reason he hadn't questioned her paternity, the reason he hadn't even suspected that she might be his? It was only a matter of time until he learned the truth. That Anne Marie was fifteen. That she'd been born eight months after he left Birmingham. Five months after she married Amery.

"No one could have handled you, Morgan," she told him. "Everyone tried. Even me. And we all failed."

"I'm not that same wild, selfish kid I was back then, any

more than you're the same shy, insecure girl. We've both grown up. Matured. Become different people." Reaching out, he ran the back of his hand across her cheek. "I would never hurt you again. I'd never use you. All I want to do is take care of you and help you. I owe you something, Beth, for the way I messed up your life. I promise that I'll do everything in my power to make sure Farraday's real killer is found. I want you and Anne Marie to be able to resume your normal life, to put this whole affair behind you."

"That's what I want, too," Bethany said quietly. "But this nightmare won't ever end for me and Anne Marie and mother and James unless we *do* find Jimmy's killer. If you can prove who the real murderer is, then you won't owe me anything. Whatever debt you feel that you owe me will be paid in full."

Chapter 6

Sunset splattered across the western sky, creating a massive finger-painted canvas of vivid, vibrant colors. Orange overlaid with gold. Lavender edged with pink. And an iridescent scarlet bleeding into the blue. An evening breeze brushed across the treetops, stirring the warm summertime air.

Morgan Kane stood on the lattice-framed wooden deck at the back of Bethany's house and breathed in the delicious aroma of sizzling steaks. The cozy, secure atmosphere of this family-style dinner within the cloistered courtyard of Bethany's backyard could easily deceive any onlooker. Anne Marie and James frolicked in the pool, while Bethany hummed Air Supply's "Making Love Out of Nothing at All," the song on the portable CD player that she'd brought out on the deck.

He watched Bethany as she raised the grill lid and flipped over the steaks, then checked on the foil-wrapped potatoes and ears of corn. She'd pulled her long, dark hair away from her face and secured it with a silver clasp. Loose sepia strands curled about her face. Lowering his gaze down the length of her slender neck and across her bare shoulders, he drank in the sight of her. Small-boned and delicate, her body rounded into feminine curves that tempted a man to reach out and touch. Did she have any idea how sexy she looked in that red halter top and sarong-style floral skirt, a hint of thigh peeping out between the side folds?

He remembered her as a soft, fragile girl with skin like silk. A tender-hearted angel who cried over sad movies and songs. The softness was gone, replaced by a strength, both physical and emotional. Only a hint of the fragility remained. In her facial expressions. In her sad eyes. But her skin looked as if it was still as smooth as silk.

Anne Marie squealed. Water splashed. Morgan turned his attention to the pool. The two teenagers tossed a huge beach ball back and forth. He glanced again at Bethany and caught her staring at him, an odd look on her face.

Was she thinking the same thing he was? That the four of them appeared to be a normal all-American family having a summer cookout. In their case, appearances were most definitely deceiving. Their foursome was comprised, not of Mom, Dad and the kids, but of an accused murderer, a former Navy SEAL-turned-bodyguard, the son of a man recently shot to death and the daughter of the accused.

Morgan was amazed by Bethany's ability to produce order out of chaos, to create warmth and love out of anger and hurt. To see her now, no one would guess that her life hung in the balance, that unless they could find Jimmy Farraday's real murderer, she might well spend the rest of her life in prison.

The very thought that Bethany—his beautiful, sweet, caring Beth—would have to spend one day in prison hurt him deeply, in the very depths of his soul. She was the last person on earth who deserved such misery. She was such a good person. A dutiful, loving daughter, not only to her own mother, but to his. And she was a wise and loving mother herself, providing her daughter with stability and security, even without a father.

He glanced around at the homey setting Bethany had produced in her fern- and flower-adorned rock patio. Festive pink tablecloths covered both black wrought-iron tables and matching pillows decorated the chairs. Candles and fresh-cut flowers graced the center of each table, which had been set with pink and green ceramic dinnerware and pale green goblets. Colas in a silver ice bucket sat on the teenagers' table; a bottle of wine awaited the adults.

Suddenly he was taken back twenty years or more to the garden parties his mother used to give. Huge affairs with hundreds of guests milling around the manicured grounds at their Redmont estate. Claudia had been blessed with an abundance of style and excellent taste, but her old, genteel Southern family had been practically penniless. The Morgans had depended upon their daughters to marry well. Claudia had exceeded their expectations when she'd married Judge William Kane's only son. But Danielle had been unable to snare herself a rich husband, and her son, Amery, had spent his life trying to fit into his wealthy relatives' lives.

Morgan closed his eyes and allowed the pain to spread slowly from his gut to his entire body, then he took a deep, cleansing breath and released the hurt. He could not change the past. He could not undo the damage he'd done. All he could do now was take care of Bethany, and then, when she was truly free, walk away and leave her unharmed by his desire. If only he could have seen years ago, before he'd left Birmingham, what he saw now. If only he could have seen Bethany for the woman she was and not as a potential duplication of his mother.

He'd been so wrong about so many things. His errors in judgment had cost him the one thing he had discovered—too late—he wanted most.

Reminding himself that this modest garden, this small patio, this intimate dinner bore little resemblance to his mother's elaborate affairs, he absorbed the ambience of the moment. Only the beauty of the surroundings and the impeccable good taste of the hostess were similar.

This was a family affair. But not his family. Regretfully he admitted to himself that they could have been his. Just as Bethany could have been his woman forever, Anne Marie could have been his child.

When he left Birmingham sixteen years ago, he hadn't wanted a wife or children. Or so he'd thought. And once he'd lost Bethany, he'd never again considered a permanent relationship with another woman. Now it was too late. He was too old, too set in his ways. If he'd ever been capable of truly loving a woman, he'd lost that ability long ago. He might put his life on the line repeatedly. But he never took a chance with his heart.

And his gut instincts told him that Bethany might have become stronger, wiser and more cautious, but she could still be easily hurt. No matter how much he wanted her, he had no right to pursue her. No matter how tempted he was to try to break through the barriers she'd built around herself, he had to be careful not to let his passion overrule his common sense.

But heaven help him, he had to have her, common sense be damned! He'd never wanted another woman as much as he wanted Beth.

"Hey, Morgan, aren't you coming in for a swim before dinner?" Anne Marie called out to him as she climbed out of the water and up onto the pool's deck.

Smiling, he waved at her. "Not now. Maybe after dinner."

James lifted his muscular body out of the pool and reached for a beach towel lying across the back of a wrought-iron chaise longue. "Hey, Anne Marie tells me that you used to be a Navy SEAL. I bet you can swim like a fish, huh?" The boy eyed Morgan's shoulder holster.

"I do all right." Morgan grinned at the boy, wondering if the kid had any idea just how adept he really was in the water. James couldn't imagine what it felt like to swim in liquid ice off Alaska. He knew nothing of being part of a team that had to carry a 150-pound rubber raft through treacherous waters and overcome every barrier between them and their objective.

"I've heard that SEALs go through something called Hell Week, kind of like fraternities put guys through." James shook the moisture from his dark hair, then vigorously rubbed the towel over his arms and legs.

There was no way he could explain to this eighteen-year-old high school senior what Hell Week meant to a SEAL, Morgan thought. It was the rite of passage to becoming a warrior. Time never forgotten, etched in a man's memory forever, as was the number for his class.

Hell Week taught a man how to turn off pain and focus on his mission, a lesson he should apply to his present situation. He had to turn off the pain of wanting a woman who had told him that she would fight her attraction to him with every breath she took. He needed to focus on his mission—protecting Bethany and proving her innocence.

"I think fraternities are a bunch of bull." Anne Marie dried off her long, slim legs, then wrapped the huge blue-and-green-striped towel around her hips. "And sororities aren't much better. I don't think I'm even going to consider a sorority when I go to college."

"Whatever you do, don't tell Grandmother or Nana." Bethany pinched off a twig from the grape cluster on the fruit plate beside the wine bottle. "They'll expect you to join either Nana's or Grandmother's sorority."

"Mum's the word for the next four years," Anne Marie said. "No need to upset either of them before it's absolutely necessary. You won't mind will you, Mama, if I don't join your sorority?"

"No, sweetheart, I won't mind at all." Bethany shifted the small grape cluster from one hand to the other. "I want you to make your own decisions and live your own life. You know I'll back you up, whatever you do."

Walking over to Morgan, James nodded toward the shoulder holster he wore. "Do you wear that thing all the time? It makes you look like a cop or something."

"Couldn't you remove it?" Bethany asked. "Just for this evening. After all, I hardly think I'm in danger in my own backyard."

No, she probably wasn't in any danger in her own backyard. Morgan doubted any of Jimmy Farraday's fans would risk arrest just to harass his accused murderer at her home. And the real killer was undoubtedly too smart to get up close and personal, without a damn good reason.

"I'm sorry it bothers you," he said. "But it's necessary." He undid the holster, removed it and laid it on the table. "I'll take it off if it makes you feel more comfortable, but I want it close by."

"Just in case, huh?" James asked.

"Yeah, just in case," Morgan said.

The CD changed from *Air Supply's Greatest Hits* to Christopher Cross belting out the pulse-pounding "Say You'll Be Mine." James pulled Anne Marie into his arms and danced her around the patio. Bethany popped several grapes into her mouth, then dropped the cluster on the table. Clapping her hands in time to the rhythm, she laughed as she watched the kids cavorting playfully.

Morgan couldn't keep his eyes off Bethany. God, but she was

beautiful, her face aglow, her eyes sparkling, her lush body undulating to the music's beat. Without thought, without care, he grabbed her and drew her into his arms. She stared up at him with startled eyes, but allowed him to lead her into a dance. As her breasts brushed across the lower part of his chest, her nipples hardened. Sucking in his breath, he spread his open palm across her spine. The tips of his fingers bit into the top edge of her buttocks.

Lowering his head, he nuzzled her neck and whispered in her ear. "Ah, Beth. I want you."

Her body tensed. She pulled away from him. He cursed himself for a fool. He'd ruined a perfectly beautiful moment. Don't push her, you idiot, he chided himself. Coax her. Seduce her. Win her over slowly. Don't rush. Even if it kills you by slow degrees.

"I think the medium-rare steaks should be ready," Bethany said.

"That's mine and yours, Morgan," Anne Marie said. "I can't believe Mama and James want theirs burned to a crisp."

"We don't want ours burned, do we, Bethany? We just want ours cooked, not still bloody inside," James said.

"Right." Bethany lifted the grill hood. "Anne Marie, you and James go get the slaw out of the refrigerator and bring the salt and pepper. I forgot to bring the shakers out here."

The moment the teenagers went inside, Bethany turned on Morgan. "Don't ever touch me like that in front of my daughter!"

"What are you talking about?"

"I'm talking about the way you were pawing me. The way you were doing all that heavy breathing in my ear." Bethany glared at him. "How can I teach Anne Marie the wisdom of restraint and abstinence if she sees me allowing some man to practically make love to me in front of her?"

"I was hardly making love to you in front her. And I wasn't pawing you." Huffing loudly, he turned his back to her. Dammit, he had not been pawing her! All right, maybe he had held her a little too close. And maybe he had let his hand stray a little too far south. And maybe the whisper in her ear had been a little too suggestive. "I'm sorry. I wasn't thinking. I was just enjoying the feel of you in my arms, your body pressing against mine. For a few minutes there, I forgot we weren't alone."

"Please, don't forget again," she told him.

After dinner, Anne Marie helped Bethany clear the tables, while James and Morgan cleaned the grill.

"We'll be back out as soon as we load the dishwasher," Anne Marie called from the open door leading to the kitchen.

"Yeah, OK," James said, then turned to Morgan when Anne Marie closed the door.

"Hey, man, you've got the hots for Bethany, haven't you?"

"What?"

"Anne Marie told me that you and Bethany used to be an item, back before she married Anne Marie's father."

"That was a long time ago." Morgan wanted to tell this brash young boy that he was involving himself in something that was none of his business. But his own actions had created James's interest. Maybe Bethany had been right. Maybe James and Anne Marie had been aware of the way he'd been touching her.

"Look, I don't blame you. Bethany is a gorgeous woman. If she wasn't my stepsister and nearly old enough to be my mother, I'd be all over her myself." Narrowing his bright blue eyes, James frowned as he stared directly at Morgan. "Anne Marie has put you up on a pedestal, as if you were some sort of god. She's got it in her head that you're going to be sticking around permanently, that maybe you'll wind up marrying her mother."

"Did she tell you that?" Morgan asked.

"Yeah. Tonight. She said, 'See the way he's holding Mama and the way they're looking at each other.' Face it, you'd have to be blind not to have noticed. Anne Marie noticed all right, and she's convinced that you and Bethany are going to fall in love all over again. You know how romantic girls her age can be."

"Yeah, I know." Her mother had been a romantic, to whom love and sex were synonymous. "So, why are we having this man-to-man talk? Who are you trying to protect, Anne Marie or Bethany?"

"Both of them." James laid aside the wire brush he'd used to scrape the charred residue from the grill racks. "I figure Bethany's a pretty tough lady and she can take care of herself. But Anne Marie's not so tough, no matter how good a front she puts up. I know what it's like to want and need a father. I had my old man, but I'd have been better off without him. Anne Marie never knew her father, so she's let her Nana fill her head with a bunch of stories about you. And she's convinced herself that you'd make the ideal father."

"I'll talk to Bethany and have her explain the situation to Anne Marie."

"So, you're not planning on being around for the long haul, are you? You're just staying until you've found out who really killed the great Jimmy Farraday."

"That's right. And I thought Anne Marie understood. The last thing I want to do is hurt that girl." He would never forgive himself if he caused Bethany's child any grief. He had agreed to stay on in Birmingham and take this assignment in order to help Bethany, not to create more problems for her.

"Well, you'd better set Anne Marie straight. And the sooner the better. Before she has wedding invitations printed."

"I'll handle things," Morgan said. "Thanks for letting me know."

"No, problem. I like Anne Marie a lot. I don't want to see her get hurt any more than you do."

"I hope you mean that." Morgan laid his big hand on the boy's shoulder. "That little girl's got a major crush on you. You know that, don't you?"

"Yeah, I know. So?"

"When a girl feels about a guy the way she does you, it would be easy for him to take advantage of her."

Chuckling nervously, James shivered when Morgan tightened his hold on his shoulder.

"Look, I like Anne Marie. She's a sweet kid. But I know she's off limits. I'm already eighteen. A girl her age is jail bait." James's lips curved into a cocky, macho grin. "Besides, I can get what I want from plenty of other girls. You know, the ones smart enough to take care of themselves and just want to have a good time, the way I do."

"Yeah, I know all about those kinds of girls," Morgan said. "But does Anne Marie know—"

The back door swung open. "Does Anne Marie know what?" she asked.

James glanced past Morgan and smiled. "Hey, I've got to hit the road. It's going on ten o'clock and I have stuff to do tonight."

"It's not that late." Anne Marie's voice held a trace of a whine, but she smiled at James. "Do you have to go now?"

"Yeah. I've got a late date." James looked at Morgan, his eyes speaking volumes.

"Oh." The smile vanished from Anne Marie's face. "I—I guess I'll see you this weekend at Grandmother's."

"Sure thing." James turned to Bethany. "Thanks for dinner. Everything was delicious. Take care, huh? I know things are pretty rough right now, but with James Bond here—" he nodded toward Morgan "—on the case, we're bound to find out who really plugged the old man full of holes."

"I'll walk you to the door." Anne Marie followed James into the house.

The moment the teenagers were out of earshot, Morgan said, "You should talk to Anne Marie about her crush on James. If she's not careful, she could wind up getting hurt."

"I've already talked to her." Bethany blew out the candles on the table nearest to her. "She knows James thinks of her as a buddy and not as a girlfriend. She also knows that he dates other girls. But I can't dictate what Anne Marie can and cannot feel. I have no more control over her heart than she does. She loves James."

Morgan followed Bethany as she walked over to the other table and blew out the candles. "Hell, she's too young to know what love is. She's just at the age when hormones kick in and emotions go haywire."

Swirling around quickly, Bethany looked up at him and shook her head. "What she's feeling may be what you and I would call puppy love, but to her it's just as real and strong as true love. Are you so cynical and hard-hearted that you can't remember what it was like the first time you fell in love?"

"When I was Anne Marie's age, I didn't have any idea what love was." Reaching out, he slid his hand behind Bethany's head, slipped his fingers under her hair and grasped the back of her neck. "When I got a little older, I became personally acquainted with lust. I knew what it was to want a girl. To walk around aroused all the time. Just like James. But love never entered into my relationships. Not when I was a teenager.''

''And what about later, when you were older?'' Bethany held her breath, waiting for his answer.

''I've never been in love,'' he said, knowing beforehand that his admission would hurt her. He had never lied to Bethany in the past, and he wasn't going to start lying to her now. ''Not ever.''

''I see.'' She kept her gaze locked with his, her expression void of any emotion.

''I cared about you more than I ever cared for anyone. Please believe me.'' And I realized, too late, that I didn't want to lose you, that I wanted you to be a permanent part of my life.

''I do believe you.'' She closed her eyes, uncertain how much longer she could stand so close to him, listening to his confessions, and not fall apart. ''I was foolish enough to confuse sex with love. That wasn't your fault, was it? You didn't make me any promises.''

''Yes, I did.'' Tightening his hold on her neck, he drew her toward him as he lowered his head. ''I didn't realize that I was promising you anything, but I was. Every time I kissed you. Every time I caressed you. Every time I made love to you, I was making silent promises. I wasn't so stupid that I didn't know you thought love and sex were the same thing.''

She wished he would stop talking, stop venting his guilt, stop trying so damn hard to atone for the past. He had no idea what he'd done to her by leaving her alone—alone to bear his child and rear that child without him.

''Don't do this, Morgan,'' she pleaded.

''Open your eyes, Beth. Look at me.''

She opened her eyes slowly and looked up at him, a fine sheen of moisture blurring her vision.

''I'm sorry that I made you promises I didn't keep,'' he told her, his lips almost touching hers. ''I'm sorry that I left you behind when I went away. I'm sorry that I didn't take you with me.''

''But you didn't take me with you, did you? And nothing can change that fact. All the guilt in the world won't change the past. Yours or mine.'' She jerked away from him, freeing herself from his strong grasp.

''Don't you see, honey? James Farraday reminds me of myself when I was a cocky, young SOB, and Anne Marie looks at him the way you used to look at me. He cares about her, just like I cared about you. He won't mean to hurt her, but sooner or later, he's not going to be able to resist all that sweet innocence.''

''You're telling me not to trust James.''

''Look, he seems like a good kid. Probably a lot better than I was at his age. But he's cocksure of himself and he's got a lot of bitterness inside him, just like I did.''

''Surely you don't still think James might have killed his father, do you?'' Bethany asked.

Anne Marie gasped. She stood on the deck, her blue-gray eyes turning cold as she glared at Morgan. ''You can't possibly believe that James would kill his own father. How could you! He is the sweetest, nicest, most wonderful...'' Whirling around, she fled into the house.

''Oh, Lord!'' Bethany sighed. ''Why did she have to overhear us? Just stay here. I'll go in and talk to her.''

Morgan grabbed Bethany's wrist, halting her. ''Wait. Let me go in and talk to her. I'm the one she's angry with.''

''All right. But please be careful what you say to her.''

''You don't have to remind me that I don't know a damn thing about parenting. But I'm the one who made the mess, so I'm the one who should straighten it out.''

Bethany nodded in agreement.

Morgan found Anne Marie hunched in one of the Louis XVI chairs, her elbows resting on the kitchen table. Her shoulders trembled as she sobbed softly.

''Will you let me talk to you?'' he asked. ''Will you give me a chance to explain?''

For several minutes she didn't respond; she sat there gulping quietly, then slowly nodded her head. ''I'm listening.''

For the life of him, Morgan didn't know why he had the overwhelming urge to lift Anne Marie out of her chair and wrap her protectively in his arms. Her tears touched him, made him want to wipe them away and promise her that he wouldn't ever let anyone hurt her again. His need to comfort Bethany's child consumed him.

Morgan shoved his hands into the back pockets of his jeans. Leaning backward, bracing himself on the heels of his feet, he looked up at the ceiling and pondered just what to say to make things right again. "I don't think James killed his father."

Anne Marie spun around and stared at him. "Then why did Mama ask you if you still thought James killed Jimmy?"

"Because James is on our list of suspects."

When Anne Marie opened her mouth to protest, Morgan held up a restraining hand.

"Wait just a minute before you go off on another tangent. Everyone who had motive and opportunity is on that list. James hated his father and he was at the television station when Jimmy was shot."

"But James didn't kill Jimmy any more than Mama did. I know him. He'd never—"

"I tend to agree with you," Morgan said. "After spending a little time with James and talking to him tonight, I don't think he's our murderer."

"Then why don't you trust him? I heard Mama say that you didn't think she should trust James."

"Just how much did you hear?" Morgan walked over to the table, pulled out a chair and sat down beside her.

Wiping her tear-streaked face, Anne Marie squirmed in the chair until she was sitting up straight. "That's all I heard. Just that you didn't trust James and that you'd thought he killed his father."

"I don't trust the boy," Morgan admitted. "I don't trust him with you."

Anne Marie's eyes widened. Her mouth gaped. "What do you mean you don't trust him with me?" She pointed her index finger at her chest.

"I was just warning your mother to be careful and not let young Farraday break your heart." Morgan grasped Anne Marie's chin. "I suppose I was playing substitute father. I was a teenage boy once myself, you know, and...well, if I was your father, I'd keep every boy in the world away from you until you were at least thirty. Especially any of them you looked at the way you look at James."

"Oh, Morgan!" She came up out of the chair like a cannon blast and grabbed Morgan around the neck. "I'm sorry I misunderstood. I've never had a father to worry about me and try to protect me from boys. Thank you. I love the idea of your acting as my substitute father."

She hugged him, her strong young arms squeezing him affectionately. Slowly, cautiously, Morgan lifted his arms and wrapped them around the girl, returning her hug.

Hell! What had he done now? Had he created a bigger mess than the one he'd just cleaned up? No matter how much he cared about Bethany or might wish that Anne Marie was his child instead of Amery's, he couldn't allow this sweet young girl to start thinking of him as her father. His stay in Birmingham wasn't permanent. And any relationships he formed while he was here would be only temporary.

Before he had a chance to fully form his thoughts, let alone put his thoughts into action, Anne Marie grabbed his hand, pulled him out of the chair and toward the back door.

"Come on." Tugging on his hand, she led him outside onto the deck, then released her hold on him and gave him a shove down the steps. "Go on. You and Mama deserve some quiet time alone. I'm going up to my room and get ready for bed."

"Are you all right?" Bethany's concerned gaze fell on her daughter's smiling face.

"Fine. Couldn't be better. Morgan explained everything." She waved to her mother. "Good night. See y'all in the morning."

"Good night." Bethany looked at Morgan, her eyes questioning him. "And how did you perform that miracle?"

"I told her that I didn't believe James killed his father."

"Is that the truth?"

"I wouldn't lie to Anne Marie."

In her peripheral vision, Bethany noticed a shadow move across the deck. Every muscle in her body tensed. Cautiously, she glanced over her shoulder.

"Anne Marie! I thought you were going to bed."

"Sorry. I didn't mean to eavesdrop or disturb you," Anne Marie said. "I thought I'd change the CDs on the player and put on something y'all might like."

"Thank you," Bethany said. "Now, go to bed."

"I put on Mama's favorite song." Anne Marie winked at Morgan. "Something tells me that you'll recognize it the minute you hear it."

"Young lady!" Bethany glared at her daughter.

"I'm gone." Anne Marie rushed inside, slamming the door behind her.

"I don't know what she's done or why, but I'm turning off that stupid CD player."

The moment Bethany started toward the deck, the music began—the tinkling, throbbing of a piano's heartbeat. Slow and sweet and mournful. She froze on the spot.

Oh, dear God. No! Not that song. Bethany didn't think she could bear it. Anne Marie had no idea what she'd done.

She had to turn it off, had to shut out the memories before they flooded her mind and heart. Why had she ever told Anne Marie that this was her favorite song? She had never dreamed that someday she'd hear it again with Morgan.

Bob Seger's sandpaper-rough voice pleaded for her to stay, promising nothing beyond this one night as he sang "We've Got Tonight." Wrapping his arms around her, Morgan drew Bethany's back up against his chest, lowered his head and brushed his lips across the side of her forehead.

Being in his arms was such sweet torment, such unbearable ecstasy. She trembled, her body quivering from head to toe.

He knew she was remembering, just as he was, that night in his apartment, when they'd made love for the first time. He had never wanted a girl the way he'd wanted Beth. He had waited for her, been as patient as he knew how to be, coaxing her slowly to surrender to his desire. But in the end, her passion had been as great as his. And in all her sweet, loving innocence, she had given herself to him, and nothing—absolutely nothing—had ever equaled what they'd shared.

The repetitive drumbeat escalated, building the tension as the plaintive words of Seger's love song wrapped themselves around Bethany's heart and bound her to Morgan as securely as his strong arms did.

"This was our song." Morgan nuzzled her ear. "I've never forgotten the way you looked that night or the way you cried out my name...or what it felt like to be your first lover." He kissed her neck. She sighed. "Your only lover."

The music softened, the drumbeat fading to a hushed plea. Bethany's heartbeat accelerated to a deafening roar. Gradually the music swelled and expanded, growing again into a resounding combination of drum, piano and Seger's lonely lament. "Stay with me, Beth," Morgan had said that night. And she had stayed, asking for nothing more than to be with him. She had thought it would be forever. She'd been wrong.

Morgan turned Bethany in his arms, lifting her up off the patio floor until her small feet dangled in the air. She clung to his big, broad shoulders as he lowered his head and took her mouth in a breath-robbing kiss.

I have to stop this before it goes any further was the last coherent thought Bethany had before her own long-denied passion claimed her.

Chapter 7

Blossoming like a withering flower drawing in the life-giving nourishment of the rain, Bethany responded to his kiss. Her body wrapped itself around his, clinging, pressing, longing for a remembered pleasure. Opening herself up to him, she accepted his thrusting tongue inside her mouth. She trembled when he cupped her hip, drawing her intimately against his arousal.

The kiss consumed her. Consumed him. They became the kiss. The kiss became them. Joined together in the intensity of their mutual need, they hurled headlong into dangerous waters, the hazardous depths of desire.

Morgan lifted her up and into his arms without breaking the kiss. He carried her across the patio and laid her down on the wrought-iron chaise longue. Easing her onto her side, he wedged himself alongside her.

He explored her body with hungry hands, feasting on the silken feel of her soft flesh. She jerked his tan cotton shirt from beneath the waistband of his jeans and slipped her hands up and over his broad back.

Morgan broke the kiss. Both of them gulped in air. He blazed a warm, moist trail down her throat, across from one shoulder to the other, and then his tongue slid inside her halter top, dampening the crevice between her breasts. Moaning, Bethany lifted her hips, pressing her femininity against his sex. Skimming his fingertips up and under her skirt, along the satin skin of her thigh, he returned his mouth to hers, drinking in her sweetness.

While he nipped at her bottom lip, he cupped her breast, squeezing gently. "I want you," he groaned the words. "Here. Now."

His big, nimble fingers loosened the ties on her wraparound skirt just as he drew the tip of her breast into his mouth, suckling through the thin barrier of the material covering her.

Instinctively she unbuttoned his shirt in her need to eliminate any barriers between them. When she touched his lean belly, he sucked in his breath.

Longing for Morgan's possession, Bethany's body wanted to surrender, wanted to succumb to his masterful seduction. Like a dormant creature awakening from a decade of sleep, sexual desire emerged from the depths of her celibate body, ravenous, demanding and dangerous.

"Please, don't do this to me," she begged, but her hands asked for more as she stroked his chest, her fingers threading through the thicket of brown hair. Her mind warred with her body, her reasoning struggling to overpower her physical needs.

"I'm not doing anything you don't want me to do, Beth, and you know it." Gliding his hand between her legs, he fondled her. When she cried out, he captured the sound with his mouth and adeptly eased his fingers inside her red bikini bottom. "You want me. You need this as much as I do."

"We can't." She pushed halfheartedly against his chest. "I can't. Anne Marie is—"

"In her room," Morgan said. "She isn't going to disturb us. Don't use your daughter's presence as an excuse."

"Please. I—I can't let this happen." She grabbed the front of his shirt, her fingers curling around the material, bunching it into wrinkled wads.

"Why not?" He stroked his index finger across her sensitive nub and was rewarded with a rush of moisture. "You're hurting, honey. And I can ease that hurt."

She could give in so easily to what he wanted—to what she wanted. Heaven knew Morgan Kane was the one man on earth to whom she'd never been able to say no. She wanted him now more than she'd ever wanted him. Her woman's body longed for the fulfillment he alone could give her. Physical relief was easily achieved, but ease for a heart's aching loneliness, for a soul's starvation required the complexity of love and passion that she had found with no other man.

His touch tempted her almost beyond reason. But as tempted as she was, as close to the edge as he'd brought her, she could not escape an inevitable truth. Morgan Kane had nearly destroyed her once, and it had been his fault. She'd been young, naive and trusting, and he'd used her. But she was a mature woman now, a wise and cautious woman. If she allowed him to use her, cast her aside and destroy her emotionally, she'd have no one to blame but herself.

To Morgan their mating would be a physical act; to her it would be so much more. Could she give herself to him again, with no promises, without any pledge of love? Could she accept this for what it was and not want more?

No! She couldn't. She didn't dare.

Bethany shoved against him, harder and harder. "I'm not ready for this," she told him. "I can't—"

Removing his hands from her body, he rolled over and off the chaise longue. Standing up, he turned his back to her. "Deep down inside, you're still the same, aren't you, Beth? You want all or nothing. You'll deny us both what we so desperately need because you still can't separate sex from love."

No, I can't! she screamed silently. Damn you, Morgan! Damn you for making me care. She wanted to hurl herself against him, to beat her fists into his big, broad back.

Bethany eased off the chaise longue, picked up her skirt and walked away without looking back, leaving Morgan alone on the patio. Music from the CD player belted out a recent Seger hit tune, his gravelly voice filling the night air. She slammed the kitchen door behind her, then leaned back against it, her body trembling uncontrollably. Willing herself not to cry, she stood there shaking, holding all the pain inside her.

Morgan stripped off, down to his black swim briefs, tossed his clothes onto the patio floor, then dove into the pool. He swam from one end of the Olympic-size pool to the other and back again. He was aroused and hurting, in physical misery. Anger swelled up inside him, needing a release. And somewhere in the vicinity of his heart, he felt a few aching twinges. Bethany wasn't the only one who hadn't changed. Around her, he was still the same greedy, insensitive bastard he'd always been.

His sleek, superbly toned body sliced through the water. He was physically and mentally in perfect harmony with the aquatic environment, which was like a second home to him. He continued making the trek, back and forth, again and again.

Knotting her shaky hands into fists, Bethany sucked in several deep breaths, then turned around and glanced out the window. She watched Morgan's big, muscular body cut through the water, forcing onward as if battling his aqueous surroundings. Instinctively she knew that he was hurting, just as she was... frustrated by their unfulfilled desire. And he was angry, too. Angry that she had denied him.

An almost uncontrollable urge to go to him overwhelmed her. It would be so easy to open the door, walk across the patio and dive into the pool with him. As she watched him trying to exhaust himself, she laid her hand on the window frame and pressed her forehead against the pane. She could strip off her bikini and dive into the water, naked and ready for his possession. He would come to her, pull her into his arms and devour her with his mouth.

Bethany's body throbbed. Her breathing quickened. Closing her eyes to shut out the sight of him, she covered her lips with her clenched fist and moaned silently.

Pulling herself away from the window, she eased backward, her vision still focused on the man in the pool. Don't do this to yourself! Don't tempt and punish! Don't long for something that can never be yours. Morgan doesn't love you. He never did.

She raced up the back stairs and into her room, leaving her door slightly ajar. Once safely inside the privacy of her bathroom, she stripped off her bathing suit, turned on the shower and stepped beneath the needle-sharp spray. Lathering her hair, she washed and rinsed it hurriedly, then squirted scented liquid soap into a net sponge and ran it over her arms and across her breasts. Her nipples hardened to diamond points, and for one brief moment she could feel Morgan's mouth on her breast. Sensual quivers spread from her breasts to her feminine core. The desire she was trying so hard to wash away consumed her.

* * *

Morgan dragged himself out of the pool. He had hoped to exhaust himself, to drive the desire from his body and the anger from his heart. Anger turned inward on himself. But it would take many more laps in the pool to tire him enough to sleep, to enable him to rest.

He picked up his discarded clothes, lifted his gun holster from the table and went inside the house. After checking the security, he opened the refrigerator and retrieved the half-full bottle of wine left over from dinner. Even if Bethany kept anything stronger in the house, which she didn't, it would be off limits to him. He could function well enough to protect Bethany after finishing off the wine, but he wouldn't be worth a damn if he got really soused.

When he passed her room, he noticed the partially open door. If he were a gentleman, he'd knock on the door and when she responded, he would apologize for trying to ravish her. He stopped outside her room, one hand gripping the wine bottle, the other reaching for the doorknob. Easing open the door, he peered inside and drew in a deep breath at the sight of Bethany emerging from the bathroom, totally naked, her long, damp hair clinging to her shoulders.

His sex hardened instantly, and it was all he could do not to storm into the room, grab her, throw her on the bed and bury himself deeply and completely inside her.

Her full, round breasts beckoned his mouth. Her curvaceous hips and buttocks begged for his touch. And the dark triangle of curls that pointed the way to her femininity tempted his throbbing sex.

He turned and walked across the hall, his body tense and aching, his mind calling him a fool. He left the door open, but didn't turn on the light. Dumping his clothes in a heap on the floor, he swallowed hard, willing himself under control. He set the wine bottle on his nightstand, then went into the bathroom, stripped off his swim briefs and turned on the shower. As the lukewarm spray hit his aroused body, he shuddered, memories of Bethany's nakedness exciting his senses. Lathering his body, he scrubbed his skin, all the while wishing the hands cleansing his body were Bethany's and not his own. He lingered over the lower part of his body, thinking of Bethany, of thrusting, pumping, exploding. Shuddering from head to toe, he spread out his hands and pressed his palms against the ceramic wall.

What he wanted was Bethany, crying out her pleasure, calling out his name. And sooner or later he would have her again. Even if it had to be on her terms!

Bethany slept fitfully all night. Tossing and turning for hours, she finally got out of bed before daybreak. After freshening up, applying her makeup and dressing, she started downstairs, but stopped abruptly when she heard Morgan stirring about in his room. Spread out on the floor, he lifted and lowered his big body as he did push-ups. The muscles in his arms bulged as he repeated the exercise again and again, not even breathing hard.

She stood there, immobilized, watching him, mesmerized by the beauty of his perfect physique. He was naked except for his black cotton briefs that hugged his lean hips and round buttocks. Fine swirls of light brown hair dusted his legs and arms.

He'd always been a big man, long and lean and muscular, but the twenty-two-year-old she'd known and loved so long ago was gone, replaced by this prime physical specimen with a body honed by a warrior's endurance.

If he saw her watching him, he didn't let on in any way. Perhaps he was too engrossed in his exercise to notice a voyeur. She shouldn't punish herself this way, watching when she knew it would be deadly to touch.

She walked downstairs quietly, feeling her way through the dark house until she reached the kitchen. Flipping on a light switch, she crossed the room and immediately prepared the coffee machine. Checking the wall clock with her watch, she groaned when both timepieces agreed that it was 5:45. The *Birmingham News* should have run by now. She just hoped there wasn't another article about Jimmy's murder or one about her awaiting a grand jury date.

As soon as the coffee brewed, she poured herself a cup. The first cup of the morning, strong and hot, but laced liberally with sweetener and low-fat creamer. A throbbing little ache pulsed in the right side of her head. A queazy unease rumbled in her stomach. She sipped the tan brew, allowing it to trickle slowly down her throat.

How long would it be before Morgan came downstairs? How many minutes did she have until she'd have to face him? Despite sixteen years apart, they still knew each other too well to pretend. Neither of them had gotten much sleep. Morgan had been as restless with unfulfilled need as she had been. And nothing had changed with the passing of time. After nearly two decades, she still wanted him with the same mindless passion she had when she'd been a girl. And even now she was as vulnerable to his masculine allure as she'd been last night. If he came downstairs and took her into his arms, if he kissed her, if he touched her, would she have the strength to reject him again?

Sipping her coffee, she reached over and turned on the small portable television on the built-in desk in the corner. She left the sound off. No need to disturb the sweet silence until the commercial ended. She'd catch the morning weather and traffic reports before she went outside for the newspaper.

After the commercial break, Tony Hayes's smiling face appeared on the television screen. Damn! She had the TV on the wrong station. She never watched Wake Up Birmingham. Clicking the sound button on the remote control, she started to press the channel changer, but stopped suddenly when she heard Tony's heartfelt plea.

"Friends, I know you are as upset as I am that Jimmy Farraday was murdered, in cold blood, right here at WHNB." Tony's mouth broadened into a big smile. He sighed. "Never has a finer man walked the face of this earth. No one misses him as much as I do. He was my dearest friend. My mentor." Sighing again, Tony sobered and wiped an imaginary tear from his eye.

Bethany's thumb hovered over the channel button.

"Jimmy's accused murderess is free to walk the streets, to fill people's heads with her lies about a good man. I know this woman and cannot imagine what has possessed her." Tony's face reddened as he bounced around the stage like a hell-fire and brimstone preacher. "There's nothing sadder than a good woman gone bad. Nothing more tragic than for a man's daughter to turn against him.

"I'm pleading with those of you who loved Jimmy as I did, to demand justice. Swift, sure justice!"

Had Tony been spouting off this slanderous condemnation of

her ever since he'd come on the air at five-thirty? she wondered. How many of Jimmy's loyal fans had he stirred to vengeance? Surely he couldn't go on television and defame her this way. She knew that ever since she'd refused to go out with him again, after two dates four years ago, Tony had treated her coolly, but she'd never dreamed he would be so vindictive. Had he truly loved Jimmy that much? And did he really believe she killed her stepfather?

With trembling fingers, Bethany pushed the Power button, turned off the television and tossed the remote onto the table. She didn't have to listen to any more of this drivel. If Tony Hayes thought he could malign her on local television, he'd better think again. She'd call Maxine and find out if she had grounds to sue.

After setting her coffee cup aside, she unarmed the security alarm, turned on the outside floodlights and exited through the side door leading to the breezeway between the house and the garage. Breathing in the fresh, cool air that reminded her that autumn was only three weeks away, she scanned the driveway for the paper. Catching a glimpse of the plastic-wrapped roll, she grimaced. Plastic covering on the morning paper was a sure indication that rain was predicted for that day.

When she stepped off the breezeway and onto the driveway, she heard an approaching vehicle. The loud clatter-clanking of a large truck echoed through the stillness of the peaceful Forest Park community. It wasn't garbage pickup day and no one who lived in this area drove a commercial vehicle. Just as she leaned over to pick up the Birmingham News, a dump truck backed into her drive. Her heartbeat accelerated. Foreboding swirled in the depths of her stomach. Bethany blinked a couple of times, unable to believe her own eyes when the truck bed rose into the air and dumped its load onto her lawn. The stench of fresh manure filled the air, sickening Bethany instantly. Grabbing the paper in one hand, she stood up straight and covered her mouth and nose with her other hand.

She ran toward the truck, yelling at the top of her lungs. "Who sent you here? Who hired you to empty a load of manure on my lawn?"

Just as she reached the side of the truck, the driver rolled down the window, stuck out his head and spat a stream of brown tobacco juice toward Bethany. The spittle landed on her shoe. Crinkling her nose in disgust, she groaned and stepped backward.

"This here's a little present from Jimmy Farraday's friends," the burly red-haired man said.

"You cannot leave this here! Do you hear me? I'll call the police!"

The man laughed, the robust sound sending shivers along Bethany's spine. "You'd just better be glad that I didn't bury you alive in this stuff. It's what you deserve."

When Bethany reached out, intending to pound her fists against the truck door, Morgan grabbed her wrists and pulled her hands over her head. Gasping, she struggled against him momentarily, then relaxed when he walked her backward, away from the truck. He jerked the newspaper out of her clutched hand.

"You scared me to death," she told Morgan.

"Heard you had you a bodyguard," the man said. "Good thing. Somebody's liable to fill you full of lead the way you did Jimmy."

"I suggest you leave." Morgan glared at the truck driver, a deadly glint in his eye. "You've done what you came here to do."

"You're going to let him get away with this...this..." Bethany spluttered furiously. "Just look at my beautiful lawn. And the smell is horrible...sickening, and—"

"I've already called the police and given them the license plate number on this truck." Morgan glanced up at the driver, whose smile suddenly vanished. Manacling her around the waist, Morgan lifted her off her feet. "We'll get someone in here today to clean up this mess," he told her as she squirmed in his arms. "In the meantime, let's just leave our morning visitor to the police."

Bethany fought against Morgan's tenacious hold. "Let me go! If you're not going to do something, I am! I'm not letting that stupid redneck get away with this."

Hoisting her under his arm, Morgan carried a wriggling, huffing Bethany up the drive and onto the breezeway. The truck pulled out of the drive and chugged its way down the street. When Morgan set Bethany on her feet, she turned on him, her hazel eyes blazing. Planting her hands on her hips, she gritted her teeth.

"Why didn't you do something?" she demanded.

"I called the police," he said. "What else do you think I should have done?"

His question stumped her momentarily. "I don't know. Dragged him out of the truck and beat him to a pulp, I suppose."

"As angry as you are, I think you could have done that yourself, without any help from me."

Admitting to herself that she might have overreacted just a bit, she sighed loudly, then glanced down at her dirty shoe, stained by tobacco juice spittle. "He spit on my shoe. That deserved a punch in the nose."

Morgan handed Bethany the *Birmingham News.* "Here's your paper." Bending down on one knee, he grasped her ankle, lifted her foot and removed her nasty shoe. His big fingers lightly caressed her instep. She shivered. He removed her other shoe, then hooked two fingers into the back of the narrow heels. "The shoe can be cleaned. Most of the manure can be removed from the yard and the rest can be scattered for fertilizer."

"You think I overreacted, don't you?" She opened the door to the kitchen.

"I think you have every right to be upset, even angry." Morgan followed her into the house. "But yes, considering that one attempt has already been made on your life, I do think you might have overreacted to a minor irritation. The way I see it, Farraday's fans harassing you is a secondary concern. It's something I can handle."

"Well, I'm so glad you can handle it!" She stomped across the floor in her stocking feet.

He closed and locked the door behind him, then set her dirty shoes in the corner. "Harassment is something you can deal with. I'm not nearly as upset over the fact that some idiot thought he was making a statement by dumping manure in your yard as I am the fact that you went outside this house, alone, in the dark." He grabbed her shoulder and whirled her around to face him. His steel-blue eyes bored into her. "I don't want you to ever go outside this house without me. Do you understand? Not ever again."

His words were tinged with anger and fear, and she suddenly realized how foolish she'd been to venture into her own front yard without her bodyguard. Morgan was right. Harassment was a minor irritation. Manure could be cleared away; spittle could be washed off. But what if the person who'd sent her the mail bomb had been waiting outside for her instead of some stupid but harmless, loudmouthed fan of Jimmy's? She could be dead now.

Shuddering at the thought, she gazed up into Morgan's concerned face and said, "I'm sorry. You're right. I wasn't thinking."

Releasing his hold on her shoulder, he walked around her and went over to the coffee machine. "It wasn't all your fault," he told her. "No, you shouldn't have gone outside, but then you aren't accustomed to having a bodyguard. I was as much at fault as you. Maybe more. When I heard you come downstairs, I should have followed you immediately, instead of giving you some time alone."

"It wasn't your fault. How could you have known I'd go outside?"

"Under normal circumstances, I would have followed you immediately and stayed at your side. But I let my personal feelings interfere with doing my job." He removed a mug from the cabinet, filled it with coffee and set the mug on the table. "I should have known that I couldn't be objective when it came to you, and I should have foreseen what happened between us last night."

"Nothing happened."

"Who are you lying to, Beth, yourself or me?"

"All right, so something did happen. But nothing we couldn't handle."

When she neared the table, he reached up and grabbed her wrist. She hesitated, then glanced down at him.

"Can we handle it?" he asked. "Can I give you the best protection possible when all I can think about is making love to you?"

She jerked her wrist free, then quickly picked up her coffee cup and refilled it. "Are you considering quitting this job and turning it over to someone else?"

"That would be the smart thing to do, wouldn't it? But then I've never done the smart thing when it came to you, have I?"

"So, what are you trying to tell me?" Cradling her cup in both hands, she brought it to her lips.

"I let you come downstairs alone this morning because I thought you probably dreaded facing me again as much as I dreaded facing you. We know what nearly happened last night, what I wanted to happen. And I know you didn't sleep any better than I did. You tossed and turned all night wishing you were lying in my arms."

She opened her mouth to protest, but his warning glare silenced her.

"I'm not leaving, Beth. I'm staying until we find out who really killed Farraday. You might be safer with someone else, but I can't hand you over to another man. Not ever again."

Silence hung between them like a soundless, elegiac message, an unspoken, heartbreaking memory. Their gazes locked for endless moments, then Bethany turned abruptly.

She set her coffee cup on the counter, walked across the room and lifted her dirty shoes off the floor. "I'm going to take these upstairs and clean them. I'll be back down in a few minutes."

She had to escape, had to get away from his declaration of guilt. "I can't hand you over to another man. Not ever again." He knew, damn him! He knew that leaving her sixteen years ago had been tantamount to giving her to Amery. Had he known, even then, what would happen to her when he left Birmingham and then left, anyway?

Bethany stayed in her room long after she'd cleaned her shoe. She didn't want to go back downstairs and face Morgan, even though she knew that sooner or later she'd have no choice. Had she made a mistake allowing him to become her bodyguard, letting him move into her home and live with Anne Marie and her? She had thought she could deal with whatever attraction she still felt for him, thought she was strong enough to withstand any emotional assault his presence might cause. But she'd been wrong. She could no more control her desire for Morgan now than she'd been able to in the past.

She reminded herself of the reason she had opened her home

to him, why she wanted and needed him to become a part of her life. A part of Anne Marie's life. She hoped that on some level Morgan and Anne Marie would bond. If the worst happened and she was sent to prison for Jimmy's murder, then she would have to tell Morgan that he was Anne Marie's father. By that time, she prayed that he'd care too much for their child to turn his back on her.

She gasped when she heard a knock on her door. Turning quickly, she instinctively took a step backward when Morgan opened the door and walked into her bedroom.

"I just got a call." He held up his cellular phone. Lines wrinkled his normally smooth brow.

"What's wrong?" Her stomach quivered.

"Maxine called. Judge Harper has set a date for your grand jury hearing."

"When?"

"Next Thursday. Ten o'clock. Jefferson County Courthouse."

"Oh, God!" Lifting her hand to her mouth, she bit down on her clenched fist.

"You knew it was coming. Better to get it over with. There's a chance you won't have to go to trial."

"Do you really believe that? With all the evidence the district attorney has against me, I don't see how the jury could rule in my favor."

"If we can find Farraday's murderer, all the charges will be dropped against you." He crossed the room, reached out and gripped the back of her neck.

Unmoving, she stood there and stared at him, her body as tense as a coiled spring. "What are our chances of discovering who killed Jimmy by next Wednesday?"

He stroked the side of her neck with his thumb. "I won't kid you. The odds are against us. But even if the grand jury rules to hand you over for trial, it doesn't mean you'll be found guilty."

"I'm scared, Morgan. For myself. And for Anne Marie. I don't know what she'd do if I had to leave her."

Morgan drew Bethany toward him; she went without hesitation. He wrapped her in his arms; she laid her head on his chest.

"I'm not going to let you go to prison for a crime you didn't commit," he said. "I'm not going to let anyone or anything hurt you or Anne Marie. Not ever again. I promise."

"Oh, Morgan. I thought I told you not to make any promises you couldn't keep."

Lifting her chin, he tilted her face upward, then lowered his head and brushed her lips with a featherlight kiss. "I'll do everything in my power to protect you and your daughter. And that *is* a promise I'll keep."

"If I go to prison—"

He silenced her with his mouth, the kiss forceful and demanding. When he lifted his head, he said. "You aren't going to prison."

"But if I do, would you...will you keep your promise to protect Anne Marie?"

"You aren't going to prison," he repeated.

She clutched his shoulders. "But if I do, will you—?"

"I'll keep my promise."

Smiling weakly, she nodded as she swallowed her unshed tears. "Thank you."

Chapter 8

The days passed quickly for Bethany—far too quickly. Tomorrow the grand jury would convene and her fate would be decided by a group of eighteen men and women who didn't personally know her or Jimmy Farraday. They wouldn't know what a bastard Jimmy had been, what a lousy father, what a habitually unfaithful husband. And they wouldn't know that she was innocent. The prosecuter would present them with the facts. And the cold hard facts pointed directly to Bethany as Jimmy's murderer.

She knew that it would take a miracle to prevent the jury from binding her over for trial. Despite Morgan's continuous attempts to boost her morale and convince her otherwise, she realized the deck was stacked against her.

She was scared. For herself. For Anne Marie. And she was even scared that the real murderer might turn out to be someone near and dear to her. The pressure she felt on a daily basis was compounded by Morgan's presence. With every subtle glance, every unexpected touch, the tension between them increased. But she couldn't send him away, not when there was every possibility that she would have to turn over Anne Marie's care to him sometime in the very near future.

"Let's review all our information again." Morgan propped his big feet up on the paisley ottoman in front of him and re-adjusted his hips in the Chippendale armchair. "There has to be something here that can help us."

"I can't imagine what it could be." Bethany slipped off her shoes and let them drop to the floor. Bending her knees, she lifted her feet up on the sofa. "All this information proves—" she threw the file folder on the coffee table "—is that I wasn't the only one with a motive for killing Jimmy. A lot of people hated him, but I'm the one whose fingerprints were on the gun that shot him. I'm the only one who threatened to kill him the night before he was murdered. And I'm the one who witnesses will swear was at the scene of the crime a few minutes before Jimmy's body was discovered."

"You and I both know that one of the suspects on our list went into Jimmy's office, got your gun out of your purse and used it to kill Jimmy, then slipped out of his office without being seen."

"Well, that narrows it down, doesn't it?" Bethany said sarcastically. "Every suspect on our list was at the television station that afternoon. Mother was there. James was there. And of course, Tony and Vivian were both at the station."

"And Seth Renfrew," Morgan said.

"Despite what you think, I do not believe Seth killed Jimmy. My heavens, if Seth had been going to kill Jimmy, he'd have done it years ago, wouldn't he? I mean, why wait until now?"

"As far as I can see, Seth had more reason to hate Farraday than anyone else, except perhaps your mother."

Grabbing one of the numerous throw pillows on the sofa, Bethany hugged it to her. "I've told you repeatedly that I refuse to believe my own mother would allow me to go through the hell I'm in right now. If she killed Jimmy—"

"Eileen might not be thinking rationally. We both know that she's always acted first and thought about what she did later, after the fact."

"As far as I'm concerned, we can scratch Mother, Seth and James off the list." Bethany's oval nails dug into the burgundy polished cotton pillow.

"You're thinking with your heart and not your head," Morgan told her. "You love these people so you don't want to believe one of them killed Jimmy, and for all intents and purposes framed you for the murder. If we eliminate them, that leaves Vivian and Tony, and from what we've been able to find out, both of them worshipped Jimmy."

Bethany flung the pillow at Morgan. He grabbed it midair and tossed it back onto the sofa.

"But Vivian has a motive and so does Tony," she said. "Just because they were in awe of Jimmy doesn't mean one of them couldn't have killed him. Lord knows that Mother was madly in love with Jimmy and yet she hated him, too."

"All right, let's look at the facts." Kicking the ottoman forward, Morgan stood, walked over to the front window and gazed out at the gray morning sky. "Vivian and Jimmy were lovers on and off, ever since she came to work for him. Maybe he promised to divorce Eileen and marry her. Maybe he strung her along for years. She could have gotten tired of waiting, of being lied to, and killed him. But we have no evidence. Only a theory."

Glancing over her shoulder, Bethany stared at Morgan's broad back. Memories flashed through her mind. Morgan swimming laps in the pool. Morgan doing push-ups in his room. Morgan checking his gun and then strapping on his shoulder holster.

"So that leaves Tony," Bethany said calmly, while butterflies danced in her stomach. She hated herself for letting Morgan's nearness affect her so strongly. But it had always been that way. From the first moment she saw him, when she was eighteen. "Tony's only motive is that he wanted Jimmy's job. But all he had to do was wait a couple of years until Jimmy retired. He was already the heir apparent."

"Maybe Tony got tired of waiting. He wouldn't be the first prince to eliminate a king in order to acquire a throne."

A roll of distant thunder rumbled noisily. Dark, sooty clouds swirled in the sky. Morgan stuck his hands in his pockets. From the evidence they'd acquired during the last few days, Morgan couldn't see any real reason for Vivian or Tony to have murdered Jimmy. Not unless something showed up after the agency dug a little deeper into their backgrounds.

Vivian Crosby was a model citizen, except for her long-standing affair with a married man. And Tony Hayes seemed to be cut from the same cloth as his mentor—a loudmouthed sleaze, adored by his public and despised by those who knew him intimately. But just because a guy was a real son of a bitch didn't mean he was capable of murder.

"Didn't the Dundee Agency come up with any information on Vivian or Tony that might help us?" Bethany asked.

Turning around, Morgan glanced at Bethany. Dark circles under her eyes told him what he already knew. She wasn't sleeping well. He often heard her stirring about in her room in the middle of the night. He had longed to go to her, take her in his arms and give her comfort. But if he'd gone to her, she would have sent him away. She knew as well as he did that, between them, comfort would soon turn to passion.

"Dane hasn't come across anything that could help us," Morgan said. "Just general stuff. Things like Vivian was homecoming queen in high school. She's been married and divorced. No children. And Tony was born illegitimate and adopted by his stepfather when he was two years old. He did a stint in the army and he's worked at a dozen different television stations in the past twenty years. He's never been married, has no children, but considers himself quite a ladies' man."

"You don't have to tell me." Bethany grimaced, remembering her second date with Tony, when she'd had to fight him off.

"Have you had some trouble with Tony Hayes?"

"Four years ago I had two dates with him. The first one was a social function, and I actually had an enjoyable time, but the second date turned into a physical struggle. He thought that a second date meant he'd be invited to spend the night."

"So, you rejected him. Maybe he's been carrying a grudge the past four years. That would give him a motive for framing you. Now, if we could just come up with a believable motive for him to have killed Farraday."

"We're back where we started." Bethany slid her legs off the sofa and stood. "We keep going around in circles and we always come back to Mother, James and Seth."

"Despite your misgivings, we're going to have to consider all three of them as suspects."

"I thought you told Anne Marie that you didn't think James killed his father."

"I don't think he did," Morgan said. "I kind of like the kid.

But that doesn't mean I can rule him out as a suspect. Especially not since we learned that Jimmy had a million-dollar life insurance policy and James is his sole beneficiary."

"That's not a good reason." Bethany paced back and forth in front of the stone fireplace. "Mother buys James anything he wants. She adores him. Mother and Jimmy were always fighting over the way she spoiled James. Jimmy even demanded that Mother not let James have any money without his approval."

"You've just given James another motive. He hated his father. He loves Eileen and didn't like the way Jimmy treated her. Not only does he stand to inherit a million dollars in insurance money, with Jimmy out of the way, but now there's no one to censor Eileen's generosity."

"Whatever you do, don't let Anne Marie know that James is still a suspect." Crossing her arms over her chest, Bethany increased her pace to a frantic speed, marching back and forth from the round, cloth-covered table by the fireplace to the double windows, draped in green plaid.

Sweeping across the room, Morgan grabbed Bethany's arm. "Honey, will you stop pacing? You're making me crazy."

She glanced down at his hand holding her, then up at his stern face. Jerking away from him, she almost toppled over, but righted her footing before he reached for her again.

"I'm making *you* crazy!" she shouted. "I'm the one who's going out of my mind. My life has turned into a nightmare. Jimmy's fans keep sending me letters—"

"Letters you don't even see," Morgan told her. "Letters that I intercept and take care of without your being bothered with them."

"And now that I have a new, unlisted home phone number, those idiots are calling my boutiques and harassing my employees."

"Since we've had a caller ID box attached to the phones, those calls have practically stopped."

"There were people picketing my boutiques this past weekend," she said.

"And the police dispersed the picketers before they did any harm."

"Well, Tony's daily condemnation of me on television is harming me. And Maxine can't stop him because he's never mentioned my name and he always refers to me as the suspect.'' Bethany rushed out of the living room.

Morgan caught up with her in the kitchen. She stood at the open refrigerator, her back to him. He held out his hand, but let it hover over her, not quite making contact. He wanted to comfort her, but touching her would be a mistake.

''Look, honey, you have every right to be nervous, upset and even angry. But you have to stop and think. We've been investigating every aspect of Jimmy's murder for only a week now. As difficult as it is for you, you're going to have to be patient and believe that sooner or later, we'll unearth something that will lead us directly to Jimmy's real murderer.''

'''Be patient'?'' She whirled around, a package of sliced chicken in one hand and a bottle of mustard in the other. ''If I were the only one being affected by this situation, I might be able to deal with it better. But my child is suffering and I can't bear it. God only knows what Anne Marie is putting up with at school right this minute. I want to be there with her, all the time, protecting her, defending her.''

''Believe it or not, I understand how you feel,'' Morgan said. ''When we dropped her off at school, I wanted to go in with her and issue a warning that nobody had better mess with Anne Marie Wyndham or they'd be sorry.'' Morgan's mouth curved into a halfhearted grin. He'd known Bethany's child only a week and yet he felt connected to the girl and as protective of her as he was of her mother. He supposed he felt that way because Anne Marie was Bethany's child, or maybe because the girl so obviously adored him. Whatever the cause, he had to admit that he was feeling downright paternal toward her.

Bethany tightened her hold on the mustard bottle. ''If she comes home today, in tears, I don't—''

''She won't come home in tears. I guarantee it. You've raised a strong, self-confident girl. She went to school today prepared for whatever happens. My money's on Anne Marie. Something tells me that she's capable of giving as good as she gets.''

''Oh, God, I hope so.''

Bethany placed the chicken and mustard on the table, then opened the bread box and removed a loaf of whole wheat.

''What are you doing?'' he asked.

''Fixing lunch.'' She opened the loaf of bread.

"Bethany, it's only ten o'clock."

She slung the loaf of bread across the room. Slices scattered on the floor. "Dammit! I don't even know what I'm doing anymore."

Caution be damned. He had to touch her! Gripping her shoulders, Morgan kneaded softly. "You're doing fine. It's only normal that you'd be nervous and scared."

Bethany leaned her back against his chest, momentarily giving in to her need for comfort. Seeking comfort from Morgan could be dangerous. But right now, she didn't care. She needed something—someone—to hold on to and keep her from drowning in a sea of fear and self-doubt.

Morgan turned her in his arms. She looked up into his eyes and knew she was lost. He offered her everything. In his arms she could find the comfort she wanted, the protection she needed, the temporary peace her mind longed for and the fulfillment her body craved. With trembling fingers, she reached up and touched his cheek.

"Morgan?"

As if on cue, his cellular phone rang. Cursing under his breath, he eased one arm around Bethany's waist, then reached inside his jacket pocket and removed his phone.

Flipping it open, he held the telephone to his ear. "Kane here."

Bethany held her breath as she watched Morgan's face for any sign of emotion. She saw none.

"Yes. Yes," he said. "No, you're right. That gives us another motive. I'll tell Bethany, but she's not going to like it."

"What is it?" She tugged on Morgan's sleeve. "What am I not going to like?"

"We still don't have any proof," Morgan said into the phone. "Keep digging. I don't want anything overlooked." He flipped the phone closed and returned it to his pocket.

"Who was that? What am I not going to like?"

"That was Dane Carmichael. He's uncovered some information on Seth Renfrew."

"What sort of information?" Bethany's heartbeat drummed in her ears.

"Did you know that Seth had a sister who committed suicide twelve years ago?"

"We knew he had a sister who was dead, but—"

"Renfrew's sister was involved with Jimmy Farraday. When she caught him with another woman, she went home and took an overdose of sleeping pills. Renfrew was the one who found her body and the suicide note addressed to Farraday."

"Oh, poor Seth." Bethany gasped as she suddenly realized the implications. "This information gives Seth another motive for killing Jimmy, doesn't it?"

"We need to talk to Renfrew," Morgan said. "I want to look the man straight in the eye and have him deny that he killed Farraday."

They tracked Seth down at the Birmingham Country Club where he was having lunch with Eileen. Bethany dreaded the confrontation, but she knew it was necessary. She didn't believe that Seth had killed Jimmy, but she did think it odd that he had never told her about his sister's suicide or her involvement with Jimmy. Why had he kept such an important part of his past a secret?

"Bethany, darling." Eileen, dressed appropriately for a widow in a stunning black silk dress, grasped her daughter's hand. "What are y'all doing here?"

Ever the Southern gentleman, Seth stood. "Won't you and Mr. Kane join us for lunch?"

"Yes, thank you." Bethany glanced over her shoulder, seeking Morgan's approval.

Morgan assisted her into a chair and then seated himself across from Seth. A waiter arrived instantly and Bethany hurriedly ordered two iced teas and salads, all the while watching while Morgan carefully scrutinized Seth. Did he think he could detect signs of innocence or guilt just by examining Seth?

"This is my first day out since Jimmy's funeral," Eileen said. "Seth insisted that there was no reason for me to stay confined to the house."

"Her friends are here at the club," Seth said. "They all love her and have been so happy to see her. No one expects her to hide away."

"I suppose no one has been rude enough to ask if you think your daughter killed your husband." Lifting her white napkin,

Bethany shook the starched linen apart and draped it across her lap.

"None of our friends think you killed Jimmy." Eileen curled her jeweled fingers around Bethany's wrist. "Something's wrong, isn't it? Y'all didn't come here just to have lunch with us. What is it? What's happened?"

"Nothing has happened, Mother." Bethany twisted her arm until she was able to clasp her mother's hand in hers. "Morgan has just discovered some information and he needs to ask Seth a few questions."

"Ask Seth questions about what?" Snapping her head around, Eileen glared at Morgan. "Surely Seth isn't under suspicion. He is no more capable of murder than I am."

Silence dominated the table. The faint clinking of silverware and china blended with the muted conversations of the other patrons. Bethany took a deep breath. Seth's cheeks flushed. Eileen's mouth opened in a silent gasp. Morgan remained totally unmoved, his face a blank.

"Oh, I see." Eileen sat up ramrod straight in the chair. "So I'm a suspect, too."

"No, Mother, of course you and Seth aren't suspects. I know that neither of you—"

"That's not quite true," Morgan interrupted. "Bethany doesn't believe either of you killed Jimmy, but as far as I'm concerned anyone with motive and opportunity is a suspect. And unfortunately, that includes both of you."

Bethany squeezed her mother's hand tightly. Eileen jerked her hand out of Bethany's. "I did not kill Jimmy," Eileen whispered as she glanced around to see if anyone overheard their conversation. "Did I wish him dead? Yes. Often. But as odd as it may seem to you, I loved Jimmy as much as I hated him. Every time he embarrassed me, every time he disappointed me, every time he infuriated me with his conduct, he promised he'd change, that it would never happen again. And I wanted so desperately to believe him."

"You stayed with Jimmy because, despite everything, you still loved him?" Bethany asked, unable to understand how her mother could have continued loving such a worthless piece of trash.

"Yes, that was one of the reasons," Eileen said.

"What were the other reasons?" Morgan asked.

"Only one other reason." Eileen stared defiantly, proudly at Morgan. "James. I remained married to Jimmy for James's sake. That poor child needed me. He still does. I knew that if I divorced Jimmy and tried to gain custody of James, I would have to air all our dirty laundry in public."

"Oh, Mother." Bethany felt a mixture of sympathy and aggravation. Eileen had been a loving and indulgent parent, but a poor role model. Eileen Dow Farraday had always lived her life with her social position foremost in her mind. Slightly scatter-brained and often impulsive, she'd made her share of mistakes, but her greatest concern had never been to correct those mistakes, only to hide them from the world.

Morgan focused his attention on Seth Renfrew. "Did you kill Jimmy Farraday?"

Seth's pink flushed cheeks darkened. He dampened his lips with his tongue, then wiped his cupped hand across his mouth.

"I did have the opportunity. I was at WHNB at the time Jimmy was shot. But I wasn't there to see him. I'd dropped some ads by for an upcoming charity event of which I'm publicity chairman."

"I'm already aware of your reason for being at WHNB," Morgan said. "But I think it's a rather odd coincidence that you chose that day and that time to stop by WHNB."

"Seth may have had the opportunity to kill Jimmy," Bethany said, "but I know he would never let me take the blame for a crime he had committed."

Releasing an indrawn breath, Seth smiled weakly at Bethany. "Thank you, my dear, for saying that, for believing that I didn't kill Jimmy."

"Bethany may believe you," Morgan said. "But I'd like for you to convince me. If I were in your shoes, with two strong motives for killing Farraday, I'd be sweating."

"What can I say or do to convince you, Mr. Kane?"

"Explain why you never told anyone about your sister Lynda's death?"

"How did you..." Clasping his shaky hands, Seth stared down at his lap. "Of course, you would thoroughly investigate anyone you suspected."

"What's this about Lynda Renfrew?" Eileen asked. "Surely,

you're not referring to her—'' Eileen lowered her voice to a mere whisper ''—suicide, are you? Seth told me all about Lynda before I married Jimmy. He tried to warn me against marrying that womanizing jerk. But I didn't listen to him, and I've paid dearly for the past ten years.''

''Mother, are you saying that you've known all these years that Seth's sister committed suicide because of Jimmy Farraday?''

''Yes, of course, I've known. Seth and I have no secrets from each other.'' Eileen's lips quivered ever so slightly, then she smiled at her old friend. ''I know that Seth loves me, that he's always loved me.''

''I hated Jimmy Farraday more than any man on earth,'' Seth admitted. ''He destroyed my sister and he made Eileen's life a living hell. But if my love for Eileen and my need to avenge my sister's death are my motives for murdering Jimmy, why would I have waited so long? Why didn't I kill Jimmy years ago?''

''That's exactly what I told him.'' Bethany glared at Morgan, a self-satisfied expression on her face.

''I don't know,'' Morgan said. ''Perhaps the right opportunity never came along. Or maybe you'd finally taken all you could bear. You knew Farraday had come on to Anne Marie, didn't you?''

''Oh, my God!'' Eileen gasped loud enough that her outburst gained attention from people at the two nearest tables.

''Dammit, Morgan, Seth knew, but Mother didn't!'' Bethany told him.

''It's all right,'' Eileen said. ''I shouldn't be surprised, should I?'' Reaching out, she grasped Bethany's hand. ''You told me years ago that Jimmy tried to...to rape you, and I wouldn't let myself believe you. I chose to believe his explanation instead.'' Eileen turned to Morgan. ''I didn't kill Jimmy, but I wish I had. I wish I'd had the courage to rid the world of the monster I was married to.''

''I don't think Mr. Kane really suspects you, Eileen,'' Seth said. ''He didn't come here to question you.''

Bethany looked pleadingly at her business partner. ''For heaven's sake, Seth, tell him you didn't kill Jimmy.''

''I could say that I didn't shoot Jimmy, but there's no way

you or Mr. Kane would know whether or not I was lying. I could have killed him. I did have opportunity and motive. And I could be biding my time, waiting to see if you go to trial and then I could wait even longer to see if you are convicted before I confess."

"Stop it! I know you didn't kill Jimmy, no matter what Morgan believes. You care too much for me and Anne Marie to ever put me through this torment!" Bethany jumped up from her chair just as the waiter served her salad. When she and the waiter collided, the tray he carried flipped over, dumping the tea glasses to the floor. Bits and pieces of salad flew in every direction as the bowls hurled through the air.

"I'm sorry," Bethany said as she brushed pieces of lettuce and tomato off her yellow silk blouse. With tears blurring her vision, she shoved past the waiter.

Morgan called after her, and when she didn't pause in her escape, he shoved back his chair and stood. "My accusations are nothing personal," he told Seth and Eileen. "I'm just doing what I've been hired to do and that's find out who really killed Farraday. I can't afford not to follow through on every possible lead."

Before either Seth or Eileen could reply, Morgan rushed after Bethany. He caught up with her outside. The damp residue of a scattered shower glimmered on the grass and a fine mist of steam rose off the pavement. Sunshine broke through the lingering cloud cover, temporarily brightening the sky and spreading a warm radiance over the earth. When Morgan clutched Bethany's elbow, she spun away from him and walked off. He cursed under his breath, then headed after her. Every time he tried to touch her, she avoided his grasp.

"Leave me alone! Go back to Atlanta. Have your agency send me another bodyguard."

He followed along beside her as she trekked toward her Mercedes S600. Sunlight reflected off the windshield of the white coupe, hitting Bethany in the eye. Squinting, she glanced away and rummaged in her purse for the car keys.

"You're being irrational." Morgan grabbed the keys out of her hand, manacled her wrist and dragged her over to the car.

"Let go of me!" When she tried to free herself, he tightened his hold. Struggling against his superior strength, she soon tired and stopped fighting him. "Dammit, why did you have to do that to Seth?"

Morgan dragged her around the hood of the car, unlocked the door and deposited her in the passenger seat. "I'm trying to unearth the truth and sometimes that can't be done without stepping on some toes, without hurting feelings."

Bethany glared at Morgan, her jaw tight with barely suppressed rage. "The truth? The truth is that Seth Renfrew did not kill Jimmy!"

"Just because you want to believe he's innocent doesn't make it true."

Morgan closed the door, rushed around to the driver's side and got in, then sat there clutching the keys in his hand. "Renfrew never actually denied that he killed Farraday, did he?"

"I hate you for doing that to Seth." Crossing her arms over her waist, Bethany gripped her elbows. She was not going to fall apart. She wasn't going to cry. She'd already cried too much as it was. Tears wouldn't solve her problems. "I don't want you to rip apart the people I love in your quest to prove my innocence."

"Who are you really angry with?" Morgan inserted the key into the ignition switch and turned over the motor. "Are you angry with me or with yourself, because deep down inside you aren't a hundred percent sure Renfrew didn't kill Farraday?"

Bethany swung around in the seat, her hazel eyes flashing angrily. She opened her mouth, but no words came out. Clenching her jaw tightly, she sat there glaring at Morgan, her shoulders trembling as she tried valiantly not to succumb to tears.

Damn! He hated seeing Bethany like this, on the verge of tears and struggling desperately to remain in control. "I can imagine how difficult it is for you to accept the possibility that someone you care about might actually be responsible for putting you in this unbearable situation."

"Seth didn't kill Jimmy."

Morgan clutched the leather-covered wood steering wheel. "You can't be sure. Even if Renfrew had denied killing Farraday, you could—"

"When you asked me if I'd killed Jimmy and I told you that I hadn't, you believed me. Why can't you believe that Seth is innocent? I know, deep down inside—" she laid her hand over her heart "—that despite a few silly doubts on my part, Seth didn't kill Jimmy."

"I don't know Seth Renfrew, but I'll take your word for it that he's a good guy. He seems to be devoted to your mother...and to you and Anne Marie." Morgan turned his head just a fraction and glanced at Bethany. "I've learned that only a fool trusts too easily. Often things are not what they seem. That's a lesson I learned the hard way. I don't trust anyone. Except..." Turning back around, he stared out the front windshield, deliberately avoiding eye contact with Bethany. "The reason I believed you when you said you didn't kill your stepfather is because I *do* trust you. You're the only person I've ever trusted completely. I know you'd never lie to me."

Oh, dear God! Bethany wanted to die on the spot. He trusted her. She was the only person he'd ever trusted completely. He knew she'd never lie to him.

How would she ever be able to explain to him that she had lied to him for sixteen years, lied by omission? If it became necessary for her to tell him the truth about Anne Marie's parentage, would Morgan ever forgive her for a lifetime of silence?

She sat beside him, but separated herself from him mentally, putting as much distance between them as possible. She didn't dare glance his way for fear he would see the truth in her eyes.

Morgan revved the powerful V12 motor, shifted into reverse and backed out of the parking slot. Bethany sat perfectly still, only the muted sound of her breathing mingling with Morgan's pierced the utter silence within the car. Morgan crossed Montclair Road as he headed for Forest Park.

They would be home soon. Home and alone together. She couldn't face him. Not now. Not yet. His confession had not only unnerved her, but it had forced her to accept a hard truth. No matter what happened to her, she had to tell Morgan the truth about Anne Marie. Even if by telling him the truth, she destroyed his faith in her and made him hate her. Morgan deserved to know that he had a daughter.

Chapter 9

The moment they arrived at her home, Bethany rushed up the stairs, pausing only long enough to make a halfhearted excuse. "I have a terrible headache. I'm going to take something for it and lie down awhile."

Morgan wanted to tell her not to run away, not to run from him. He hadn't meant to upset her, and God knew the last thing he wanted was to ever hurt her again. But he said nothing. Standing at the foot of the stairs, he watched her until she disappeared from view. He didn't doubt that she had a headache, but he knew it wasn't the real reason she'd fled to her room. She wanted to escape from him. He understood if she was still angry with him for making her face the possibility that a dear and trusted friend might be responsible not only for Farraday's murder, but for her present predicament. What Morgan didn't understand was why, when he had explained how much he trusted her, she had suddenly gone deadly still. She hadn't so much as glanced his way during the drive home, and she'd all but run from him the second he pulled into the driveway.

What was it that had Bethany running scared, running from him? His gut instincts told him that her fear had nothing to do with Farraday's murder. No, Bethany's reluctance to face him, her urgent need to get away from him, stemmed from something far more personal. But what?

Why had his statement about her being the only person he'd ever completely trusted upset her so much? Did she realize that, despite everything that had happened between them in the past, he had always cared about her and still did? Was it easier for her to believe that he'd never cared, that not once in all their years apart had he had any regrets?

Maybe he'd forced Bethany to examine her own feelings more closely than she wanted to. Neither of them could deny the desire—stronger than ever—that still existed between them. Bethany hadn't changed so much that she had developed a cavalier attitude toward sex. No, if she still wanted him that meant that she still cared about him, perhaps even still loved him.

The thought that Bethany might still love him rattled Morgan. He knew for sure that he didn't deserve her love. He never had. And he wasn't even sure he wanted her love, not if it meant he'd wind up hurting her all over again.

After removing his jacket and tie, he went into the kitchen, opened the pantry door and glanced around. Neither he nor Bethany had eaten a bite since their early-morning coffee, juice and toast. Their salads had just arrived when Bethany ran from the country club and barreled straight into their waiter. She was bound to be starving. Maybe part of her headache was due to hunger. He wasn't much of a cook, but living alone all his adult life, a guy learned how to open cans and heat stuff in the microwave.

Bethany unbuttoned her yellow silk blouse, slipped it off her shoulders and tossed it into the dirty clothes hamper. Luckily she had ordered her salad dressing on the side, so the spots on her blouse had come from the moisture on the fresh vegetables in her salad and not any oils that could have done permanent damage.

She laughed at herself. Here she was worrying about some stupid blouse that could easily be replaced, when her whole world was crumbling down around her. She was walking on quicksand, and with every step she took, she sank deeper and deeper into the muck. If she wasn't careful, she'd get sucked under and be lost forever.

Opening the medicine cabinet above the sink, she raked through the various bottles until she found the aspirin. Good old reliable aspirin. She hadn't lied when she'd told Morgan she had a headache. Tension throbbed in her temples and shot up the back of her neck.

Downing two tablets with a paper cup of water, she closed her eyes momentarily and sighed. If only she could lie down and take a nap. If only she could find forgetfulness in sleep. Forgetfulness and peace.

She walked out of the bathroom, removed her brown gabardine skirt and laid it over the chair at her dressing table. She kicked off her brown leather heels and stripped out of her sheer hose. Wearing nothing but her yellow lace teddy, she lay down atop the beige brocade spread on her bed.

Lying there wide awake, she wondered what Morgan was doing downstairs. She'd been surprised but thankful that he had allowed her to escape so easily. Had he sensed that she needed to be alone? There had been a time when Morgan had known her every mood. But that had been in another lifetime, in a world without secrets between them.

Closing her eyes, Bethany prayed for sleep.

Morgan stood outside Bethany's bedroom. Hesitating only briefly, he balanced the tray in one hand while he reached down and opened the door. Glancing inside, he saw Bethany stretched out across the big, white, four-poster bed. Soft, pale shadows cloaked the room like a velvet cape. Captured in the blue curtains, in the beige silk bed linen and the fabric-covered chairs, the faint scent of her floral perfume lingered. Sweet. Delicate. Alluring. Like the woman herself.

His gaze moved slowly from the bottoms of Bethany's bare feet up the luscious expanse of her slender, naked legs to the delicate French-cut silk teddy that emphasized her curvaceous hips and tiny waist.

His heart thundered like a wild beast in his chest. His sex hardened instantly. The intensity of his desire for Bethany frightened him. After that first kiss in his mother's garden so many years ago, it had always been this way. Whenever he looked at her. Whenever he touched her. A wanting so deep, so primeval, so possessive that it superseded everything else, rendering him a mindless creature of pure sensation. He hadn't realized back then that no other woman would ever affect him in quite the same way. Only Beth.

He wasn't sure whether to leave the tray for her or take it back downstairs. He didn't want to disturb her rest. God knew she got little enough as it was.

Bethany heard a faint noise. It sounded like someone breathing. Drowsily opening her eyes, she glanced around the room and saw nothing out of place. Lifting her head off the spread, she looked toward the open door. Gasping, she jackknifed straight up in bed, pulled her knees up and clutched the front of her teddy.

"Sorry," Morgan said. "I didn't mean to startle you. I thought you might be as hungry as I am, so I fixed us some sandwiches."

"Thank you." Curling her feet under her, she crawled to the foot of the bed. She lifted a beige, wool-knit throw off the deacon's bench that spanned the width of the four-poster and wrapped the nubby cloth around her shoulders. "That was very thoughtful of you."

The last thing she had expected was for Morgan to walk into her room and see her practically naked. How long had he been standing in the doorway looking at her? A shudder of pure sensual awareness rippled along her nerve endings.

This room was her private domain, and no man had ever been given permission to enter. It was so like Morgan not to ask permission, to not even consider that he needed to ask. He'd always been a man who did what he pleased, when he pleased.

He walked across the room and placed the tray on the large English pedestal table in front of the oversize bow windows. Dark clouds once again obscured the sun and cast a gray gloominess on the afternoon light.

Sensing her unease, he kept his back to her. "It's nothing fancy. Just ham and cheese. Dill pickles. I found some kind of low-fat chips in the pantry. And there was iced tea in the refrigerator."

"You shouldn't have bothered bringing the sandwiches up

here.'' Bethany scooted to the edge of the bed. ''I would have come downstairs, and we could have eaten in the kitchen.''

''Hey, I don't go around fixing lunch and serving it on a silver tray for just anybody you know.'' Turning around, Morgan smiled when he looked at her. She sat there on her knees at the edge of the bed, staring at him, her small hand gripping the beige shawl where it crossed her chest. ''I wanted to do something to make up for what happened at the country club. I had no idea questioning Seth Renfrew would upset you so much.''

''I suppose I overreacted again.'' Sliding her legs off the bed, she touched the floor with the tips of her toes. ''I seem to be doing that a lot lately. My nerves are so on edge that I can't think straight anymore.''

''With good reason.''

''Seth has been more than a friend. He was a godsend when I was looking for an investor so I could open my first boutique.'' Standing, Bethany eased the beige throw down to cover her hips, tied a knot in the material at her waist and padded silently across the floral area rug overlaying the lush beige carpet. ''He's been like a big brother to me and an uncle to Anne Marie. And of course, he's stood by mother through thick and thin.''

''I don't doubt that Seth is a good man.''

Morgan turned the Provincial accent chair so that it faced the pedestal table. Gripping the wood-trimmed back of the chair with one hand, he held out his other hand to Bethany, inviting her to sit. After seating her, Morgan rounded the table and eased his big body down on the chair opposite her. He handed her a paper napkin, then lifted a glass of tea and offered it to her.

Willing her hand not to tremble, she reached out and took the glass. Their hands touched for a fraction of a second, but it was long enough to send a jolt of electric awareness through Bethany. She should ask him to leave. She should tell him that he'd had no right to desecrate the sanctity of her bedroom with his masculine presence.

Glancing over the rim of her glass as she sipped the cool, sweet tea, Bethany noticed that Morgan seemed to be avoiding eye contact with her. His gaze traveled over the room, inspecting each piece of furniture, each lamp, each pillow, each picture on the wall.

Was he as unsure of himself as she was? Was he as afraid of

what might happen between them? He knew as well as she that their being alone like this, in her bedroom, with her only partially dressed, was inviting trouble.

"Is that a picture of Anne Marie?" he asked.

"I have a dozen pictures of Anne Marie scattered around the room. Which one are you talking about?" She followed his line of vision to the oil portrait hanging over the mantel on the wall opposite her bed. She drew in her breath on a soft, hushed gasp. "Yes, that's a portrait I had done of her when she was six years old."

Would he see, Bethany wondered, how much Anne Marie looked like him in the portrait? From the steely blue-gray eyes, to the square jaw to the gold of her long hair? And would he notice the small pendant around her neck, the oval diamond sparkling against the ruby red velvet dress?

Scooting back his chair, Morgan stood and walked across the room to inspect the portrait more closely. There was something about the picture that beckoned him. When he stood directly in front of the fireplace, he suddenly realized what it was about the portrait that had caught his eye. Anne Marie was wearing the small diamond pendant necklace that he had given Bethany for her twentieth birthday, only a week before he'd left Birmingham.

Pain hit him square in the gut, as if he'd received a hard blow from a strong fist. How many times had he wondered how different his life might have been if he'd given Bethany an engagement ring instead of the necklace? But the necklace had been as close as he'd come to declaring his feelings for her. He had cared, cared deeply, but not enough to make a lifetime commitment. Not until it had been too late. He'd been such a smug, overconfident, young fool!

Lifting his hand to the canvas, he traced the thin gold chain that circled Anne Marie's neck and fell to her chest. Balling his hand into a fist, he closed his eyes and allowed the memories to wash over him. The way Bethany had looked lying in the middle of his bed, wearing nothing but the necklace. Her arms open wide. Her body accepting his with wild passion. Her heart giving him all her love.

Bethany laid her hand on his back. Morgan tensed at her

touch. He hadn't heard her cross the room, her bare feet silent on the thickly cushioned floor.

"You kept the necklace," he said, not turning around. "I'm surprised you didn't throw it away."

"Perhaps I should have. But I didn't." Easing her hand up his back, she squeezed his shoulder. "I gave the necklace to—" she almost said *our daughter* "—Anne Marie. It's her favorite piece of jewelry."

"Does she know I gave it to you?"

"No, she doesn't know." She had told Anne Marie that her father had given the necklace to her on her twentieth birthday. But Anne Marie didn't know that Morgan was her father.

He swallowed hard. As deep, dark, primitive emotions almost choked him, Morgan turned and grabbed Bethany's upper arms. Damning himself for a fool, he gave himself over to the urgent tide of desire that washed away his common sense.

Instantly recognizing the animal hunger in his eyes, Bethany opened her mouth to protest, to tell him that this couldn't happen, that she didn't want it. But the lie died a silent death on her lips. Temptation burned hot and wild between them, enticement beyond bearing, having grown stronger and stronger each time they had resisted.

Guilt and fear had kept her celibate for twelve long, lonely years. Fear of trusting another man, of caring enough to give herself and being betrayed. And guilt that she might actually find happiness with another man when she had sent her husband to his death. Did she have a right to love, to happiness, even to sexual fulfillment, when her inability to truly give herself to her husband had driven him to suicide? The authorities had called it an accident, but in her heart, Bethany knew the truth.

When Morgan drew her closer, she threw up her arms, wedging them between their bodies in one final attempt to stop the insanity before it went any further. Flattening her palms against the front of his shirt, she felt the harsh, rapid beat of his heart. An all-consuming desire spread through her body like a wildfire through dry kindling, burning away her resistance.

He knew the moment she stopped fighting, the moment she admitted defeat to a passion neither of them could control. He sensed her acceptance of the inevitable. Tightening his hold on her arms, his fingers bit into her tender flesh. Her moaning gasp alerted him to the damage his strength was capable of doing and he instantly loosened his grip and eased his hands down her arms to her waist.

She stood perfectly still, caught by his mesmerizing stare, while he untied the knot at her waist, pulled the wool throw away from her hips and dropped it on the floor.

"I'm afraid," she admitted, her breath raspy. "I don't know if... It won't change anything. Afterward...we'll still be the same."

"We've fought it long enough, honey," he said. "The longer and harder we've fought against it, the stronger it's become." Lowering his head, his breath feathering across her lips, he closed his eyes and breathed in the sweet, heady aroma that was uniquely Bethany. She shivered when he slipped his arms around her and buried his face against her neck. "The only way to appease the beast is to feed it." He murmured the words against her throat.

Nodding agreement, she tugged at his shoulder holster. Lifting his head, he took both of her hands and laid them flat on his chest. "Unbutton my shirt."

With nervous fingers, she began the task. Morgan removed his holster and laid it on the mantel behind him, then turned and eased his hands around Bethany's hips. Cupping her buttocks he lifted her closer, close enough so that she felt the hard ridge of his sex straining against the front of his slacks.

Parting his pale blue shirt, she exposed his broad, hairy chest. Bethany trembled as her hands made contact with his skin. He was hard and hot, his chest muscles toned to perfection. She combed her fingers through the thicket of brown curls, seeking and finding his tiny male nipples. He drew in a deep, harsh breath when she raked her nails across the peaked nubs.

"Beth, honey, you're tormenting me." He slipped his hand up inside her lace teddy and kneaded her hip.

Clutching his shoulders, she lowered her head and flicked her tongue across his nipple. The moment her moisture touched his skin, he shivered. Lightning fast, he captured the back of her head in his hand and threaded his fingers through her long dark hair. Curling several sepia strands around his fingers, he pulled them tight, forcing her to turn her face toward his as he swooped down and took her lips. Hot and wet and savage, his mouth conquered hers. All the while he held her head with one hand, he used the other to slip the satin straps of her teddy down her arms and drag the lace garment to her waist.

The moment he freed her breasts from their confinement, he pulled her forward, into his bare chest. She moaned with sheer agonized pleasure as her nipples tightened painfully when they pressed against his hair-roughened chest.

Deepening the kiss, Morgan spread his hand open across the hollow of her back and urged her closer, until the apex of her thighs nestled against his rigid shaft. A sharp, tingling sensation radiated from her breasts to her feminine core, moistening her body in preparation. Her nipples ached with the need to be touched, to be laved, to be suckled.

Morgan jerked the teddy over her hips, allowing it to pool into a yellow lace cloud at her feet. Easing her a few inches away from him, he surveyed her, drinking in every luscious feminine inch of her naked body. He reached out and lifted her round full breasts into his hands, caressing tenderly. Then he rubbed the backs of his thumbs across her nipples. She tossed back her head. Her hair cascaded down across her shoulder blades like a coffee brown waterfall. She sighed, the sound sharp and breathless, wanting more, needing more.

"It's all right, babe. I'm going to make the hurt go away." Caressing her, his touch wildly erotic, he eased his hands down her rib cage and around, dipping one of his hands between their bodies. He speared his fingers through the triangle of dark hair and cupped her intimately, then when he eased his finger over her sensitive kernel, he encompassed one begging nipple with his mouth.

Bethany fell apart, her whole body becoming a throbbing, aching mass of need. She felt herself building toward a climax as he suckled one breast and then the other, his touch masterfully fondling her. It had happened too quickly. She'd been too hungry. She wanted to tell him, to beg him not to let it end so soon, to make this wild pleasure go on and on forever.

She cried out as fulfillment claimed her. Trembling from the force of her release, she clung to Morgan. He lifted her into his arms and carried her across the room and laid her down on the bed. As the aftershocks rippled through her body, she watched while Morgan tore off his clothes and threw them haphazardly on the floor. Within seconds he eased himself down on top of her, bracing his big body with his arms. Waiting, wanting, her passion ignited anew by the very sight of him, large, hard and gloriously male.

"I want you." The words rushed out of his mouth on a harsh, heated breath as he wedged his knee between her thighs and opened her up for his invasion.

She reached for him, digging her nails into his buttocks, encouraging him to take what he wanted. "Take me. Please, Morgan. I want you, too. So very much."

He eased his finger inside her, retrieving her moisture, preparing them both for his possession. Shivering and whimpering, she arched her back, lifting her hips off the bed, inviting him in.

Groaning with savage satisfaction, he plunged into the depths of her receptive body, but stilled instantly when she cried out and bit her nails deeper into his taut buttocks. Realization hit him suddenly. Bethany hadn't been with a man in twelve years, but even when they had been lovers, taking all of him into her body had never been an easy feat.

"It's all right, honey." He soothed her with kisses and tender caresses as he eased himself, inch by inch, deeper and deeper into her body.

For a moment, Bethany felt impaled as he embedded himself inside her, but gradually her body became used to the pressure of his fullness.

He lifted her hips as he plunged to the hilt, filling her completely. Once she had adjusted to him, he eased himself out by slow degrees and then thrust again, repeating the process until she writhed beneath him, crying, moaning, pleading.

He felt her tightening around him, urging the inevitable explosion. She clung to him, absorbing every ounce of pleasure from their wild mating. He hammered into her until, with one final lunge, he erupted, just as she spiraled out of control for a second time.

His shouted grunt was that of a powerful male animal in his prime. She lay beneath him shivering uncontrollably as her pleasure continued on and on until only the fluttering shock waves of completion echoed through her body.

Falling to her side, he drew her into his arms and kissed her full on the mouth, loving the sweet, salty taste of the sweat that dampened her upper lip. Running his hand up and down her arm, he nudged her other shoulder with his nose, then planted a soft kiss on the same spot.

"You are the sweetest thing I've ever known," he whispered. "It has never been like this with anyone else."

"Only with me?"

"Yes, Beth. Only with you."

Sighing with satisfaction, she cuddled in his arms and drifted off to sleep. He lay there for a long time and watched her while she slept, thinking how peaceful she looked, how completely sated. In a little while he closed his eyes and rested.

Awakening with a start, he sat straight up in bed. He heard a car door slam. Checking his watch, still strapped to his wrist, he realized how late it was. James had probably dropped Anne Marie home after school. Hell, he couldn't let her walk in on them, couldn't let her find him naked in her mother's bed. He shot out of the bed, jerked on his navy-blue slacks and slipped into his shirt. After gathering up his shoes, socks and underwear, he grabbed his holster off the mantel and rushed out into the hall and toward his room.

Standing just inside his bedroom, he heard the front door unlock. Damn! He'd have to hurry. Rushing about frantically, he washed off quickly and dressed in fresh clothes. Just as he slipped into his brown loafers, he heard Anne Marie's footsteps on the stairs. Strapping on his holster, he walked out into the hallway at the exact moment Anne Marie lifted her hand to knock on her mother's closed bedroom door.

"She's asleep," Morgan said.

Anne Marie gasped and jumped simultaneously, then turned to face him. "Oh, Morgan, you scared me. I just wanted to talk to Mama and let her know that I survived the first day at school."

"She'll be glad to hear all about it." Morgan grabbed Anne Marie by the elbow. "But later, OK? Bethany hasn't been sleeping well at night. She really needs this little nap."

"Yeah, you're right. I can fill her in on the details of my day later. How was your day? Anything significant happen?"

Tugging on her elbow, Morgan steered her away from Bethany's room. ''Why don't we go downstairs, find us a snack and exchange notes? You tell me about your day and I'll hit the highlights of mine.''

''Sounds like a plan to me.''

Anne Marie followed him downstairs to the kitchen. While he filled glasses with ice and poured them each a cola, she retrieved a bag of corn chips from the pantry.

She tossed him the chips. ''Here. Open these. I'll get the ketchup.''

''Ketchup?''

''Yeah, I know. Nana and Grandmother think it's disgusting, but I love to dip my chips in ketchup.''

She pulled a bottle out of the refrigerator, lifted a bowl from the dishwasher and squirted ketchup into it. Plunking the bowl down on the table, she returned the ketchup to the refrigerator.

Morgan watched, fascinated, even a bit bewildered as Bethany's daughter munched on ketchup-coated chips. He'd eaten his chips with ketchup since he'd been a kid. His mother had never known. She had seldom shared meals, let alone snacks, with him when he'd been a child. Retrieving a chip from the bag, he reached over and dipped it in the ketchup. Anne Marie stared at him, a look of surprise on her face. He repeated the process with several chips.

''Don't tell me that you like ketchup on your chips!''

''Never eat them any other way.''

''Gee, I think it's really cool that you and I are so much alike.''

''And how are we alike except for our food preferences?'' Morgan asked. ''Ketchup on chips. And medium rare steaks.''

''Well, Nana always told me how much I was like you. She said I reminded her a lot of you. The food I liked. The music I liked. Even being good at sports. Nana said that I was more like you than I was Amery, even though he was my real father.''

Her real father. Why did the fact that Amery was her father still bother him so much? What difference did it make after all these years? He couldn't go back and change the past, no matter how much he wanted to.

What should be concerning Morgan wasn't that Amery was Anne Marie's father, but that the girl was beginning to think of him as a substitute father. He had promised himself that when he left Birmingham this time, he wouldn't leave behind any broken hearts. Not Bethany's. And most certainly not Anne Marie's.

"Hey, we are cousins, aren't we?" Morgan lifted his glass of iced cola in a salute. "We must have inherited a lot of the same Morgan genes."

Anne Marie studied Morgan intently while she nibbled on corn chips and sipped on her cola. "You're very good-looking. I can see why Mama fell in love with you first. You know, before you left town and she and Amery got married. Just think, if you'd stayed here instead of going away and joining the Navy, you and Mama would have gotten married and I'd be your daughter."

Morgan fiercely clutched the glass in his hand, then realized what he was doing just in time to keep from breaking the glass. No matter how much he wished Anne Marie was his, she wasn't. He couldn't let the girl concoct some kind of fantasy world where he would marry her mother and they'd become one big happy family. It wasn't going to happen. "Yeah, well, I didn't stay. I didn't marry your mother. And you're Amery's daughter, not mine."

Sighing forlornly, Anne Marie said, "Yeah, I know."

After downing several large gulps of cola, Morgan set his glass on the table, reached over and grasped Anne Marie's chin. "I thought you were going to tell me how you slew the dragons at school today."

Brightening instantly at his teasing comment, she grinned. He gave her chin a playful squeeze, then released her.

"I really didn't slay any dragons, but I did keep my cool all day. Mama would have been so proud of me. No matter what anybody said, I didn't cry and I didn't get angry and holler at them. I just ignored them. I did like Mama always said I should do." When he stared at her quizzically, she laughed. "You know, Mama always says to consider the source."

"Consider the source, huh?"

"I just turned my nose up in the air and acted as if I was better than them," Anne Marie said. "And after today, I sure do know who my real friends are. Would you believe there were quite a few girls who stuck up for me?"

The kitchen door swung open and Bethany breezed into the room. Morgan noticed that she was freshly showered. Damp, dark tendrils that had escaped from her loose ponytail curled about her face.

"Mama! Did you have a good nap?" Anne Marie jumped up from the table and ran to meet her mother. Giving Bethany a big hug, she grabbed her mother's hands and dragged her over to a chair. "Sit down. I have to tell you everything. I was strong and fearless and I didn't shed one tear and I didn't yell at anybody."

Sitting down at the table, Bethany glanced at Morgan, and for one brief moment her heart stopped. She suddenly felt too warm, her skin too tight for her body, as she recalled the exquisite pleasure they'd shared only a short time ago. She prayed that what she felt didn't show too plainly on her face, that her daughter wouldn't suspect what had happened.

Morgan forced himself not to stare at Bethany, not to allow his gaze to linger too long on her face and body. Just looking at her was enough to arouse him. He knew that if Anne Marie hadn't come home, Bethany could have awakened in his arms and they would be upstairs in her bed right now, making love again.

"Mama, Melanie Harden is now my new best friend." Propping her elbows on the table, Anne Marie stared straight at Bethany. "She sat with me at lunch and whenever we overheard anybody saying something hateful, she gave them the evil eye. And once she even told Tiffany Lang not to ever expect to be invited to any of her parties. Not ever again. And you know Melanie's parties are the best. I mean everybody wants to be invited."

Morgan watched the interchange between mother and daughter, strongly aware of the bond of love and trust and commitment that existed. He was an outsider, a privileged outsider, looking in on a private moment, allowed to be a temporary part of this family circle.

Anne Marie had all but invited him to become her father. She was hungry for a paternal force in her life, a man for her mother and a dad for her. But this type of life-style was alien to him. He was a loner, a man without any real ties. He had chosen the life he wanted to live sixteen years ago and he hadn't changed his mind. He still wanted no part of the world he'd left behind, the world of social position and wealth. The phony artificial life his parents had lived held no appeal for him. And even though Bethany had not turned out to be a carbon copy of Claudia Kane, she still lived in the same world, still moved in the same circles and she had raised her daughter to be a member of that elite society.

He had to make sure that both mother and daughter understood that when this job was over, he'd be gone. He wouldn't let anything or anyone lure him back into the life he'd hated. No matter how much the thought of being Bethany's lover appealed to him, and no matter how much he wished that Amery's daughter was his, he would never stay in Birmingham.

Once they proved Bethany's innocence and she was a free woman, he would leave. And even if he asked her to go with him this time, he didn't think she'd give up the life she'd built here. Sixteen years ago, the girl who had loved him so completely would have followed him to the moon. But Bethany was a different person now, a woman with a business, a teenage daughter and obligations she couldn't walk away from so easily.

No matter how much they still wanted each other, still cared for each other, Morgan didn't see any forever-after in their future.

Chapter 10

"There's no way to get her out of here without taking her straight through the reporters," Maxine Carson told Morgan. "They're everywhere. At the back entrance that leads to the park and at the entrance facing Twenty-First Street, too. And they're filling up the building."

"Dammit! I knew I shouldn't have let you come to the courthouse today." Bending down on his haunches in front of Bethany's chair, Morgan reached out, took her quivering hands in his strong, steady grasp and gazed into her eyes. He saw his own concern reflected there in the depths of her gold-flecked eyes. And he saw more. He saw her fear.

Bringing her hands to his lips, he kissed them, longing for a way to ease her pain and erase her fear. "Don't worry, honey, I'll get you out of here and safely to the car."

Smiling weakly, she looked at him, but he had the oddest feeling that she was looking right through him, past him and into her future. A future she couldn't bear to imagine.

"I know you'll get me out of here." Freeing her hands from his grasp, she reached up and caressed his cheek. "I'm sorry getting me out of here is going to be so difficult. I probably shouldn't have come to the courthouse, but I had to. Even though I couldn't be in the courtroom, I needed to be here when the grand jury made their ruling."

Maxine paced the floor, her sharp three-inch heels clinking at an allegro beat. "Well, I can't say I didn't expect it. We knew all the evidence was against us. The prosecutor had everything on his side."

"Yes, I suppose it shouldn't have come as a great surprise that the grand jury indicted me." Bethany's voice possessed a trancelike calm. "I had hoped, not only for my sake, but for Anne Marie's and Mother's and...I can't bear the thought of what my daughter is going to have to go through. This situation is already intolerable for her."

"Have you considered sending her out of town somewhere until after the trial?" Maxine asked. "Maybe a boarding school in Europe?"

"No!" Bethany and Morgan said simultaneously, then looked at each other and smiled sadly. The understanding that passed between them formed a bond, and in that one moment, Bethany knew that if the time came, her daughter would be safe in Morgan's care.

Stopping abruptly, Maxine glared at Bethany and Morgan. "Well, it was only a suggestion. By your reactions, you'd think I'd said send her to Siberia."

"Anne Marie needs to be here, in Birmingham, with family," Bethany said. "I don't want to miss one day with her. If—if I'm convicted—"

"You're not going to be convicted!" Maxine shouted. "You didn't kill Jimmy Farraday, and I'm going to find a way to prove it."

Rising to his feet, Morgan brought Bethany up out of the chair, then slipped his arm around her waist. "The best way to prove it is for us to find the real killer."

"Well, if Eileen or Seth killed Jimmy, now would be the perfect time for a confession," Maxine said. "Before your arraignment."

"When will the arraignment be?" Bethany asked.

"It's usually a week or two after the grand jury hands down the indictment." Opening the door leading into the hallway, Maxine searched the milling crowd. "At least no one has discovered where we are. Not for the time being. Remind me to send Bob a bottle of Jack Daniels as a thank-you for letting us hide out here in his office."

"I'll have to be present at the arraignment, won't I?" Bethany rested her head on Morgan's chest.

"We'll have to appear before the court that will try your case. The judge will apprise you of the formal charges against you, set a trial date and consider our request not to revoke your bail." Maxine closed the door, shutting out the loud hustle and bustle of reporters, spectators and frenzied Jimmy Farraday fans that crowded the halls and lined the front steps and the sidewalks at every exit.

Bethany slumped against Morgan, thankful for his powerful presence, as all the possible realities of the situation hit her. "Do you think that could happen? Is there a chance I might have to stay in jail until after the trial?"

"There's always a chance, considering the seriousness of the charges, that the judge might—"

"It won't go that far," Morgan said. "I don't care what I have to do, I'll find Farraday's murderer before the trial."

The outer door flew open and slammed shut with a resounding bang. Holt Perdue, a junior partner in Kane, Walker and Carson, panted like a woman in labor. His beet red face clashed with his salmon pink tie and his pale blue eyes. Dots of sweat covered his forehead and upper lip.

"God, it's a madhouse out there. I've never seen so many reporters!" Holt pulled a handkerchief from his coat pocket and wiped the moisture from his face. "The natives are restless. Tony Hayes has a news crew here from WHNB, and he's been stirring up the crowd while they wait for Bethany to come out. The police have had to block off traffic along Twenty-First Street."

"We'll have to try to take her out the other way, through Lynn Park," Maxine said. "If necessary, call a taxi to take her home, and we'll get someone to pick up her car later."

"Before y'all make any plans, there's something you should know," Holt said.

"What should we know?" Morgan asked.

"Mrs. Farraday is giving an interview to Tony Hayes out on the front steps." Holt looked directly at Bethany. "Anne Marie and James are with her."

"Oh, God, no!" Bethany gripped the sleeve of Morgan's jacket. "What was Mother thinking coming here and bringing those children?"

"I'd say Eileen is acting on instinct, as usual," Maxine said. "I'm sure, in her own mind, she has a good reason for showing up and bringing Anne Marie with her."

Morgan knew he couldn't be in two places at once, but right this minute he wished he could split himself in two. He needed to get Bethany safely out of the courthouse and away from the reporters and Farraday fans. But he knew that she wouldn't go anywhere as long as her daughter was in the midst of the madness. He couldn't whisk Bethany to safety and rescue Anne Marie at the same time. He'd give a year's pay to have Hawk at his side right now.

Releasing her hold on Morgan, Bethany took a deep breath. "Morgan, give Holt the keys to my Mercedes. He can get the car and have it waiting for us." When Morgan hesitated, she prompted, "Go ahead, give him the keys." When Morgan handed the young lawyer the key chain, Bethany told Holt, "Bring the car out of the parking deck and around in front of the Criminal Justice Building on Eighth Avenue the minute you see us break through the crowd."

"Bethany, this is insanity," Maxine said. "Farraday's fans will eat you alive if you go out through the front entrance."

"I'm not leaving my daughter out there to face only God knows what." Bethany looked up at Morgan's stern, somber face. "You can handle this, can't you? You can get me to Anne Marie and—"

"Let's go." Cupping her elbow in his big hand, he urged her toward the door. "Have the car waiting for us, Perdue!"

"Holt, tell the reporters that Bethany will be coming out the back way." Maxine opened the door and ushered her colleague into the hall. "It could divert some attention away from us." Stepping outside, she watched while Holt approached a bevy of reporters. "They're following him. Let's get out of here while the gettin's good."

With Maxine on one side of her and Morgan on the other, Bethany said a silent prayer for courage as they marched down the hall. They made it halfway to the front entrance before a newspaper reporter recognized Bethany and hurried along behind her, shooting out questions like bullets from a machine gun.

As more people moved in on them, Morgan reached inside his jacket and checked his shoulder holster, revealing its presence to the onlookers. No matter how much he wanted to, he couldn't use his Sig as a means of crowd control, but it didn't hurt to simply give people a glimpse of his weapon.

As they drew nearer the entrance, the crowd that pressed in around them grew heavier. Morgan burst through the front doors, his big body draping Bethany's like a shield as he drew her closer to his side.

Eileen Farraday, the picture of mature loveliness, stood on the top step, speaking into a microphone held up in front of her by Tony Hayes. Eileen had one arm around James's waist and the other around Anne Marie's. Seth Renfrew, who stood directly behind Eileen glanced in every direction, as if searching for someone. The moment he saw Bethany, he frowned and shook his head in warning.

Bethany stopped dead in her tracks. "What does Mother think she's doing?"

For several minutes, no one seemed to notice Bethany as all eyes focused on Eileen.

"You have something you want to tell Jimmy's fans, Mrs. Farraday." Tony Hayes swept his arm through the air in a grand gesture. "Your husband's fans are surrounding you here at the courthouse, and out there across the state of Alabama." Tony smiled into the camera. "They are waiting to hear whatever you have to say to them."

"Thank you, Tony." Eileen laid her hand on Tony's arm and patted him affectionately. "I know that you loved Jimmy, too, and his death has been a tragedy for all of us."

"God love you, Mrs. Farraday." Shoving James aside, Tony hugged Eileen. "Please, tell us how you feel about your daughter being indicted for Jimmy's murder."

"My daughter is innocent," Eileen proclaimed. "I believe in her and I support her completely."

"Despite all the evidence against her and all the cruel accusations her lawyers have made against Jimmy, defaming a fine man, you still defend her?" Tony bowed his head for a dramatic moment, then lifted it again to show the world the tears in his eyes. "How like a mother to love her child despite all that she's done."

Eileen grabbed the microphone out of Tony's hand with a swift adeptness that seemed to surprise the heir to Jimmy's television throne.

"I know that someone else killed my husband," Eileen said in a strong, sure voice. "I am putting up a reward of fifty thousand dollars to be given to anyone who has information that will lead us to the real murderer and help us convict him or her."

The crowd went wild, with shouted cheers and jeers, and a chorus of both praise and condemnation. Two fistfights broke out in the throng that covered Twenty-First Street North directly in front of the gray stone courthouse. Reporters representing every news agency in the state and nation swarmed around Eileen, firing questions at supersonic speed.

"Well, she's done it now," Maxine said. "That reward will bring out every crazy in the state."

Morgan glanced over Bethany's head, trying to discern the best course of action for rescuing Anne Marie, who still stood beside her grandmother. Suddenly Seth Renfrew whispered something in Anne Marie's ear and drew her away from Eileen. The two of them eased backward, through the heavy crowd. Noticing what was happening, James followed them.

Seth brought Anne Marie safely to her mother. Bethany reached out and grabbed her child, pulling her into her arms.

"Oh, Mama, I'm so sorry. I can't believe the jury indicted you."

Seth glanced over at Morgan. "You'd better get them out of here immediately, while Eileen still has all their attention. I'll take care of things here."

"Thanks," Morgan said, then spoke directly to James. "Can you help me get them out of here?"

"Just tell me what to do," James said.

"You and Anne Marie are going to go out directly in front of Bethany and me," Morgan said. "Keep one arm around Anne Marie and use the other one to push through the crowd if they move in too close. Don't look right or left and don't stop for anything. Just keep moving straight ahead. Get out on the sidewalk and head directly for Eighth Avenue. Holt Perdue has Bethany's car waiting for us."

Following Morgan's instructions to the letter, James circled Anne Marie's waist in imitation of Morgan's hold on Bethany, and when Morgan gave him a signal, James led Anne Marie through the crowd. While Eileen maintained her place in the spotlight and a few reporters cornered Maxine Carson, the foursome slipped through the mob of reporters, fans and onlookers. They made it to the corner of Twenty-First Street and Eighth Avenue before a group of irate Jimmy Farraday fans surrounded them, blocking their way.

"Don't stop," Morgan told James. "Don't even slow down. Plow right through them if you have to."

When James obeyed Morgan's command, the hecklers moved aside just enough for the four of them to pass through. All the while the group shouted threats and accusations, and one person tossed an empty aluminum can, hitting Morgan's shoulder. He didn't even flinch.

Bethany prayed for escape, wanting nothing more than to get her child to safety. Once again she thanked God for Morgan's presence, for his strength, upon which she depended. Fate had brought him back into her life when she needed him so desperately.

Holt Perdue whipped the white Mercedes coupe out of the parking deck and up in front of the Criminal Justice Building the minute Morgan motioned to him.

The foursome rushed across the street, the crowd on their heels. Holt jumped out of the car. James shoved Anne Marie into the back seat and crawled in beside her. Morgan pushed Bethany into the car on the driver's side. She scooted over quickly, her breath ragged, her palms clammy and damp. He dove into the car, slammed the door and revved the motor. Within seconds, he maneuvered the Mercedes through the heckling onlookers and out of downtown Birmingham. Heading southeast, toward Red Mountain, to home.

Morgan drove through the intricately carved iron gates that guarded the road to his mother's estate on Argyle Road. He had intended taking Bethany and Anne Marie straight home to Forest Park, but Bethany had insisted on telling Claudia, in person, that the grand jury had indicted her.

"I know that I could phone Claudia and tell her," Bethany said. "But I'd rather be there with her when I tell her." And I need time alone with Claudia to discuss how I'm going to go about telling you that Anne Marie is your daughter.

Ida Mae's face paled the minute she opened the front door. "Come on in. The phone's been ringing off the hook, but I've caught it every time. She don't know." Ida Mae grabbed Bethany's hands. "I knew you'd come tell her yourself. Oh, Miss Bethany, it's a sad day when a woman as good and kind as you is accused of murder."

Bethany hugged the old woman. "Is Claudia in her room?"

"Yes, ma'am. I've had the devil's own time keeping her up there and explaining to her why the phone hasn't stopped ringing."

When Anne Marie started up the stairs, Bethany called out to her. "Wait, sweetheart. I want to go up and see Nana by myself. Later, after I've talked to her, you can come up and see her before we go home."

Gazing at her mother questioningly, she asked, "Is something wrong? Something you're not telling me?"

"No. I—I just need some time alone with Claudia. I want to discuss plans for your future, in case—"

Anne Marie rushed toward her mother. "No, please, don't even think it. You won't be convicted. They can't send you to prison. I'd die without you."

Morgan glanced away, unable to bear the agony he saw on Bethany's face and the terror on Anne Marie's. He noticed James looking down at the floor while he nervously shuffled his feet.

Grabbing her daughter's shoulders, Bethany forced a smile. "We will hope for the best, but we must prepare for the worst."

"Mama..."

"Ida Mae?" Bethany called to the housekeeper, who stood close by, wiping her eyes with the edge of her apron.

"Would you take the kids into the kitchen and fix them a snack and make Morgan a pot of coffee?"

"I most certainly will," Ida Mae said.

Bethany gazed into Morgan's concerned eyes and without saying a word conveyed her feelings to him. Please, dear God, let him understand.

"Come on." Morgan slipped his arm around Anne Marie's trembling shoulders. "You're going to have to be strong and brave for your mother now. Let her do what she needs to do."

Turning to watch as Bethany headed up the stairs, Anne Marie called after her. "Mama, let me know when I can come up and see Nana."

Pausing briefly, Bethany glanced over her shoulder at her daughter and nodded affirmatively, then hurried up the stairs and down the hall to Claudia's room.

Easing the door open, Bethany stepped inside the opulent bedroom. "Claudia?"

"Come in, dear. I've been expecting you."

Bethany turned her head sharply toward the sitting area where Claudia rested on a tufted velvet settee in the corner between two towering floor-to-ceiling windows. Late-afternoon sunlight shimmered on the decorative gilded drapery rods that stretched the silk side panels to the edge of the fourteen-foot-high ceiling.

"How are you feeling today?" Bethany asked as she laid her purse on top of the sleek glass Muvano table.

"The news isn't good, is it?" Claudia held out her thin, frail hand.

Grasping Claudia's hand, Bethany sat down in the highly decorative Louis XVI armchair to her right. "The grand jury indicted me for murder."

"Oh, my dear, dear Beth." Claudia clung to Bethany's hand, her clasp weak. "Morgan will find Farraday's murderer. He and that agency he works for are the best in the business. We must never give up hope."

"I'm hoping and praying that Morgan can find the real murderer," Bethany said. "But I have to be prepared to stand trial and perhaps even serve time in prison."

"I refuse to believe that will happen." Tears welled up in Claudia's eyes. "Before I'll let that happen, I'll have Morgan whisk you out of the country and into hiding. I'll—"

"Don't get upset." Bethany patted Claudia's hand. "No matter what happens, I can face it, as long as I know that Anne Marie is in good hands. If—if your health wasn't so...you know there is no one I'd rather have take care of Anne Marie than you. But you're not well enough to take on the responsibility. And having Mother do it is out of the question."

"You're going to tell Morgan the truth, aren't you? You're going to tell him that he's Anne Marie's father?" Releasing her hold on Bethany's hand, Claudia leaned back against the cushions on the settee and sighed deeply. "He'll hate me then, more than he already does."

"He doesn't hate you," Bethany said. "And there's no reason why he should blame you for not telling him about Anne Marie. I'm the one who chose to keep her a secret from him, after we found out where he was. Even after Amery died, I was the one who convinced you and Henderson not to tell Morgan the truth."

"When do you plan to tell him?"

"I'll tell him before the trial starts. If I'm convicted, I want to be certain that Morgan will take on his responsibilities as Anne Marie's father." Bethany leaned over the edge of the chair toward the settee. "You should see them together now that they've gotten to know each other. She adores him. And he's very protective of her."

"They're so much alike. They'll do just fine together."

"At first, Morgan may hate me for keeping the truth from him all these years," Bethany said. "But he can't blame me for something that's his own fault. He left me and never came back. Anne Marie, though, is so innocent, so blameless. I just don't know how she's going to feel about me when she learns that I've lied to her about her father her whole life."

"She may be upset at first," Claudia said. "But she loved Morgan before she ever met him. I gave him to her with all my silly little Morgan stories. And she loves you, my dear. She knows what a good mother you've been. Once you and Morgan explain the entire situation to her, she'll understand."

"What will I do if Morgan refuses to stay in Birmingham? What if he takes Anne Marie out of the state? If I go to prison and he has custody of her, he could keep her away from me, never let me see her."

"Morgan would never keep your child from you. Whether he realizes it or not, he loves you. He always did and he still does."

"You're wrong, Claudia. Morgan never loved me. He wanted me. He cared for me. He even needed me to a certain extent. But he never loved me. If he had loved me, he would have taken me with him when he left Birmingham. He knew I would have gone to the ends of the earth with him."

"My dear, there is something I must tell you." Claudia eased to the edge of the settee and looked pleadingly into Bethany's eyes. "It's something I never knew. Something none of us knew. If we'd had any idea that—everything would have been so different. You wouldn't have had to marry Amery. And Anne Marie would have been raised as Morgan's child, and—"

Bethany grabbed Claudia's arm. "What are you talking about?"

"He came back for you."

A cold, deadly chill encompassed Bethany's body, as if she'd suddenly been trapped in an arctic storm. "What do you mean he came back for me?"

"Morgan told me, the day he read in the newspaper about your being arrested." Claudia laid her hand over Bethany's. "A few months after he left Birmingham sixteen years ago, he realized that he wanted you with him. And he came home to get you. He went to your house and was told you were at the church."

"Oh, please, God. No. No." Terror so stark, so painfully devastating that it threatened to devour her tunneled through Bethany's heart. "Morgan came back to Birmingham to get me on the day I married Amery."

"Yes." Tears trickled down Claudia's delicately wrinkled cheeks. "He stood outside the church in the rain and watched you and Amery come out of the church and get into the white limousine."

"Damn him!" Bethany hit her knee against the glass table when she bounded out of the chair. "Damn him for coming back and damn him for not taking me away from Amery. If he'd loved me, he wouldn't have cared that I married Amery. He would have understood why. He would have..."

Bethany burst into tears. Tears she'd held inside her for far too long. She cried not only for the foolish young girl she'd been, not only for faded dreams and lost chances, but for Morgan, who had stood outside the church in the rain. And for Amery who had tried so hard to make her love him and had died so tragically. And for Anne Marie who'd spent the first fifteen years of her life without her real father. And even for

Claudia. Poor, sick, lonely Claudia. They had all lost so much. Lost what could never be retrieved. Precious moments gone forever. Shared pleasures never experienced.

Claudia eased her frail body off the settee and walked over to Bethany, placing her hand on Bethany's back. "He's never understood why you let your mother and Henderson and me talk you into marrying Amery only a few months after he left town. When you tell him that Anne Marie is his child, he'll know why you married his cousin."

Bethany turned, opened her arms and hugged Claudia, tenderly stroking the old woman's back as they both cried.

"I wonder what's keeping Mama so long." Anne Marie sipped on the lemonade she'd helped Ida Mae prepare. "You don't think Nana is sick or something, do you?"

"I'm sure Bethany would have called us if Mother was sick," Morgan said. "I imagine Mother is upset over the news of Bethany's indictment and Bethany is trying to reassure her."

"Who's going to reassure Mama?" Anne Marie swirled around on the swivel bar stool. "Gee, Morgan, I thought surely by now you'd at least have some leads on the real killer."

Before Morgan could reply, James piped in. "Hey, when a guy's got a list of suspects a mile long, it takes a while to narrow it down. Let's face it, my old man made more than his share of enemies."

"Well, you'd never know it by the way that horde of fans of his was acting at the courthouse today. You'd think Jimmy had been Godalmighty!"

"Anne Marie Wyndham!" Ida Mae scolded. "Watch your mouth, young lady."

Morgan clamped his big hand down on Anne Marie's shoulder. "I promise you that I will do everything possible to keep your mother from ever going to trial, let alone being convicted and sentenced to prison."

She looked at him adoringly. "I know you'll save Mama. I just wish saving her wasn't taking you so long."

"You and I are going to have to keep up a brave front for Bethany," Morgan told her. "If she thinks we're worried, then—"

The insistent ring of Morgan's cellular phone interrupted. He removed the phone from his jacket pocket, flipped it open and said, "Kane here." His brow wrinkled.

Anne Marie slid off the bar stool and eased over beside him. James set his glass of lemonade on the bar and focused his attention on the conversation.

"Damn! I'll tell her," Morgan said. "Knowing her, she'll want to come straight over."

"What's wrong?" Anne Marie tugged on Morgan's sleeve. "What happened?"

Morgan motioned for her to wait, then said into the telephone, "So you caught them. How many were there? Yeah, thanks for getting in touch with me so quickly. Will you wait around until we get there? OK. Fine. I'm sure Bethany will want to ask you a few questions."

The minute Morgan slipped his phone back in his pocket, Anne Marie grabbed his arm. "What happened?"

"Some of Farraday's fans broke into your and your mother's home and ransacked the downstairs before the police could get there."

"Oh, no! This is all Mama needs."

"Didn't the security alarm go off?" James asked.

"It went off and alerted the police and scared all the neighbors," Morgan said. "But it didn't deter the men who broke in. It seems they'd all been celebrating Bethany's indictment and had one beer too many."

"Who was that on the phone?" Anne Marie asked.

"Detective Varner," Morgan said.

Bethany walked into the kitchen, her eyes puffy and damp from crying. "What's this about Hal Varner?"

"How's Mother?" Morgan asked Bethany.

"She's all right. I told her that I'd been indicted. We discussed the future and the past and— Did I understand you to say something about Hal Varner calling you just now?"

"Mama, please, don't get upset." Anne Marie rushed to her mother's side.

"What's going on?" Bethany asked.

"Some of Farraday's drunken fans broke into your house and ransacked the place," Morgan told her, and when she didn't even blink an eye, he marveled at her composure. "The police arrived in time to apprehend three of them. They weren't in any condition to run."

"I want to go home, now," she told Morgan, then turned to Ida Mae. "Please don't say a word about this to Claudia. I put her to bed before I came downstairs, so you should check on her in a little while and make sure she takes her medication."

"I always do," Ida Mae said.

"Why don't you kids stay here?" Morgan suggested.

"No, if Mama's going to look at the house, then I'm going, too!" Anne Marie clasped her mother's hand.

"We'll all go and see how much damage there is," Bethany said placidly.

Morgan knew that there was something wrong with Bethany, something bothering her that had nothing to do with the break-in at her house. She was far too calm and controlled for a woman who'd just lived through the worst day of her life and had suddenly discovered that her home had been vandalized.

What had happened upstairs between Bethany and his mother? If he asked Bethany, would she tell him? And if she was willing to tell him, was he sure he really wanted to know?

Hal Varner met them the minute they pulled into the garage at Bethany's Forest Park home. Several neighbors still milled around in the street and one black-and-white was still parked in the driveway.

Bethany didn't wait for Morgan to get out and assist her. She jumped out of her Mercedes and headed up the sidewalk.

"Mrs. Wyndham?" Detective Varner called to her. "One of the intruders broke out a window in the kitchen and crawled in, unlocked the door and let the others in. It's quite a mess in the downstairs. You might not want to—"

Stopping halfway up the sidewalk, Bethany glanced over her shoulder. "Did you catch all of them?"

"We arrested three of them, but we figure a couple more got away. The three we caught were too drunk to run."

Bethany walked up to the open front door, then stepped into the foyer. Morgan followed her. She halted, her body tensing the moment she glanced into her living room. Coming up behind her, Morgan grasped her shoulders and drew her back up against his chest.

James's eyes widened in shock when he walked into the house. "Holy cow!"

"Oh, Mama. Mama." Anne Marie stood in the foyer beside James and shook her head back and forth, then suddenly turned pale. She grabbed James's hand and whispered, "I think I'm going to throw up."

James put his arm around Anne Marie's shoulder. "Come on. Let's go back outside."

Bethany could hardly believe her eyes. Utter, complete, desolate destruction. Drapes torn down from their rods. Pictures and mirrors ripped from the walls. Lamps thrown onto the floor, their broken fragments scattered on the carpet. Tables overturned, pillows strewed, gashes sliced in the sofa and chairs. The brass fire poker pierced the oil painting above the mantel.

"I'm leaving an officer here overnight, Mrs. Wyndham." Hal Varner stood in the open front door. "It's not regulation, but under the circumstances... Well, you'll need to get somebody out here first thing in the morning to repair the broken windows and—"

"Thank you, Detective," Morgan said when Bethany made no reply, indeed didn't acknowledge either Varner's presence or his. "I'll see that someone's here bright and early."

"I'm sorry about this," Varner said. "I'd like to lock up that Tony Hayes along with those three we arrested here tonight. He might have loved Jimmy Farraday like a son loves a father, but that doesn't give him the right to incite these pea-brained bastards to take the law into their own hands."

Bethany stepped over the debris in the floor as she made her way across the room. Morgan watched her as she picked something up off the carpet. Clutching the retrieved object in her arms, she returned to his side, looked up at him with cool, dazed eyes and said, "We'll spend the night at Mother's. She has more than enough room for all of us."

"All right, honey," Morgan put his arm around her shoulders. "Come on. Let's get out of here."

Holding the retrieved object in one hand, Bethany reached up and caressed Morgan's cheek with the other. He laid his hand over hers, pressing the tips of her fingers into his cheekbone.

She held up a lopsided bright green clay pot with the word Mommy painted in red across one side. "Anne Marie made this for me in her second-grade art class. For Christmas. It isn't broken." Tears gathered in the corners of Bethany's eyes and trickled down her face. "See. Not a scratch on it." Bethany clung to the disfigured little pot as if it were solid gold. "Where is she? Is she all right? I want to show her that her little Christmas vase is all right."

"She's outside, honey," Morgan said. "She got a bit sick to her stomach when she saw the mess, but James is taking care of her."

"I should be taking care of her. I'm her mother. I've always taken care of her." Bethany allowed Morgan to pull her into his arms, but she didn't loosen her tenacious hold on the green and red pot. "I've loved her since the moment I found out I was pregnant. Everything I've done, I've done for her. Always. Please, Morgan, tell me that you believe me, that you know why—"

"Hush, honey, hush. Everything is going to be all right. I'll take care of you and Anne Marie. I'll handle everything. I promise."

"Oh, Morgan." She cuddled close to him, absorbing his strength. "I've told you over and over again not to make promises that you can't keep."

Chapter 11

Morgan hovered in the corner, a dark shadow in the sunny yellow bedroom in Eileen Farraday's home. He had stood silently by while Bethany cared for her emotionally distraught child. The day's events had been too much for Anne Marie, the vandalism of her home tipping the scales. He had wanted to do something—anything—to help ease Anne Marie's distress, but she had wanted no one except her mother. And he had felt helpless, still felt helpless. He was supposed to be their protector, the man who would keep them safe and secure. But there wasn't a damn thing he could do to change what had happened. Bethany had been indicted for Jimmy Farraday's murder, and the man's idiot fans had vandalized her home.

Bethany lifted the embroidered silk shawl off the foot of the bed and covered her sleeping child. All the love in her heart showed plainly in her eyes as she gazed down at her daughter. A tight knot formed in Morgan's throat as he watched Bethany caress Anne Marie's cheek.

Bethany was a woman who loved completely, with every fiber of her being, holding nothing back, giving all. She had loved him that way once, and he'd been too young and foolish to realize what a rare and precious thing Bethany's kind of loving was. Whether it was mother love or sexual love, Bethany loved with all her heart.

He glanced over at the chair where Bethany had placed her purse. The lopsided little green and red vase that Anne Marie had made in second grade sat beside the leather shoulder bag. He shuddered, remembering the fanatical way Bethany had clung to that stupid clay pot, almost as if it were a lifeline. Nothing had mattered to Bethany, absolutely nothing, except what her daughter's gift represented: a lifetime of love and sacrifice she'd given her child and that child's love and devotion in return.

"She's asleep." Easing off the side of the bed, Bethany stood. "She's exhausted. Poor baby. This has been such a horrendous day for her."

"She'll be all right after a good night's sleep," Morgan said. "We'll be able to talk to her tomorrow and make her understand that everything is going to be all right."

Bethany stared at Morgan, her eyes questioning him. "*Is* everything going to be all right?"

"Of course it is," he told her, unwilling to believe he wouldn't be able to save her. "I'm not going to let you go to prison."

Stepping away from the bed, Bethany staggered. She grabbed the edge of the nightstand in an effort to steady herself. The Chinoiserie lamp on the nightstand tottered precariously. Bethany swayed forward, reaching for the lamp.

Realizing Bethany was on the verge of collapsing, Morgan bolted across the room. Catching her around the waist, he supported her body as she righted the lamp. "You're dead on your feet, honey. Let me take care of you."

She turned in his arms and gazed up into his piercing gray eyes. The way she looked at him spoke to him as loudly and clearly as any vocal response could have. For a split second she wondered if he had understood her silent message, but when he swept her up into his arms, she knew he had heard her heart's plea. Yes, take care of me. Hold me and love me and comfort me. Make the world go away. Just for tonight, let's pretend that neither the past nor the present exists.

She wanted to forget that he had left her sixteen years ago, alone and pregnant. And she wanted him to forget that he had come back for her and found her married to his cousin a few months later.

She clung to him as he carried her across the room, out into the hall and into the guest bedroom that Eileen had assigned to him. He closed the door behind them, shutting out the world, closing them off from the day's events and from tomorrow's worries.

Morgan knew that, despite her strength and determination, despite the way she'd held herself together for her daughter's sake, Bethany was ready to collapse. Emotional collapse as well as physical. Something more than being indicted for murder and having her house vandalized haunted Bethany. Something had happened between his mother and her, something that had thrown Bethany into an emotional turmoil she couldn't quite handle. He had no idea what that something was. He didn't need to know. Not now. Not tonight. All he needed to know was that Bethany needed him.

He flipped the wall switch. Subdued lighting from two huge, stone-based lamps illuminated the autumn-leaves textured wall and softened the rich hues of moss greens, golds and reds that dominated the large, masculine bedroom. He carried her past the sleigh bed and straight through to the adjoining bathroom.

"Morgan?" She questioned his actions when he entered the bathroom, turned on the wall sconces and set her down on the bench in front of the marble vanity.

"You need some tender, loving care, Beth." He knelt in front of her and removed her shoes, his big hands incredibly gentle as they massaged her feet. "This has been the day from hell. I want you to put everything out of your mind and relax and let me take care of you. Just for tonight. As if there were no tomorrow."

His words mirrored her thoughts. They had tonight. What would a few stolen hours of bliss hurt? Somehow she knew instinctively that Morgan needed her as much as she needed him. Tomorrow she would face all the ugly, bitter truths. Her indictment for murder. Her vandalized home. Her fears for Anne Marie's future. Her guilty heart, realizing more now than ever what an unforgivable mistake she'd made in marrying Amery.

When Morgan caressed the calves of her legs, easing slowly upward, Bethany reached down and tunneled her fingers through his long, golden hair. With his hands spread out over her knees, he looked up at her.

"Just for tonight." With those three words she placed herself in his care, trusting him to give her the pleasure and the peace her heart and body craved.

He lifted her enough to ease his hands up and under her skirt. He grasped the waistband of her panty hose, slid them over her hips and down her legs. Closing her eyes, she threw back her head and abandoned herself to the luxury of Morgan's loving attention.

With indulgent ease, as if he had all the time in the world, he undressed her. Unbuttoning her blouse slowly, he caressed her breasts through the thin silk, then unhooked and discarded her bra. His fingers plucked at her nipples, insistent yet gentle. Bethany sighed as sensations of sheer feminine delight rippled through her body. Within minutes, he divested her of all her clothing, and she sat before him, gloriously beautiful in her nakedness.

He removed his own clothes quickly and adeptly, then lifted Bethany into his arms, opened the frameless glass door and walked into the enormous marble-tiled shower. After adjusting the faucets and turning on the water, he guided her down the full length of his big, aroused body, allowing her to feel every throbbing inch of him. The warm spray hit their bodies like a thousand heated, massaging, cushioned needle pricks. Clinging to Morgan's shoulders, Bethany stood on tiptoe to reach his neck. Pressing her damp breasts against his hairy chest, she kissed his throat. Morgan groaned. His hardened sex pulsated against her belly.

Holding her securely around the waist, he pushed her gently away from him. She moaned when their bodies separated. He lifted the bar of soap from its niche in the shower wall and began a slow, intimate exploration of her body, lathering every silken centimeter of her wet, naked flesh. When her knees weakened, she tightened her hold on his shoulders. Giving her a gentle shove, he pushed her against the shower wall, bracing her there as he lowered his mouth and covered one breast while he pinched the nipple of her other breast with his fingertips. She squirmed as sexual twinges radiated from her breasts and through the core of her femininity.

Moving downward, he licked a hungry trail across her stomach, over her navel and on to the edge of the dark triangle at the apex of her thighs. He kissed her there, as the water cascaded over him, drenching him. When he slipped his hand between her legs and parted her thighs, Bethany gasped and trembled.

"Oh, Morgan...please...ah..."

His knees rested on the tiled shower floor. His big hands cupped her, spread her, opened her up for his marauding mouth and deadly hot tongue. The moment his lips kissed her intimately, she whimpered. With her hips pressed into the warm marble surface, she flattened her palms against the wall on each side of her, trying to steady her trembling body.

While his mouth made passionate love to her, he reached up to capture her breasts, heightening every sensation as his tongue and fingertips worked in perfect union. As she moaned and writhed, her body squirming against the marble wall, Morgan devoured her with his raging hunger. She cried out, shuddering with the force of her release. He drew every ounce of fulfillment from her, until she collapsed in his arms. Lifting her, he turned off the water and carried her out of the shower.

Bethany felt as if her bones had turned to liquid. She allowed Morgan to take care of her as if she were totally helpless. He set her on the vanity stool and wrapped a towel around her head, securing her long dark hair in the turban. With infinite patience for a man boldly aroused, he rubbed a large towel over her arms, her legs, her breasts, her hips and then eased the towel between her thighs and patted her intimately.

Desire spiraled anew within her. She reached out and caressed his chest. He sucked in a deep breath. His big hand shook when he grabbed her wrist and drew her fingers toward his sex.

"Touch me." He guided her hand, and when she encircled him, he threw back his head and groaned like a wounded animal.

With moisture still clinging to his hairy chest, legs and arms, Morgan picked Bethany up off the vanity stool. "I want to make love to you all night," he said, then captured her mouth in a heated, tongue-thrusting kiss. She wrapped her arms around his neck, accepting and then participating in the ravaging kiss.

Morgan carried her into the bedroom, laid her in the middle of the bed, atop the topaz gold sheets, and came down over her. His lips covered hers as he lowered his body. He parted her legs and sought entrance into her hot, damp depths. With his mouth eating at hers, sucking, nibbling, consuming, he lifted her hips and rammed into her. She cried out from the earth-shattering sensation of having him buried deep inside her.

Every muscle in his body tensed as he willed himself under control. The pleasure was almost beyond enduring. Simply sheathing himself within the tight fist of her womanhood brought him to the brink. But he wanted to make this loving last, at least long enough to bring Bethany to fulfillment once again.

When he withdrew from her, she whimpered, clinging to him, trying to bring him back inside. He plunged again, then withdrew and delved deeply. Stilling his movements as quivers of impending release warned him how close he was to losing himself, Morgan placed his lips over her breast and drew one tight nipple into his mouth.

She squirmed beneath him. Shudders of excitement trembled through her. She lifted and lowered her hips, then lifted them again, telling him of her need.

The moment he felt her tightening around him, her feminine mound pressing harder and harder against him with each upward thrust of her body, Morgan gripped her hips and jackhammered into her repeatedly. She cried out as fulfillment claimed her, the force of her release like a magnificent explosion that went on and on and on.

With one final lunge, Morgan emptied himself into her. Spirals of pleasure spread through his body, a thousand electrical currents of erotic sensation. A deep, hard groan surged from his throat in a long, tormented rumble.

Falling to her side, he eased her up toward the row of pillows at the head of the bed, then reached down and brought the multicolored blanket up to cover them. Bethany lay in his arms, the aftershocks still rippling through her body. When he caressed her arm, she shivered, her skin ultrasensitive.

Neither of them spoke. No words of love were exchanged. No promises for the future. No mention of tomorrow. They belonged to each other. Body and soul. But only for tonight. For the few precious hours between now and dawn.

As if afraid tomorrow would never come or perhaps afraid that it would come too soon, Morgan and Bethany slept briefly only to awaken again and again to seek each other in the darkness and claim the ecstasy they could find in no one else's arms.

The first time Morgan woke, moonlight streamed through the thin beige curtains. Wavy shadows danced across the bed. Bracing himself on one elbow, he turned and gazed down at Bethany, who slept peacefully at his side. He had buried his feelings for her so deep inside that he'd been able to pretend she meant nothing to him. But the moment he saw her again, all pretense vanished in the wake of the gut-wrenching emotions she brought to the surface.

He could not stop his hand as it reached out and touched her, his fingertips gliding over her face, down her throat and across her delicate shoulder. She roused, her eyelids fluttering as she opened her eyes and looked up at him. She smiled, and a hard knot of desire formed in his belly. She draped her arm around his neck and drew him to her, inviting him to take what he wanted.

"Beth, I don't ever want to hurt you again." He eased the covers off her naked body and caressed her satiny flesh. "I'm so very sorry that I left you, that I—"

She cut off his words with a kiss that ended all rational thought. Curling herself around him, she urged him to action. He took her quickly, losing himself inside her welcoming warmth.

Hours later, just as the dawn light spread a mingled pink haze across the horizon, Bethany woke to find Morgan's big, heavy arm draped across her. Easing out of his hold, she sat up in the bed, resting her back against the headboard. He mumbled incoherently in his sleep and turned over onto his back. The topaz sheet and multicolored blanket slipped below his waist, revealing his broad chest and narrow hips. Bethany sucked in her breath at the sight of him. Big. Hairy. Muscular. Powerfully male.

The first faint light of day illuminated the room with a soft, pale glow. She looked at him, drinking her fill. How many long, lonely nights had she dreamed of a moment like this? She had spent her lifetime loving Morgan Kane. She had tried to deny her true feelings, to pretend that she hated him, that she never wanted to see him again. But now she knew the truth and the truth broke her heart anew. Morgan had come back to Birmingham for her sixteen years ago. He had come back the day she married Amery.

If only she'd been older, wiser, stronger, she would have fought her mother and Morgan's parents. She would have gone against their wishes and refused to marry a man she didn't love. How different things might have been if only she had waited. She could have saved herself from a loveless marriage. She could have prevented Amery's tragic death. And she could have given Anne Marie her real father long ago. It was a wonder Morgan didn't hate her. But he didn't.

He might not love her, but he still cared. And he still wanted her.

Bethany flung the covers to the foot of the bed. Morgan stirred, but didn't open his eyes. She leaned over him, breathing in the smell of him, that strong, unique scent that was Morgan's alone. She ran the tip of her index finger across one tiny male nipple. Morgan groaned. She repeated the process. He groaned again. When she replaced her finger with her tongue, Morgan threaded his fingers through her long, dark hair, gripped the back of her head with one hand and grabbed her hip with the other.

Dragging her over on top of him, he surged up and into her, taking her by surprise. She gasped as he filled her fully.

"Morgan." Her breath caught in her throat. "We—we need to talk. I have to explain—"

"Later." Clutching her hips, he lifted her up and then settled her back down onto him. "Much later."

And the ride of her life began, slow, sensuous and steady at first. And then as a thick heaviness descended upon her, she fought it, tried to conquer it, by riding him harder and faster. With each stroke of his sex deepening and expanding, taking her completely, the tension inside her tightened.

She had lived without this wild ecstasy for far too long, without this magnificent man she loved to the point of madness. She didn't know if she'd ever get enough, not even if they found a way to make their passion last forever.

Late that evening, they stood in the middle of her living room in Forest Park and assessed the day's accomplishments.

Exhaustion weighed heavily on her shoulders, draining her of the last ounces of strength she possessed. The day had been long and tiring and she'd tried to do far too much. Morgan massaged her shoulders. She relaxed against him.

"It'll take weeks to get this place back to normal," she said, surveying the partially restored order of the room. "So many small things will have to be replaced and the sofa needs re-upholstering and—"

"It's been less than twenty-four hours and we've accomplished a lot. We'll get it all done," Morgan said. "One day at a time. As soon as we get things straightened out enough to suit you, we can move back in."

"I should give Mother another call and let her know we've already eaten." Bethany nodded to the empty pizza carton on the coffee table. "I should have gotten over there in time to have had dinner with Anne Marie."

"She understands how busy you've been today." Morgan guided Bethany to the overstuffed plaid chair, sat down and pulled her onto his lap. "I believe it's a bad idea to follow through with your plans for a fashion show at the Galleria Sunday afternoon. Think about what happened to Lisa. She's lucky to be alive and recovering so well."

"I thank God that she didn't die and that she'll be out of the hospital soon."

"I don't want to take any chances of something like that happening again," Morgan said. "You're going to be front-page news for weeks, and every nut case around is going to be hounding you, especially since Eileen posted that reward."

"My mother never ceases to amaze me. I can't believe she actually gave a personal interview to Chris Hammond of the *Birmingham News* and another to that Grayson guy from the *Post Herald.*" Bethany turned, slipped her arms around Morgan's neck and laid her head on his shoulder.

"I've warned her that it would be a mistake to take Tony Hayes up on his offer and be his guest on Wake Up Birmingham." Morgan kissed her temple, then rested his jaw against the top of her head.

"Just because you've warned her against doing it doesn't mean she won't surprise us all and show up on Tony's show one morning. And if she does, she'll think she's helping me in some way."

"Cancel the fashion show," Morgan said, nuzzling her ear.

"No. I can't. I refuse to give in to my fears and let what's happened in my life make me run scared." She sought his lips.

He didn't try to reason with her, telling himself that there would be time enough later to bring her around to his way of thinking. The kiss soon got out of control and they went at each other like a couple of wild animals, lost to their own primal needs.

An hour later, they freshened up, dressed and locked the front door just as the security guard Morgan had hired to watch the house pulled up in the driveway. After giving the guard his instructions, Morgan hurried Bethany to her Mercedes. It was after nine and he knew she was eager to get to her mother's and see Anne Marie. Mother and daughter had talked on the phone three times since Anne Marie arrived at her grandmother's after school, but only face-to-face contact would be enough for Bethany.

"I wish we had time to stop by and see Claudia," Bethany said when Morgan pulled the car out of the driveway. "But since we're already running late, I'll just phone her again. She worries about me."

"Mother's maternal attitude toward you and Anne Marie never ceases to amaze me," Morgan said.

"Claudia is in many ways the same woman she always was, but she has changed. Losing you altered her priorities. If you'd give her half a chance, you might discover that you actually like your mother now."

When she'd talked to Claudia this morning, Morgan's mother had wanted to know if she and Morgan had discussed his return to Birmingham sixteen years ago. When Bethany had told her that they hadn't, Claudia had wanted to know when Bethany was going to tell Morgan that he was Anne Marie's father.

Soon. Very soon. Before the trial. Maybe even before the arraignment. She had kept father and daughter apart long enough. She owed it to both of them to reveal her secret. To give Morgan his daughter and present Anne Marie with the father she should have had since birth.

As close as she and Anne Marie were, as easily as she often read her daughter's mind, Bethany had no idea how she would react to the news that Morgan was her father. She prayed that her daughter wouldn't hate her, that she would find it in her heart to understand and forgive.

But Morgan was a different matter entirely. She had no illusions, no false hopes that he would ever forgive her.

No matter what happened, she knew what she had to do. She had no other choice. Not really. She'd kept her secret far too long. It was past time to end the lie.

"You're awfully quiet, honey." As they passed under a streetlight, Morgan stole a glance at Bethany. She had knotted herself tightly in her seat and stared out the window as if in a trance.

"I was just thinking." Thinking about when, where and how I would tell you the truth about Anne Marie.

"You mean you were worrying," he said.

"You must admit that I have a lot to worry about."

"I wish I could make it all go away, every worry you have. But all I can do is keep you safe and continue trying to find out who killed Farraday." He eased the Mercedes coupe along the road, keeping to the posted speed limit. "Sooner or later, something's got to give. The real killer can't afford to sit around safe and secure. It's only a matter of time until we zero in on him or her. Dane Carmichael is running an extended check on every suspect, and I've decided to call in another agent."

Her heart jumped to her throat. "Why would you call in another agent?" Was he going to leave? After all they'd shared, could he simply walk away again?

"I can't guard you twenty-four hours a day and do all the investigating that needs to be done. I've become too personally involved to be objective, and my first priority is taking care of you. I need someone on the scene whose top priority is solving the mystery of Farraday's murder."

"But you've done everything possible to—"

"Not enough," he said sharply. "Dammit, honey, I'm sorry. I didn't mean to snap at you. I'm angry with myself. I haven't acted like a professional. I've gotten too wrapped up in your life. I care too much about you and Anne Marie. I should have already called in someone else."

"Then you aren't leaving town and you won't turn your bodyguard duties over to someone else?"

"No way would I trust your life to anyone else."

"Then the other agent will—"

"He'll do what I should have already done. Concentrate more on Farraday's murder. Somebody has got to know something. The day Farraday was shot, someone saw something that he or she doesn't even know they saw. I should have already talked to everyone who was at the station that afternoon. Dane can run a background check on every employee and still come up with nothing."

The dark road lay ahead like a curling snake, the blackness shattered only by the occasional glare of oncoming headlights. Morgan damned himself for a fool. He'd promised Bethany that he would not only protect her but prove her innocence. And he'd already let her down by not admitting sooner that he couldn't handle this job alone. He'd call Hawk tonight and have him catch the first flight out of Atlanta in the morning.

Bright headlights from behind the Mercedes struck the side-view mirror. Morgan muttered a vulgar oath under his breath.

"I hate it when someone drives too close behind like that," Bethany said. "Especially on these dark mountain roads."

"It would help if they'd dim their—"

The offending vehicle bumped the Mercedes's back end. Bethany gasped. Morgan cursed loudly, then eased his foot down on the accelerator. The car behind them picked up speed, quickly catching up with them. The driver rammed them from behind again, more forcefully the second time. Morgan gripped the steering wheel with white knuckled ferocity.

"That was no accident," he said. "Someone's playing games with us."

"What do you mean?"

Morgan tried to escape, but the faster he drove, the faster their attacker pursued them. Bethany gripped the seat with both hands. Her heartbeat drummed in her ears. Morgan maneuvered the Mercedes with expert skill, but the increased speed created havoc as he took the next sharp turn in the road.

"Someone's playing a deadly game, and we're their prey," Morgan said.

Coming up beside them, the driver slammed the side of his vehicle into the Mercedes, shoving it off the road. The white coupe skidded in the loose gravel on the shoulder. Morgan whipped the steering wheel around, cutting directly back into their attacker.

"Hang on," Morgan told her.

Bethany held her breath, nodding agreement, but unable to utter a single word. Fear clutched her stomach like an angry fist.

Bouncing back, the driver of the other car sideswiped them again, forcefully shoving them off the road and over the side of the embankment.

The Mercedes went down, down, down. The beam from the headlights bobbed up and then down as the car hit rough ground. A clump of trees hovered below like giant black demons lying in wait, ready to slaughter them.

Bethany heard herself screaming, but the sound seemed to come from a distance, like a terrified echo reverberating in the wind.

Dear God, they were going to die!

Chapter 12

Slamming his foot on the brake pedal, Morgan stopped the Mercedes only inches from the cove of trees blocking the descent down the mountainside. The headlights blasted the towering pines and the two ancient oaks, creating bizarre-shaped shadows. The sudden jolt threw Morgan and Bethany forward, the protective band of their seat belts the only barrier between their bodies and the windshield.

Bethany gulped in air at a frantic pace. Her heartbeat roared in her head like a cyclone. "Oh, dear God. Dear God." She repeated the prayerful chant again and again.

Killing the motor, Morgan drew up the emergency brake and sat very still for a brief moment. Focusing, centering his mind, he took control. Unsnapping his seat belt, he turned to Bethany. Even in the shadowy darkness he could still make out the terrified look on her face. Her eyes stared sightlessly straight ahead. Her breathing bordered on hyperventilation. Her body shivered, the quivering slight but noticeable.

After undoing her seat belt, he ran his hands up and down her trembling arms. "Are you all right?"

Not responding by word or action, Bethany sat there like a frozen statue on the verge of crumbling into pieces.

Grabbing her by the shoulders, he turned her toward him and shook her gently. "Bethany, snap out of it. We're safe. We didn't wreck."

"I—I thought we were going to die," she said. "What happened? Who ran us off the road?"

"Come on, honey, we need to get out of the car. I'm not sure how secure we are. I don't think the car is going anywhere, but just in case it does, I don't want us to be inside."

Reaching across Bethany, he opened the glove compartment, removed a flashlight and then eased open the passenger's side door. "Get out, but be careful. We're on a fairly steep slope, it's dark and you could easily fall."

When she hesitated, he gave her a gentle shove and said, "Go on, honey. I'm right behind you."

Willing herself to move, Bethany clutched her shoulder bag to her chest and climbed out of the car and onto the uneven ground. Her knees buckled. Her foot slipped on some loose pebbles. She cried out, grabbing at the darkness surrounding her. Suddenly a pair of strong arms encompassed her, lifting her before she fell, setting her back on her unsteady feet.

"Come on, Beth." He held her firmly around the waist. "We're not that far from the road."

Turning on the flashlight, he pointed its beam toward the highway above them. The faint, narrow light cut an illuminated pathway through the high grass, weeds, scraggly shrubs and bushes. Together they climbed the slope, through the underbrush, Morgan's hold on Bethany never wavering as he guided her to safety. When they reached the shoulder of the road, Morgan sat, pulling Bethany down with him. She was slightly winded; he wasn't even breathing hard.

The gravel gouged into her buttocks through the thin material of her cotton slacks. Reaching beneath her, she swept away a handful of rocks. Grunting as she squirmed, she settled more comfortably onto the cleared area.

Morgan jerked his cellular phone from his pocket, flipped it open and dialed. Bethany grabbed his jacket sleeve.

"Who are you—" she asked.

"Varner? Yeah, this is Morgan Kane. Someone just ran Bethany Wyndham and me off the road up here on Red Mountain.

No. We're okay. Just a bit shaken. No, we don't need an ambulance. We need a wrecker and a ride home."

Bethany clutched Morgan's arm as he listened to Detective Varner. A dozen questions bombarded her mind. Who? Why? Jimmy's killer? Because they were closer to discovering his or her identity than they realized? Or had it been someone attacking them for some other reason?

"It was no accident," Morgan said. "Somebody wanted us to plunge over the side of the mountain. Yeah, I got a good look, but it's dark and I'm only guessing. A red Porsche. Late model."

Bethany gasped. No, it couldn't have been. Surely Morgan was mistaken. It had all happened so quickly and it was very dark on this stretch of road. How could he be sure the car that had run them off the side of the mountain was a red Porsche?

"I can't identify the driver, but I'm pretty sure about the car," Morgan said. "Yeah, I know someone who drives a car just like it."

"Morgan!" Bethany refused to believe it was possible.

"James Farraday. Yeah, you'll need to check it out."

Bethany only half listened while Morgan gave Hal Varner their location. Her mind was totally absorbed in the knowledge that the attacking vehicle had been a red Porsche. Surely it was a coincidence that James drove an identical car, a present from Eileen when he turned sixteen. She refused to believe that her young stepbrother was capable of anything so sinister.

Morgan returned the phone to his pocket, then slipped his arm around Bethany's shoulder and drew her to his side. "Varner's sending out a wrecker and an ambulance. I couldn't convince him we were all right. He said he'll be here as soon as possible."

"Is he sending someone over to Mother's to check on James's car?" she asked.

Morgan held the flashlight like a candle, shooting the light straight up, casting a shady glow across his face. "I can't be a hundred percent certain it was James's Porsche," Morgan said. "But it was one just like his."

"But James would never—"

"I don't want to believe that boy is a killer any more than you do. I like him. But... There's no point in jumping to conclusions. The car might not have been James's. And even if it was his car, there's no proof that he was driving it."

"You didn't get a glimpse of the driver, did you?" Bethany laid her head on Morgan's shoulder. "It was too dark." Morgan was right. Neither of them should jump to any conclusions. If the car that ran them off the road belonged to James, then someone else must have been driving it. She had to hold on to that thought. She would not allow herself to think anything else. She loved James. And more important, Anne Marie loved him.

"What do you mean, she isn't here?" Bethany glared at her mother's tear-stained face. "How could you have let her slip out of the house? It's dangerous out there for her all alone. People know her face. They know she's my daughter. My God, Mother, you had her at your side at the courthouse yesterday when news crews from across the country were there."

"I had no idea Anne Marie would do something so foolish as to leave the house without asking my permission." Eileen puckered her perfect little mouth into a pout as she dabbed at her eyes with a lace handkerchief. "When she stayed such a long time upstairs, I went to check on her and that's when..." Eileen burst into tears, her slender shoulders trembling. "I found the note. It was addressed to you."

Eileen held up the piece of crumpled notebook paper in front of her. Bethany grabbed it out of her mother's hand.

Mama,

Don't be upset, but I just couldn't miss this chance. Melanie called and asked me to go out with her tonight. She has her own car and just got her driver's license. She knows where James hangs out on Friday nights. She's seen him there before, so we're going to follow him. I didn't tell Grandmother because I knew she'd go into hysterics. I promise we'll be home by midnight. If I'm lucky, maybe James will bring me home.

Love, A.M.

"Damn!" Bethany handed the note to Morgan. "I can't imagine what possessed her. Anne Marie has never done anything like this before in her whole life.''

Morgan scanned the note quickly, folded it and stuck it in his pocket. ''So James isn't here.'' Morgan glanced at Eileen. ''Where is he?''

''I don't know. Not for sure. He's eighteen, you know, and a very social young man,'' Eileen said. ''He always has plans on weekend nights.''

Detective Varner cleared his throat. ''Sorry to interrupt, but we're going to have to find young Farraday's car.''

''What is he talking about?'' Eileen's gaze traveled from Bethany's face to Morgan's, and then she turned to Seth Renfrew, who stood at her side.

Seth patted her tenderly on the back. He looked at Hal Varner. ''What's this about James's car?''

Morgan glanced from Seth to Eileen. ''The car that ran us off the road tonight was a red Porsche.''

Gasping, Eileen clutched her blouse, her ring-adorned fingers centered over her heart. ''You can't mean you think James is the person who tried to...tried to... No!''

Bethany grabbed her mother's shoulders and shook her soundly. ''Don't go all to pieces. Not now. I want you to think. Do you have any idea where James might be? We have to find him. And we have to find Anne Marie.''

Eileen crumpled into a heap, bowing her head, wringing her hands and weeping uncontrollably. Seth pulled her away from Bethany and into his arms, cuddling her, stroking her back and shoulders as he whispered comforting words.

Glancing over Eileen's head, he looked Morgan square in the eye. ''James and I have had a few man-to-man talks, if you know what I mean. He thinks of me as an uncle, a confidant. I've made a point of taking an interest in James. During one of our one-bachelor-to-another talks, he confided in me that he often drives to the WHNB station, parks his Porsche and goes off with some friends.''

''Do you know where they go?''

''To Southside, somewhere around the Five Points area,'' Seth said.

''Oh, dear God!'' Bethany grabbed Morgan's arm. ''If Anne Marie and Melanie have gone to Southside, there's no telling what kind of trouble they've run into. There are all kinds of clubs and hangouts down there. Weirdos and druggies and—''

''We'll call Melanie Harden's parents and find out what kind of car she's driving,'' Morgan said.

''James may have left his car at the TV station as he's done in the past,'' Seth told Detective Varner, then returned his gaze to Morgan's stoic face. ''He has mentioned a place called the Purple Fizz. It seems no one checks IDs very closely there.''

Standing in the WHNB parking lot, Bethany watched the police wrecker tow James's badly damaged red Porsche. Morgan clamped his hands down on her shoulders. Pivoting her head slightly, she glanced up at him.

''This can't be happening,'' she said. ''James's car was used to run us off the mountain, and Anne Marie slipped out of the house to chase off down to Five Points after him. I know James wasn't driving his car. I can't believe he tried to kill us any more than I can believe he could have killed his father.''

''We're going to have to pick the boy up for questioning,'' Hal Varner said. ''If he doesn't have an alibi for the time of your accident, then I'm afraid he's going to be in a lot of trouble.''

''He's going to be in a lot of trouble regardless,'' Morgan said. ''If anything happens to Anne Marie, he'll have to answer to me.''

Snapping her head around, Bethany stared at Morgan. Not only the protective attitude his words conveyed but the deadly, controlled tone of his voice revealed the paternal feelings Morgan had for Anne Marie. He had sounded just like a worried father.

''Why are you blaming James?'' Bethany asked. ''He didn't exactly invite Anne Marie and Melanie to follow him.'' She turned to Detective Varner. ''Please, if you don't need us anymore, may we leave? I have a child out there somewhere who could be in danger.''

A classic black Pontiac GTO pulled into the parking lot, screeching to an abrupt halt. Tony Hayes opened the door and stepped out. Holding a large paper bag in one hand, he threw up his other hand in greeting.

"Well, hello, Bethany, what are you doing here?" Tony glanced at Hal Varner. "What's going on? I noticed a wrecker pulling James's car, or at least I think it was James's car."

"What are you doing at the station this time of night?" Bethany glared at Tony. Slick Tony. Smooth-talking, cocky Tony, with his silver-streaked dark hair and his bedroom blue eyes. He was every bit the womanizing bastard Jimmy Farraday had been. Two peas in a pod.

"Oh, I was working on a special tribute to Jimmy. Vivian's been helping me. She and some of the crew stayed here to finish up. I had a dinner engagement, so afterward, I decided I'd bring Vivian and the gang some supper.

"So now you know why I'm at the station, how about telling me what y'all are doing here? Was that or was that not James's car?"

"It was young Farraday's car," Detective Varner said. "His red Porsche was involved in an accident earlier tonight."

"Is James all right?" Tony asked. "Is he in the hospital?"

"James is fine," Morgan said. "We aren't sure he was even driving the car."

"Look, we're wasting time standing here explaining things to Tony," Bethany said. "I want to go find Anne Marie. Now!"

"You two go ahead," Varner said. "I'm going to stay here and question everyone at the station. Maybe somebody saw something that can help us."

"Come on, honey, we'll find Anne Marie." Morgan led Bethany to the green Aston Martin convertible they'd borrowed from her mother.

"Hey, Kane," Varner shouted. "If you find James Farraday before my men do, give me a call."

Morgan nodded to Varner, then put Bethany in the convertible. He slid into the driver's seat and closed the door. He stole a quick glance her way. She sat there rigid as a statue, her small hands folded in her lap. He suspected she was clasping her hands to prevent them from shaking.

He reached over, slid his hand beneath her dark wind-blown hair and caressed the back of her neck. "We'll find Anne Marie. Don't worry. And when we find her, I'm going to lock her up and throw away the key."

"She has never done anything like this before." Bethany

looked at Morgan, all the fear and sorrow she felt showing plainly on her face. "I don't know. Maybe it's this wild crush she has on James, or perhaps her new friendship with Melanie Harden. Of course, having her mother indicted for murder and the story being front-page news has turned her world upside down."

Morgan drove the convertible out of the parking lot and onto the highway, taking Bethany's directions on the quickest way to get from WHNB to Five Points. He didn't know how much more Bethany could take without falling to pieces. Her nerves were wound so tightly, now, that he expected her to snap at any time. Over the years, Bethany had developed into a strong woman, but even the strongest had their breaking point. If she had one weakness, it was her daughter. She loved her child more than anything on earth. Amery's child.

He hated himself for the selfish thought. Jealous not only that Bethany had given Amery a child, but that she loved that child with such passionate devotion. It doesn't matter, he told himself, who her father was, Bethany would love Anne Marie the same. It's because Anne Marie is her child that she loves her, not because she's Amery's.

And you could love her for the very same reason. Because she's Bethany's.

They cruised the Southside streets, concentrating their search mostly in the Five Points area. Down University Boulevard, onto Ninth Avenue, then Tenth Avenue and Eleventh. If the Purple Fizz existed, it was well hidden.

"Hell! You'd think a canary yellow, twin-turbos Audi would be easy to spot." Morgan slowed the convertible to a snail's pace, scanning every side street as they passed, checking parking areas, while Bethany searched in vain for Melanie Harden's car.

"We don't even know for sure that Anne Marie is down here," Bethany said. "Just because James told Seth that he comes down here sometimes doesn't mean this is where he came tonight."

"You're right," Morgan admitted, apprehension building steadily in his gut. "But my instincts tell me that James is enough like I was at his age that he gets his kicks out of walking on the wild side."

"Well, my daughter is not old enough to walk on the wild

side. I've protected her from the seamier side of life, and I can't bear to think what my arrest and indictment have done to her. She'll never be the sweet, innocent child she was before all this happened to us."

"You can't blame yourself. What's happened to you isn't your fault. And sooner or later, Anne Marie has to grow up. You can't protect her from the real world forever."

"Well, she could have spent the rest of her life without being exposed to— Look! Down that street. See that sign."

Morgan took a sharp right, then pulled the Aston Martin to a halt, momentarily blocking traffic. The sign read Purple Fizz with an arrow pointing toward a small parking area between two buildings.

"How the hell did we miss that the last go-around?" he grumbled.

"I don't like the looks of that place."

Purple neon lights flickered on and off around the double doors of a small one-story building. Loud hard-rock music permeated the air. A swarm of people crowded the parking area, most with either a cigarette in their mouth or a beer bottle in their hand, some with both.

"There's a yellow Audi," Morgan said, nodding to the small, sleek automobile that was half-hidden between a battered, rusty van and a shiny, new half-ton Chevy truck.

Morgan pulled the car into a parking space straight across from the Audi, killed the motor, checked his shoulder holster and then turned to Bethany.

"If that's Melanie's car, then they're probably inside the club." He unhooked his safety belt. Bethany did the same. "Let's check out the license plate number on the car first, then we'll storm the walls and get those girls out of that dump."

With only one security light in the whole parking lot, visibility was limited. The pulsating purple neon lights sent out flickering waves of illumination that cast a lavender glow over everything they touched. A half moon beamed down from a clear, black sky.

Morgan bent over, checked the license plate on the Audi and groaned. "This is Melanie's car."

"How could those girls do something so stupid?" Bethany clung to Morgan's arm.

"Because they're teenagers," Morgan said. "I remember thinking that I was invincible. Nothing could hurt me. Danger simply wasn't a reality."

"But Anne Marie has always been so much like me. She's never been a risk taker like—" Bethany caught herself before she compared her daughter to Morgan.

Draping his arm around her waist, Morgan led Bethany across the parking lot. "You took the biggest risk of your life, honey, by falling in love with me. If you'd been smart, you would have run from me as far and fast as you could have."

"What you're saying is that Anne Marie is doing just what I did, risking everything for love."

Loud voices and a thundering crash directly across the parking lot grabbed Morgan's immediate attention. Instinctively he shoved Bethany behind him and surveyed the scene. A small group of people, mostly men, made a semicircle around two young guys squaring off against each other.

The black-haired youth with his back to them looked familiar. James Farraday! Crouched and ready to attack. Damn that boy! What kind of mess had he gotten himself into with these tough-looking characters? Morgan wondered.

"It's James!" Bethany gasped as she peered around Morgan's side. "Oh, God, look! There's Anne Marie and Melanie."

Morgan's heart stopped beating for a split second when he saw Anne Marie standing to one side of the semicircle, a terrified look on her face. The pint-size redhead grasping Anne Marie's hand had to be Melanie Harden.

"I don't like the look of this," Morgan said. He'd been in his share of fights over the years. As a boy and as a man. As an untrained civilian and as a skilled warrior.

He retrieved his phone from his jacket, handed it to Bethany and repeated the number for her to call. "Get in touch with Hal Varner and let him know we've found James."

When Morgan took a tentative step forward, she grabbed his arm, halting his advance. "What are you going to do?"

What was he going to do to? This wasn't a combat situation where the kill or be killed motto held true. This was a street fight between two equal, unarmed participants. He thought it best not to interfere, to let the boys fight it out, as long as no one was in any real danger.

He could easily whisk Anne Marie and Melanie away, but he thought the girls should witness the fight. Maybe it would scare a little sense into them.

"Please, don't do this," Anne Marie yelled. "Just let Melanie and me leave. We don't want to go with you and your buddies."

James's opponent, a lean, wiry teenager with curly brown hair, leered at Anne Marie, his lips curving in a cocky smile. "Hey, baby, if your boyfriend wins this fight, you and Red there can leave with him. Otherwise, you two are going with us."

"She's not going anywhere with you, B.J." James snarled, baring his teeth in a show of deadly defiance.

Bethany finished her brief conversation with Hal Varner, then slid Morgan's phone into the pocket of her dirty, wrinkled cotton slacks.

"Do something, Morgan, before they start fighting."

Bethany started to walk around Morgan, but he caught her wrist and jerked her backward. "Right now, this is James's fight."

"What are you saying? Surely, you don't intend to allow those boys to beat each other to a pulp, do you?"

Before Morgan could reply, B.J. let out a blood-curdling yell and went into a typical karate stance. Not to be outdone, James repeated the action. With hands, arms and legs in motion, the two young men began an uncoordinated battle dance that resulted in little more than evasion tactics. Apparently both boys knew a few karate moves, but it took only a few seconds for them to exhaust their limited repertoire of skilled maneuvers.

Apparently tired of getting nowhere fast, B.J. charged, tossing the first punch, but James dodged the blow and quickly retaliated with a right cross. B.J. staggered backward, but recovered and came at his sparring partner again, this time landing a blow to James's midsection.

Anne Marie cried out, but when she tried to rush toward James, Melanie restrained her.

Bethany pulled against Morgan's hold on her, but when he clamped his hand down on her shoulder, she stopped struggling and glared at him. "I want you to stop them," she told him. "Now!"

"Not yet," he said.

Both boys were breathing hard, panting as they tried to stare each other down. Then they went at it again, James getting in several hard punches and one quick, adept move that sent B.J. to the ground.

"Now end it," Bethany said.

"Not yet."

"Not yet! Then when?"

One of the men in the semicircle smashed the neck of his beer bottle against the concrete curb, then tossed the jagged glass weapon to B.J.

"Here, you go, B.J. Let's make this fight interesting. Show the rich kid how we do things down here," the guy said.

"Now?" Bethany asked in exasperation.

"Now," Morgan said.

B.J. grinned wickedly, obviously aware that he had the advantage with a weapon in his hand. James didn't flinch when B.J. eased up off the ground, holding the broken bottle in front of him. Preparing to defend himself, James waited for the first lunge of the deadly sharp glass. But the first strike never came.

Bethany watched in amazed silence. Everything happened in a split second. If she'd blinked, she would have missed Morgan's assault. Like an accelerated ballet, Morgan entered into the fray and before anyone knew he was even there, he knocked the beer bottle out of B.J.'s hand and spun the boy around and into a choke hold.

"Morgan!" Anne Marie screamed. "You saved our lives." Jerking free from Melanie, she ran over to James. "I was so scared. Are you all right? Thank God Morgan showed up when he did."

Bethany rushed toward her daughter. Morgan turned B.J. to face his circle of admirers, letting every man there see how helpless their buddy was. Morgan's jacket had caught behind his shoulder holster and the leather sheath and handle of the shiny Sig were in plain sight.

"Fun's over, boys and girls. Everybody move along," Morgan told the crowd.

B.J. grunted, trying but unable to speak. Sweat coated his pimpled face.

When the crowd didn't dissipate fast enough to suit Morgan, he glared at them, a deadly glint in his eyes. Curving his lips, he snarled silently. Within seconds the parking lot emptied and only six people remained.

"Bethany, take the girls and y'all get in Melanie's Audi and head straight to your mother's," Morgan said.

"What about you and James?" Bethany asked.

"James and I will wait for Hal Varner." Morgan released his dangerous hold on B.J., shoved him toward the flashing neon-lit doors of the Purple Fizz and laughed when the boy came back at him.

"You got a death wish, boy?" was all Morgan said, but B.J. halted and backed away slowly, then turned and all but ran into the Purple Fizz.

"Mama, why does—" Anne Marie said.

"Not one word, young lady," Bethany warned. "You are in big trouble."

"But why did Morgan call the police? And why did he let B.J. go and not James?" Anne Marie's voice combined an unpleasant whine with a soulful plea.

"Go home with your mother, Anne Marie," James told her. "You had no business following me down here. This is no place for a girl like you."

Anne Marie nodded as tears filled her eyes. Bethany led the girls toward Melanie's car. Morgan waited until Bethany and both girls were in the Audi before he turned back to James.

"Look, Morgan, I didn't invite her down here," James said. "Hell, I don't even know how she knew where I was."

"I realize that," Morgan said. "Believe me, if I thought you'd brought her down here or invited her, B.J. would never have gotten the first blow."

James's face paled. "Well, if you know it wasn't my fault that she was down here, why'd you sic the police on me?"

"Your fight with B.J. has nothing to do with why we're waiting for Hal Varner."

"I don't understand."

"Do you have an alibi for where you were between nine and nine-thirty tonight?" Morgan asked.

"Why do I need an alibi?"

"Because somebody driving your red Porsche tried to run Bethany and me off the side of the mountain tonight a little after nine."

"Oh, God.... It wasn't me. I swear it wasn't."

"For the sake of everyone involved, I sure as hell hope you can prove it wasn't you." Morgan's steel gray eyes glinted, his quick, hard perusal frightening in its intensity. "Because if it was you, you'll have to answer to me."

Chapter 13

"It's them!" Anne Marie ran to the front door and swung it open wide. "They're here."

Bethany rushed behind her, as anxious as her daughter to see Morgan and James, to have them home safe and sound. Bethany walked out onto the front porch and eased up beside Anne Marie. Slipping her hand into her daughter's, she squeezed tightly.

Stars twinkled in the dark night sky. The porch lights illuminated the stone steps, the walkway and several feet of manicured lawn. A cool breeze caressed Bethany's bare arms. She shivered. Dawn was only a couple of hours away.

She glanced at Anne Marie's tear-streaked face and recognized the look of adoration in her child's eyes as she gazed longingly at James Farraday. Could other people see that look on her own face whenever she stared at Morgan? Maybe for Anne Marie it was only puppy love, only young love, but it was love all the same, and perhaps even more intense for its innocence.

Morgan's big hand rested on James's shoulder as the two men came up the walkway. Letting out a deep breath, Bethany said a silent prayer of thanks.

"How's Eileen?" James asked as he climbed the stone steps

to the porch. "Does she know the truth? Does she know I wasn't the one who tried to run you and Morgan off the road?"

"She never believed you did." Anne Marie hurried down the steps, then halted abruptly when she came face-to-face with James. She strained forward, but didn't reach out and touch him. "Grandmother and I knew you couldn't have done anything so awful."

Bethany wasn't surprised that James's first thoughts had been of her mother. The boy loved Eileen dearly. If he'd been her own son, he couldn't have been more devoted.

"As soon as Morgan called from the police station and told us that your alibi checked out, Seth gave Mother a sleeping pill and put her to bed," Bethany told James. "Come on in. You both look exhausted." She gazed into Morgan's cool gray eyes and for a brief instant they exchanged a poignant look.

Bethany knew that Morgan was as relieved as she that James hadn't been the one who'd tried to kill them. But with James no longer a suspect, they were left with a deadly, unanswered question. Who had *borrowed* James's car and run Morgan and her off the side of Red Mountain?

Morgan glanced upward from where he stood on the steps, past Bethany and straight at Seth Renfrew, who stood in the foyer, just inside the open front door. Looking back over her shoulder, Bethany caught the odd look in Seth's eyes. Fear? No, not fear. Supplication.

In that one moment, as she watched Morgan's visual assault and Seth's retreat, she realized that Morgan was once again questioning Seth's guilt or innocence. With James eliminated as a suspect, Morgan was already altering the list, considering the other possibilities. And Seth seemed to be at the top of that list.

Morgan and Seth stared at each other, an accusation issued and a denial returned. Anne Marie and James gazed at each other, love and comfort offered and reluctantly rejected.

"It's nearly four o'clock." Bethany's words broke the peculiar silence that hung in the air. "It's been a long, difficult night for all of us. Come on inside."

Morgan waited at the bottom of the steps. Anne Marie followed James up and onto the porch. He paused momentarily and when Bethany opened her arms, he went into her motherly embrace.

"I'm glad you weren't hurt tonight." James pulled away from Bethany. "I hope the police find out who stole my car."

"I hope they do, too," Bethany said. "Perhaps when they do, they'll also find your father's murderer."

James nodded, then glanced over at Anne Marie. "I'll talk to Anne Marie and make sure she never does something else as stupid as she did tonight. She won't ever again be in danger because of her crush on me."

Bethany saw the tears glimmering in her daughter's eyes and knew the agony her child felt. Love rejected was like a mortal wound, the pain almost unbearable. James was trying to do the right thing, the honorable thing, but in doing so, he was breaking Anne Marie's fragile young heart.

James walked inside, nodding halfheartedly at Seth as he passed him on his way through the foyer. Reaching out, Seth patted him on the back, then stepped away from the front door and waited for the others to enter the house. James took the stairs two at a time in his haste to go upstairs. Bethany suspected he would stop by Eileen's room and check on her.

Bethany wrapped her arm around Anne Marie's trembling shoulders. "Oh, Mama!" Anne Marie turned, falling into her mother's arms. Crying as if her heart would break—as if it was indeed already broken—she clung to Bethany. "I made such a mess of things, didn't I?" Anne Marie lifted her face from her mother's shoulder. "He doesn't care anything about me. Not that way. I should have known. He—he's always treated me like a kid."

"Come on, sweetheart. Let's go upstairs and go to bed."

"I wish I could sleep for ten years and wake up when I'm twenty-five." Anne Marie sniffled as she pulled out of Bethany's embrace.

She led Anne Marie into the house, pausing momentarily when she glanced at Seth. "Talk to Morgan," she said. "Make him understand that you would never do anything to hurt me or mother or Anne Marie."

"I'm not sure my powers of persuasion are that strong, my dear." Seth smiled weakly. "Your Mr. Kane doesn't trust anyone, except perhaps you. He's not going to take my word for anything, I'm afraid."

"Does Morgan think Seth was the one who—" Anne Marie asked.

"No, of course he doesn't," Bethany said. "It's just that Morgan—"

"I can speak for myself." Morgan hovered in the doorway, his massive shoulders filling the wide space.

Bethany gasped. Anne Marie jumped. Seth knotted his hands into fists at his sides.

"Morgan, you mustn't think Seth is the one who killed Jimmy or that he tried to run you and Mama off the road tonight," Anne Marie pleaded. "If you knew him the way we do, you'd know he couldn't harm anyone."

"Thank you for that vote of confidence," Seth said. "Now, little girl, you must go on upstairs to bed and get some rest. And so must your mother. Why don't you two take care of each other and stop worrying about me?"

"Morgan, promise me that you won't be mean to Seth." Anne Marie looked Morgan straight in the eye.

"All I'm going to do is ask Seth a few questions," Morgan replied.

"When you finish questioning Seth, I'd like to see you for a few minutes before you go to bed," Bethany said.

Morgan nodded agreement. Bethany led Anne Marie up the stairs quickly. Morgan turned his attention to Seth, who closed and locked the front door.

"Would you care for a brandy, Mr. Kane?" Seth asked. "Or perhaps some Scotch?"

"Scotch will be fine," Morgan said, and followed Seth into the study.

Seth turned on the light, illuminating the masculine, wood-paneled room. Going straight to the bar, he lifted a bottle of Scotch, poured a liberal amount into two glasses and held one out to Morgan.

Morgan accepted the glass, lifted the liquor to his mouth and drank slowly, allowing the hard, aged whiskey to slide down his throat, warming a trail to his stomach.

Standing behind the bar, his drink untouched, Seth looked directly at Morgan. "I'd rather you didn't bother Eileen with a lot of unnecessary questions. I can tell you whatever you need to know."

"Where were you between nine and nine-thirty last night?" Morgan swallowed another gulp of Scotch.

"When Eileen found Anne Marie's note, she called my house, but didn't get an answer," Seth said. "Then she called me on my cellular phone. I was out driving around Birmingham. When I'm restless and have a lot on my mind, I often just get in the car and drive for a hour or two, until my head clears."

"So, you were out just driving around when Bethany and I were run off the road?"

"I don't have an alibi for that thirty minutes," Seth admitted freely. "It was before nine when Eileen called me and I didn't arrive here at her home until well after ten o'clock. I was all the way across town and traffic was heavy. It always is on a Friday night. So, you see, Mr. Kane, if you can't take my word that I didn't steal James's car and deliberately try to run you and Bethany off the mountain, I'm afraid you'll have to keep me on your list of suspects."

"Who besides you, Eileen and James knew that Bethany and I were at her house tonight? Someone knew where we were. And the only way they'd know what time we left Bethany's and what route we took was if they waited near Bethany's house and followed us."

"I'm not sure who else might have known." Seth pondered the question for a moment, then snapped his fingers as he remembered something. "Eileen mentioned that Vivian Crosby had stopped by earlier in the afternoon and had asked about Bethany and how she was coping with the indictment and the break-in at her house."

"Did Eileen tell Vivian Crosby where Bethany would be last night?"

"I'm sure she did. Vivian has been very supportive of Eileen since Jimmy's death and Eileen has...well, you know how Eileen loves attention. She knows that Vivian was quite fond of Jimmy, so she'd have no reason to suspect her in his death. Vivian's been stopping by on a fairly regular basis."

"I'll double-check Vivian's whereabouts," Morgan said. "But according to Tony Hayes, Vivian was at WHNB last night, along with several other members of the Wake Up Birmingham crew, preparing a special tribute to Jimmy."

"Then Tony has an alibi for that time, too?"

"Tony had a dinner date, or so he told us. I'll have to verify his story."

"So, you've narrowed your suspects down to the three of us?" Seth asked. "To Vivian, Tony and me?" Seth lifted his glass of Scotch off the bar.

"Unless there's someone else out there that we don't know about." Morgan finished off his drink, set the glass on the bar and walked toward the door. Pausing just before exiting the study, he glanced over his shoulder. "Don't be guilty, Renfrew. Please, don't be guilty."

Seth's face paled. He clutched the crystal glass so tightly that it cracked and broke, splattering liquor over his hand. Morgan walked out of the study, leaving the door open behind him.

Morgan sat down on the top step of the stairs, removed his phone from his pocket and dialed Hawk's private number.

"Whoever the hell this is, you'd better have a damn good reason for calling me in the middle of the night," Hawk growled into the phone.

"Who is it?" a feminine voice asked.

"Hawk, it's Kane. Tell your lady friend that it's business."

"Your timing is the pits," Hawk said.

"I need you in Birmingham as soon as possible. Can you be here before noon?" Morgan asked.

"I'll check in with Dane and then be on my way by sunup. I should be there before brunch."

"Tell Dane to set a fire under all the investigators digging into Renfrew, Vivian Crosby and Hayes."

"Will do."

Waiting in Morgan's room, Bethany paced back and forth. The minute she heard his footsteps in the hallway, she ceased her repetitious trek and met him at the door.

"How's Anne Marie?" he asked.

"She cried herself to sleep," Bethany said. "Her world has turned upside down the past few weeks and now her heart is broken."

"James had to do what he did, say what he said." Reaching out, Morgan grasped Bethany's shoulders and backed her into the bedroom. Lifting his foot, he kicked the door closed. "Anne Marie isn't old enough for a love affair. You've got to give James credit for realizing that fact."

"I know he did the only thing he could, under the circumstances. I just wish Anne Marie didn't feel things so deeply."

"The way her mother does?" Morgan drew Bethany into his arms.

She wedged her hands between them, separating their bodies. "Did Seth have an alibi for—"

"No."

"He didn't do it. I know Seth, and he isn't capable of murder."

"Everyone is capable of murder, given the right provocation," Morgan said.

"Seth would never harm me."

"Can we leave this discussion for later? Our arguing about Seth Renfrew's possible guilt or innocence isn't going to change either of our minds. You believe in his innocence. I'm keeping him at the top of my suspects' list, along with Vivian Crosby and Tony Hayes. And as far as I know right now, Renfrew is the only one with a motive."

"Concentrate your investigation on Vivian or Tony, not Seth!"

"Let's drop this for now, honey. I'm tired. You're tired. We can discuss this more rationally when we've both had some rest." What he wanted—what he needed—was to bury himself deep inside Bethany, to take her hard and fast and lose himself in the pleasure of possessing her once again. He wanted to taste her sweet lips, to savor the feel of her body wrapped around his.

Jerking out of his hold, she backed away from him. "All right. We'll talk about this later. I'll leave you alone so you can go to bed." The blood rushed through her body as her heart pounded loud and fast, thundering in her ears. The last thing she wanted was to leave Morgan. She desperately wanted—desperately needed—to make love to him, to give and receive the ultimate pleasure.

He grabbed her wrist and yanked her up against him. "You're not going anywhere. Not for a long time. Not until I say you can go." Narrowing his gaze, he stared at her with hungry eyes.

Her stomach quivered. Her hands shook. Caught in his mesmerizing stare, she took in deep gulps of air. Her breasts rose and fell with each labored breath. Her nipples peaked.

She gasped when he took her mouth in a hot, devouring kiss. Standing on tiptoe, she wrapped her arms around his neck and yielded to the power of her own desire. She could not deny the overwhelming longings that commanded her every action.

With a haste born of passion, Morgan stripped her clothes from her body, all the while kissing her, touching her, aiding her as she yanked off his jacket and unbuttoned his shirt.

"I want you." He growled the words, his need a wild, burning rage within him. "I want to—"

Bethany cut off his words of need with a tongue-probing kiss. Clinging to him, pressing her throbbing breasts against his naked chest, she rubbed herself intimately against him.

He backed her up to the bed, bent his head and suckled her breast. She moaned with pleasure, then pulled his shirt loose from his pants. When she unbuckled his belt and unzipped his slacks, he shoved her down on the bed, then hurriedly removed his holster and laid it on the floor. He divested himself of the rest of his clothes, tossing them haphazardly onto the floor.

The moment he came to her, big, hard and fully aroused, Bethany pulled him down on top of her, then urged him to turn over and allow her the dominant position. He turned, lifting her, taking her with him.

Lying flat on his back, Bethany straddling him, he grinned. "Is this the way you want me, honey?"

"Yes," she said. "Just like that."

She kissed him, then nibbled at his mouth. When he reached up to grab her, she manacled his big wrists and threw his arms above his head, holding him down as she rubbed her breasts across his hairy chest.

When he groaned deep in his throat, Bethany smiled, loving the feeling of power she possessed. "Just lie there. Don't touch me. Not yet."

"You're running this show, honey. Do whatever you want to me."

She began a sensual assault that soon had Morgan regretting that he'd agreed to her demands. She covered every inch of his body with her marauding mouth, her hot, enticing tongue and her tormenting fingers.

He realized that the glorious attention she gave him came from her own desperate need, but when she eased downward and flicked her tongue over him, he ceased to think coherently. Easing her hand under his buttocks, she used her fingers to excite him, while her mouth pleasured him, quickly bringing him to the edge of fulfillment.

When he felt himself losing control, he pulled her upward, then flipped her onto her back and thrust into her. She met him lunge for lunge, returning to him all that he gave her. Their mouths mated with the same wild urgency while they tossed and tumbled, consumed by the fury of their passion. Their climaxes came simultaneously, so perfectly in tune were their hearts and minds and bodies.

As the aftershocks of completion rippled through them, Morgan lifted Bethany in his arms, eased under the covers and held her close, whispering her name, his lips caressing her damp neck.

Bethany clung to him, afraid that time was running out. She would take all that he offered now, knowing there might well be no tomorrow for them.

What the hell was all that noise? Morgan roused from a deep sleep, his eyelids fluttering as he tried to open his eyes. Bethany's breasts pressed against his back. Her slender arm draped his waist.

She groaned. Awakening slowly, Morgan realized that his cellular phone, inside his coat that lay on the floor, was ringing insistently. And someone was knocking on the door.

Rising to a sitting position, he tossed the covers to the foot of the bed and gave Bethany a gentle shake. She groaned again, then opened her eyes to narrow slits.

"What is it?" she asked. "What's that awful sound?"

"Wake up, honey." He gave her another gentle shake. "We've got company. Someone's knocking on the door, and my cell phone's ringing."

She shot straight up, totally oblivious to her nakedness. "What if it's Anne Marie? How will I ever explain—"

"Morgan!" Eileen Farraday's soft, sweet, Southern voice demanded in a loud whisper. "Morgan Kane, wake up. There's a man downstairs who says you sent for him."

The phone continued ringing. "Dammit!" He crawled out of bed, rummaged through their discarded clothes until he found his jacket, then lifted it off the floor. He picked up his rumpled shirt and tossed it to Bethany. "Here, honey, put this on and go calm your mother down before she wakes the whole house."

Bethany slipped into the shirt, buttoning it quickly, then jumped out of bed and ran to the door. Easing it open just a fraction, she peeped out at her mother.

"Bethany?" Eileen's mouth gaped, forming a horizontal oval. "I should have known."

"What do you want, Mother?"

"It's nearly eleven o'clock."

"We didn't get to bed until dawn," Bethany said. "What's this about some man being downstairs waiting on Morgan?"

Morgan answered the phone. "Kane here. Could you hold for just a second?" He hissed at Bethany. Widening her eyes questioningly, she glanced back at him. "It's probably Hawk. I called him before I came to bed last night. Tell Eileen that no matter how intimidating he looks, he's not in the habit of killing anyone before noon."

Bethany grinned, then forced a mock frown as she glared disapprovingly at Morgan. Turning back to her mother, she said, "Mr. Hawk is an associate of Morgan's. Why don't you have Mrs. Volz serve him some breakfast while he's waiting?"

"Bethany, the man has a ponytail hanging halfway down his back and a gold earring in his ear and a tattoo on his hand and...and he looks foreign. I mean he speaks perfectly good English, without an accent, but he looks Mexican or Cuban or Indian...or something."

"The man is Morgan's colleague. They work together. Morgan sent for him."

"He drove up on a motorcycle." Eileen issued that last bit of information as if it was the final damnation.

Annoyed to the point of screaming, Bethany sighed loudly. Releasing some of her exasperation, she reached out into the hallway and grabbed her mother's arm. "Go downstairs and invite Mr. Hawk for breakfast. Put on your best Southern belle act and keep him entertained until Morgan comes down."

Morgan tried to ignore Bethany's conversation with her mother. "Sorry about asking you to wait, Varner. Things are a bit hectic around here this morning."

"I have some news that I thought you'd want to hear immediately," Hal Varner said. "I'm at Carraway Medical Center."

"What happened?" Morgan retrieved his slacks from the floor.

"The paramedics brought in a man who was found at the WHNB studio. He was in one of the stalls in the men's rest room. The guy's been beaten. He took several hard blows to the head and shoulders."

"Is he still alive?"

"Barely," Detective Varner said. "He's in a coma. The doctors aren't giving very good odds on his recovery."

"Have you ID'd him?"

"Name's Linc Prescott. He's some sort of roving reporter. He's only been at WHNB a few months."

"What's your take on the attack?" Morgan asked as he wriggled into his slacks.

"No suspects. Nobody saw a thing. But the doctors say he was probably beaten and left unconscious several hours before anyone found him."

"Could there be a connection between this man's beating and the attack on Bethany and me last night?" Morgan zipped his slacks.

"Your guess is as good as mine, but I've got a funny feeling in my gut about this one," Varner admitted. "If Linc Prescott saw who stole James Farraday's car last night, then our murderer might have struck again. This time to protect himself."

"Or herself."

"I'm posting an officer outside the ICU. As long as Prescott's alive, I'll keep him guarded. We might get lucky and he'll come out of the coma and identify his attacker."

"I may send someone down to check things out and wait around to see if Prescott regains consciousness," Morgan said. "His name's Hawk. He won't interfere. He'll keep a low profile."

"I wouldn't allow you so much leeway, Kane, if I didn't believe Ms. Wyndham was innocent of Farraday's murder."

"I'll owe you one when this is all over and the real killer's behind bars. Thanks, Varner." Morgan flipped his phone closed and slipped it into his slacks pocket.

Bethany slammed the door shut and turned to face him. With flushed cheeks and shimmering eyes, she gritted her teeth and groaned as she shook her fists.

"My mother can be such an idiot! From the way she's acting about your associate, you'd think Attila the Hun had invaded Mountain Brook."

Morgan chuckled. "Well, your assessment isn't far off, honey. Don't blame Eileen too much. You haven't seen Hawk. The man's quite formidable. Your mother isn't the first person he's put the fear of God into."

"Well, I'm sure Mother will find a way to deal with Mr. Hawk. I've never seen a man yet that Eileen Dow Farraday couldn't charm, if she set her mind to it." Bethany draped her arms around Morgan's neck and planted a kiss on his chin. "Who was that on the phone?"

"Hal Varner."

Bethany's heart skipped a beat. She stared quizzically at Morgan.

"A reporter named Linc Prescott was found in the men's bathroom at WHNB earlier this morning. He'd been hit in the head. He's in a coma at Carraway."

"I know Linc Prescott. He and Tony are big buddies. Jimmy liked Linc. I remember him saying that Linc would be his second choice to take over Wake Up Birmingham."

"Well, somebody didn't like Linc," Morgan said. "Maybe the guy saw or heard something he wasn't supposed to."

"You think there's some connection between Linc's assault and the attack on us last night, don't you?"

Morgan drew her hands from around his neck, lifted them to his lips and kissed her knuckles. "It's possible. Varner and I both have a hunch that this Prescott guy saw whoever stole James's Porsche last night."

"And that person certainly didn't want Linc to tell anyone."

"We're only guessing. It could be there's no connection.

We'll just have to wait and hope Prescott comes out of the coma long enough to tell us who tried to kill him."

After a quick shower and a change into clean clothes, Morgan went into Bethany's room and hurried her along. She barely had time to apply her lipstick and secure her hair with a gold clasp before he rushed her downstairs.

They found Eileen entertaining her guest over brunch in the dining room. Obviously Eileen had gotten over her initial fear of their intruder. She was bestowing her million-dollar smile on him and mouthing off some nonsense about being unable to speak one word of Spanish.

Morgan had been right, Bethany thought. Hawk *was* formidable. Big, dark and deadly, with piercing black eyes and an aura of danger that reminded her of a predatory animal. All he needed to give a believable performance as Dracula was pale skin, fangs and a black cape. Instead he was dressed in black jeans and a black cotton shirt, with a pair of black leather boots covering his big feet.

The minute she and Morgan entered the dining room, Hawk stood, gave her a quick visual survey, then lifted a large envelope off the table.

"Dane sent this. The information was faxed to the office during the night." Hawk handed the envelope to Morgan.

"Sit down and finish your breakfast." Morgan took the envelope out of Hawk's hand, then turned to Bethany. "Honey, would you mind getting me a cup of coffee?"

"Would y'all like Mrs. Volz to serve your breakfast now?" Eileen asked.

"Just coffee right now, Mother, thank you. And I can get it myself." Bethany watched Morgan as he unclasped the large manila envelope and slid out the report his employer had sent.

She poured Morgan a cup of coffee and carried it to him.

"Just put it down there on the table." He quickly scanned the pages of the report.

Bethany set his coffee on the table, then returned to the buffet and prepared herself a cup. Coming back to the table, she smiled at Hawk when she pulled out a chair and placed her coffee next to Morgan's.

"Hello, I'm Bethany Wyndham. I'm afraid Morgan didn't take time for introductions." She held out her hand.

Hawk clasped her hand firmly in his and brought it to his lips. She gasped in surprise at the Continental gesture. Gazing into his shiny, dark eyes, she suddenly realized that this man was most definitely not what he seemed to be.

"Gabriel Hawk. At your service, Ms. Wyndham." His voice was deep, dark and sensual.

Morgan slammed the report down on the dining table. "Have you read this?" he asked Hawk.

"I looked it over at the office before I left this morning," Hawk said. "Interesting bit of information on Tony Hayes."

"Tony?" Eileen and Bethany spoke simultaneously.

"Interesting all right," Morgan said. "But not damning. It explains why Farraday made him his heir apparent at WHNB, but it doesn't give Hayes a motive for murder."

"That depends on whether there was more to their relationship," Hawk said. "Maybe their happy reunion was all for show."

"How about cluing us in on what y'all are talking about?" Bethany glowered at Morgan. "Mother and I would like to know what this interesting information is."

Morgan glanced at Eileen, who sat rigidly in the Georgian-style armchair at the head of the table. "Did your husband ever tell you that he was Tony Hayes's father?"

Eileen's face paled. She clutched the white linen napkin lying in her lap. "No, he—he never told me."

"Tony is Jimmy's son?" Bethany asked.

"It seems Farraday got his teenage sweetheart pregnant and then deserted her before the child was born." Morgan tapped his index finger on the report. "She later married, and her husband adopted Tony and raised him as his son. But right before Tony's mother died a few years ago, she told him the truth about his real father."

"And Tony came to Birmingham to find Jimmy." Bethany shook her head sadly. "He showed up out of nowhere four years ago, and within two weeks of staring work at WHNB, Jimmy brought him on Wake Up Birmingham as his cohost. I wonder if Jimmy knew that Tony was his son and that's the reason he helped make him a local celebrity and decided to hand over the show to Tony once he retired.''

''There's only one way to find out,'' Morgan said. ''I think we need to pay Tony a visit this morning and ask him a few questions.''

''How does Tony being one of Jimmy's bastard children give him a motive for murdering Jimmy?'' Eileen asked.

''That fact alone doesn't give him a reason,'' Morgan told her. ''But I'll lay odds that we don't know the whole story, and that when we do, Tony Hayes may have reason to wish he'd never come to Birmingham.''

Chapter 14

Riding his powerful Harley-Davidson, Hawk followed them out of Mountain Brook. Bethany watched his reflection in the mirror on the passenger side of the car. The wind whipped through his long, black ponytail that hung past his shoulder blades.

"If you don't stop looking at Hawk, I'm going to get jealous," Morgan said teasingly.

"He's a fascinating man. I don't think I've ever met anyone like him."

"Yeah, he's one of a kind, all right."

"But he's not you." Bethany ran the back of her hand across Morgan's cheek. "There's never been anyone else for me, but you." And I'm afraid there never will be.

"Damn, woman, you pick a fine time to talk dirty to a man. Right in the middle of freeway traffic."

Bethany giggled, surprised, yet relieved that despite everything, she could still find humor in her life. Thanks to Morgan. Dear God, how could she bear for things to change once she told him the truth about Anne Marie? Could she survive his hatred? And he was sure to hate her when he found out that she'd kept him and his child apart for all these years.

Glancing in the side-view mirror again, she saw Hawk veer off to the right, exiting the highway on his way to the medical center.

"How long will Hawk stay at the hospital?" she asked.

"A while," Morgan said. "I want him there if Prescott comes out of the coma anytime today."

"And what if Linc doesn't come out of the coma, or what if he dies?"

"Then we may never know for sure if there's a connection between the attack on him and Farraday's murder or our near-death experience last night."

Bethany shifted in the leather bucket seat of Morgan's Ferrari. He had insisted on picking up his car at her house, where it had been parked in the garage since the day he moved in with her. "It's as if things have gone from bad to worse in the past forty-eight hours."

"And they're going to get even worse before they get better. We've narrowed down the suspects, which means that we're closing in on the real killer." Morgan kept his vision focused on the highway ahead as he guided the sleek, black Ferrari through noontime Birmingham traffic. "Unless Eileen and James have figured out a way to be in two places at once, then neither of them could have been driving the red Porsche that tried to run us off the mountain last night. So that leaves only three known suspects."

"Are you sure that the person who stole James's car is the same person who killed Jimmy?"

"Reasonably sure. Unless one of Farraday's fans stole the car, and that's not likely. Whoever borrowed the Porsche knew two things that only one of our three remaining suspects would've known."

"What two things?"

Morgan glanced at Bethany. Her long, sable hair fluttered about her face as the speeding wind from the open windows cooled the car's interior. "First, whoever ran us off the road was following us. He or she knew we were at your house and was waiting for us."

"What's the other thing?"

"Seth, Tony and Vivian would have known that after James accidently locked his keys in his car for the third time, Jimmy had him keep a key hidden in a metal container under the Porsche.''

''How did you know—''

''James told me.''

''Yes, of course.'' Absorbing the information Morgan had given her, Bethany sat quietly.

''If as Hal Varner and I suspect, Linc Prescott knows who *borrowed* James's car, then the killer is probably running scared. If Prescott regains consciousness, it'll all be over for him...or her.''

''You don't think they'll try again to kill Linc, do you? I mean, there's no way anyone can get past the guard outside the ICU, is there?''

''Hawk's presence will be double security against any unauthorized person getting anywhere near Prescott,'' Morgan said. ''He'll detect anyone acting in a suspicious manner.''

''So Hawk is going to protect Prescott, and you're going to protect me.'' Bethany breathed deeply, willing her unsteady nerves not to unravel. ''Oh, God, Morgan, I'm scared.''

''So am I, honey. So am I.'' He exited the freeway and headed west toward the television studio. ''Having sense enough to be scared can keep you alive. Knowing that there's danger can prepare you, can make you careful. I'm going to be at your side, twenty-four hours a day until Farraday's real killer is caught.''

''But why, at this point, when there's a good chance he is going to be caught, would Jimmy's killer try to harm me? What reason would he have now?''

''It's possible that we aren't dealing with a totally rational person,'' Morgan said. ''Don't forget that whoever killed Jimmy had no problem letting you take the rap for the murder. They might have even set you up to take the fall.''

''It's obvious that whoever killed Jimmy wanted to see me convicted of the murder?''

''That's exactly what I'm saying. They've killed once and tried to kill a second time. There's no reason to believe they wouldn't try again, if in their warped mind, they had a reason.''

Within fifteen minutes, Morgan parked his Ferrari in the WHNB parking lot. They caught Tony Hayes and Vivian Crosby just as they were leaving.

Tony Hayes halted on the sidewalk, his body tensing when he saw Bethany and Morgan. Then he flashed them his brilliant, for-my-TV-fans smile.

"Well, why am I not surprised to see you two show up here?" Tony asked sarcastically.

Tony reminded Morgan of a television evangelist—smooth, slick and charismatic, with a touch of country-boy charm. Morgan's tried-and-true instincts warned him that Hayes was probably his father's son in every sense of the word.

Vivian glared daggers at Morgan. "Wasn't it bad enough that the police were here all morning, questioning us, putting everyone through the third degree?"

Vivian Crosby had probably never been pretty. Her nose was too big and her jaw too square for classic beauty. But Morgan guessed that ten years ago, before she'd let her bosomy figure expand, she might have been sexy. With her frosted platinum hair, bright red lipstick and heavy makeup she resembled a middle-aged Kewpie doll.

"I'm afraid I need to ask y'all a few more questions," Morgan said. "Would you mind if we used your office, Tony?"

"We don't have to answer any of your questions," Vivian said. "You can't make us cooperate with you."

Tony grasped Vivian's elbow. "Now, Viv, if you act like that, Mr. Kane will think we have something to hide." Tony opened the glass door leading to the studio lobby, gave Vivian a gentle push inside and then held the door open for Morgan and Bethany..

Tony showed them into his office. Bethany hesitated momentarily in the doorway. "When did you move into Jimmy's office?" she asked.

"A couple of days ago," Tony said. "After the station had new carpet installed. Bloodstains don't come out very easily."

"I wish you wouldn't mention the bloodstains," Vivian snapped. "I keep seeing Jimmy lying there on the floor in a pool of blood." Whirling around, she gritted her teeth and glowered at Bethany. "Why did you have to kill him? He was very fond of you, you know. He talked about you a lot."

Bethany shivered at the memory of how much and in what way Jimmy Farraday had liked her. She would never forget having to fight him off only a few short months after he married her mother. If her knee hadn't made contact in just the right spot, enabling her to escape, Jimmy would have raped her that night.

"Won't y'all have a seat?" Tony indicated the chairs in front of his desk.

Morgan assisted Bethany into a red vinyl chair, then sat down beside her. "We're not here to discuss Farraday's murder," Morgan said.

"I suppose you're trying to find a link between Jimmy's murder and the attack on Linc." Tony shook his head, not a strand of his lacquer-coated black hair moving. "I can no more imagine anyone harming Linc than I could imagine someone killing Jimmy." Tony gazed directly at Bethany. "A person would have to be filled with hate to do something so terrible."

Vivian stood ramrod straight, her hands clutched in front of her in a prayerful gesture. Tony sat down in the enormous swivel chair behind Jimmy Farraday's desk.

"What about you, Tony?" Morgan focused his gaze on the man he questioned. "Would a man hate a father who had deserted him before he was born? Hate him enough to kill him?"

Tony's face flushed. His jaw tightened. And then suddenly he smiled. His whole body relaxed. "So, you've unearthed my little secret. I suppose it was only a matter of time until the truth came out."

"What are you talking about?" Vivian snapped her head around and glared at Tony.

"It seems Mr. Kane has discovered that Jimmy Farraday was my biological father."

"Jimmy was your—" Vivian stared round-eyed and open-mouthed at Tony. "Why...why didn't you ever tell anyone? Did Jimmy know? Of course he knew. That's why he took you under his wing. Oh, Tony, no wonder his death has been so difficult for you."

"Did you hate Jimmy Farraday?" Morgan rephrased his original question to Tony.

"Hate Jimmy? Good Lord, man, I loved Jimmy." Tony closed his eyes. "He was my father and my best friend." One lone tear trickled down Tony's cheek.

"Are you saying that you had no hard feelings toward a man who deserted you before you were born and never tried to contact you?'' Morgan asked. ''A man who gave his name to another son? A man who left a million dollar insurance policy to that son?''

''My parents were very young and they made a mistake,'' Tony said. ''Yes, naturally, I felt some bitterness toward my father, but once I found him and he welcomed me into his life and found a place for me in his heart, it was easy to forgive him.''

''Why didn't Farraday ever publicly recognize you as his son?''

Morgan watched Tony carefully, catching the barely noticeable way his body tensed, the telltale tightening of his jaw. Tony clutched his left hand into a fist, then released it, and repeated the process several times.

''It was something we discussed, but decided it would serve no purpose other than to sully Jimmy's reputation.''

Bethany could not repress the loud ''Ha!'' that burst from her mouth. ''I'm sorry,'' she said. ''But Jimmy Farraday's personal reputation was that of a lying, cheating, womanizing bastard.''

''And that's why you killed him, isn't it?'' Vivian said. ''Because you were jealous that other women adored him. You wanted him all to yourself. I know about you and Jimmy. He told how you wouldn't leave him alone.'' With outspread, clutching hands, Vivian sprang at Bethany, but Morgan restrained her. She fell apart, crumpling over into Morgan's arms like a rag doll. He eased her down into the chair he'd just vacated. Covering her face with her hands, Vivian wept uncontrollably.

Bethany almost felt sorry for Vivian. Her actions clearly showed her deep love for Jimmy Farraday. But a person could both love and hate at the same time. Her love for Jimmy wasn't proof that she didn't kill him.

''Look, I know you're trying to do your job, Kane,'' Tony said. ''You're doing everything you can to prove that someone other than Bethany killed Jimmy. Well, I wish you luck. I'd like to think Bethany didn't kill my father, but... Look, poor Vivian has been through enough lately. I'm afraid finding out that someone tried to kill Linc this morning has sent her over the edge.''

Tony got up, rounded his desk and put his arm around Vivian's plump shoulders, consoling her with gentle little pats.

"Where were you two this morning when Prescott was attacked?" Morgan asked.

Gasping loudly, Vivian looked up at Tony. "Is he insinuating that you or I tried to kill Linc?"

"Yes, I do believe he is," Tony replied.

"Where were y'all?" Morgan repeated.

"I'll tell you what we told the police," Tony said. "We were both at our apartments, in bed, asleep. Weekend mornings are the only mornings that we get to sleep in. The rest of the week, we're up before four o'clock and at the station by five."

"Last night, y'all were here working very late on some sort of tribute show in Farraday's memory," Morgan said. "Just how late was it when everyone left?"

"Why don't you talk to that Detective Varner?" Wiping her tearstained face, Vivian smeared her heavy makeup. "We've gone over these same questions with him time and time again. We left here right after midnight, just as soon as Detective Varner finished grilling us about someone trying to run you two off the road in James's stolen car."

"While James and I were at police headquarters last night, Hal Varner filled me in on the results of his questioning everyone here at WHNB." Morgan's lips curved into a smirky grin. "It seems you both had alibis. Tony, you were having an intimate dinner at your apartment with someone you barely knew, a lady whose last name you can't seem to recall, therefore the police can't find her to verify your story. And Vivian, it seems that a little before nine last night, you had a sick headache and had to come in here, in Jimmy's office, and lie down. You were all alone for over an hour. No one saw you from nine o'clock until after ten."

"I think it's time for you and Bethany to leave." Huffing out his chest, Tony glowered at Morgan. "Neither Vivian nor I have done anything wrong, and there's no reason for us to endure any more of this cross-examination."

"Fine." Morgan glanced at Bethany, who nodded and immediately stood. "Just remember one thing. There's a good chance that Linc Prescott will come out of his coma and be able to tell us who tried to kill him."

Without another word, Morgan whisked Bethany out of Tony's office, down the corridor and out into the lobby of WHNB. Once outside, he slowed his gait and eased his fierce hold on Bethany's arm.

"Someone is lying." Blood rushed through Morgan's body, pumping quickly through his heart. Anger welled up inside him, threatening his cool control. He never allowed emotions to cloud his judgment, never allowed his heart to interfere with his actions. But dammit, he couldn't remain an impersonal investigator in this case. It just wasn't possible.

"Neither of them really has an alibi for the time James's red Porsche ran us off the road." Bethany allowed Morgan to help her into his Ferrari.

He got in on the driver's side and sat there for a few minutes. "Tony or Vivian or Seth killed Farraday. And whoever killed Farraday stole James's car. Linc Prescott saw who took the Porsche, and our killer knew Prescott could identify him—or her—so he had to silence Prescott."

"Not Seth."

"We don't know what time Seth left Eileen's this morning, and we don't know for sure he went straight home."

"I refuse to believe it was Seth," Bethany said. "Even if he had killed Jimmy, he would never have tried to hurt me. But I think Tony is capable of just about anything. He's that much like Jimmy. And Vivian hates me enough not only to want to frame me, but to kill me."

"My instincts tell me that it's going to come down soon," Morgan told her. "A few days. A few weeks. Even sooner, if Prescott comes out of the coma."

"After I finish getting everything ready at the boutique for tomorrow afternoon's fashion show, I'd like to stop by the hospital and visit Lisa for a while this evening. And then maybe we can drop by the ICU and check on Linc."

Bethany stood in front of the open French doors that led to a small private patio off the side of the den at Claudia Kane's home. Sunset burned into the sky with hot, vibrant, multicolored flames, searing the blue with red and orange. A cool evening breeze trickled across Bethany's skin like invisible fingertips caressing her. She breathed in the fresh night air, crisp and chilly, edged with the promise of autumn soon to come.

A deep shroud of sadness draped around her, weighing her down, warning her that the end was near. Her life had changed so quickly, going from peaceful contentment to erratic, pulse-pounding chaos. In a few short weeks, everything she'd spent the past sixteen years building had crumbled down around her like a city ravaged by war.

No matter what happened in the future, even if she lost everything, she wouldn't change the days and nights she'd spent with Morgan. Perhaps she didn't deserve lasting happiness. Losing Morgan and even losing Anne Marie might well be her punishment for sending Amery to his death. If there was forgiveness in this world, any fairness at all, then she could hope she would live through this present ordeal and eventually rebuild her relationship with her daughter. But there would be no tomorrows for Morgan and her. Once she told him the truth about Anne Marie, there would be no hope for them.

"It's getting a bit chilly out there, isn't it?" Claudia walked up beside Bethany. "I love the nights when they start cooling off like this."

Glancing at Claudia, Bethany smiled. "Are Anne Marie and Morgan still playing billiards?"

"Oh, yes." Claudia laid her hand on Bethany's shoulder. "He's teaching her the finer points of the game. I stood in the doorway and watched them for a while. A blind fool could see that they're father and daughter, but Morgan doesn't see it."

"No, Morgan doesn't see it," Bethany said. "But I think he senses it, on a subconscious level. He's very paternal around her. I think he's going to be a good father."

"Then you're going to tell him soon, aren't you?"

"I plan to tell him before my arraignment." Bethany walked out onto the patio. "I keep putting off telling him because I can't bear to lose him again."

"Oh, Beth, dear child." Claudia lifted her shawl from where it rested about her arms and draped it around her shoulders, then stepped out onto the patio.

"I know that he doesn't plan to stay on in Birmingham. And I realize that our relationship is only temporary, but...I want every day, every moment that we can share. It will end soon enough as it is.''

''You're lovers again,'' Claudia said matter-of-factly. ''You and Morgan have always loved each other. You were meant to be together. Once he gets over the initial shock of learning that he's Anne Marie's father, I'm sure y'all will be able to work things out and make a life together.''

''I love Morgan.'' Bethany gazed up at the clear black sky, focusing on the brightest star, making a wish she knew would never come true. ''But Morgan has never told me that he loves me. Not sixteen years ago and not now.''

Claudia reached out and grasped Bethany's hand. They stood together on the patio, listening to the quiet nighttime sounds of nature. There had been a time when she had hated Claudia for forcing her into marriage with Amery, but that hatred had died long ago. Over the years, their individual memories of Morgan and their love and devotion to Morgan's daughter had brought them together. And Claudia's constant support and caring had endeared her to Bethany.

''So there y'all are.'' Anne Marie held Morgan's hand as the two entered the den. ''Did you know Morgan is a pool shark? I mean he's the absolute best, even better than Papa Henderson, and he was great.''

Anne Marie flew out onto the patio and hugged her nana. Claudia's face crinkled into soft lines when she smiled. ''And how badly did he beat you? I'm sure he didn't let you win a game. He always did whatever he had to do, even cheat, to keep from losing.''

''Actually, he did let me win,'' Anne Marie said triumphantly. ''But only once.'' She turned to her mother. ''Thanks for moving in with Nana until our house is ready again. I just don't think I could have stayed another night at Grandmother's. Not with James living there. Not after what happened last night. I really made a fool of myself.''

''We'll only be here a couple of days,'' Bethany said. ''I'm hoping we can move back home by mid-week. Until then Morgan can continue giving you billiard lessons.''

''She's already quite a good player,'' Morgan said. ''She told me that Father taught her how to play when she was a small child.''

"Your father adored Anne Marie," Claudia said.

"Even if I was a girl." Anne Marie shrugged, then slipped her arms through Morgan's arm and hugged up to him. "I'll bet you aren't like Papa Henderson was, are you, Morgan? It wouldn't matter the least little bit if you had a daughter instead of a son, would it?"

Morgan slipped his arm around Anne Marie and hugged her to his side, then kissed her on the forehead. "I'd rather have a daughter just like you than have half a dozen sons."

Biting down on her bottom lip so hard she broke the skin, Bethany tasted her own blood. Tears gathered in her eyes. She fled to the edge of the patio, where steps led to a brick walkway that connected to the massive gardens in back of the house.

"Where are you going, Mama?" Anne Marie asked.

"I thought I'd take a walk before I go to bed." Despite the tears threatening to choke her and the knot tightening in her stomach, Bethany spoke calmly, not a tremor in her voice.

"Want me to come with you?" Anne Marie took a tentative step forward.

Bethany didn't reply; instead she hurried away as if she hadn't heard her daughter's question.

Morgan clasped Anne Marie's wrist. "Maybe your mother needs to be alone for a while."

"Maybe she'd rather have you go with her than me," Anne Marie told him, and when Morgan didn't move, she gave him a shove. "Go on. Go after her."

"Anne Marie, why don't you see me upstairs to my room?" Claudia said. "I'm getting tired. We can stop by the kitchen and get a snack, then go on up. I'll tell you about the first time your...the first time Morgan played billiards with Papa Henderson."

Morgan waited until his mother and Anne Marie went inside before he followed Bethany. He found her at the back of the house, on the trail leading to the pond.

"Beth! Wait, honey," he called out to her.

Hesitating momentarily, she glanced over her shoulder. "I need to be by myself. Please, go away."

He heard the tears in her voice, even though he could not see her face clearly in the shadowy moonlight. His mind told him to respect her request and leave her alone. She would be safe inside the walls of his mother's estate. It would take a battalion of trained commandos to get past Claudia's state-of-the-art security system. But his heart told him that the last thing Bethany really wanted or needed was to be alone.

"You don't want me to leave," he told her.

She ran down the trail. He stood and watched her flee as if she were afraid of him. He rushed after her, calling her name. Ignoring his pleas, she ran faster and faster. He caught up with her by the pool, overtaking her just as she reached the miniature gazebo nestled in a grove of trees on the far side of the pond.

He swung her around in his arms. She went limp, her arms hanging lifelessly at her sides, her head bowed. With one arm supporting her, he reached out with the other and gripped her chin between thumb and forefinger. Forcing her face upward, he made her look at him.

The moonlight coated the garden in pale gold and illuminated the tears in Bethany's eyes, making them glimmer like liquid diamonds.

"Honey, what's wrong? Why did you run away from me?"

How could she tell him and make him understand how deeply what he'd said to Anne Marie had affected her? Morgan already cared for Anne Marie. Once he knew she was his daughter, he would love her. He would take care of her.

And he would hate Bethany for keeping him and his child apart. No matter what she did, no matter what happened, one thing was certain. She was going to lose Morgan again.

Bethany grabbed Morgan's hands and pulled him inside the small, wooden gazebo. Draping her arms around his neck, she pressed herself against him.

"I realize that we don't have a future together," she said. "I know that when this is all over, you're going to leave Birmingham. But I want you to know that—"

He laid his big index finger over her lips, silencing her. "I'm not so sure anymore what I'm going to do when this is all over. I'd like to promise you that we have a shot at living happily ever after, but I'm afraid I don't believe in fairy-tale endings."

"Neither do I. I haven't in a long, long time."

"Then all we can do is take things one day at a time and make the most of every moment."

"I love you, Morgan." She gazed into his steel-gray eyes and watched them warm and soften to a smoldering blue. "I've always loved you, and I always will."

Capturing her face in his big hands, he swooped down and took her lips in a kiss of pure raw passion. She responded with desire equally as strong and a need that brooked no obstacles to its fulfillment. While he ate at her mouth, his tongue probing, his teeth nibbling, Morgan cupped her buttocks, lifting her up and against his throbbing sex.

She clung to him when he eased her down to the floor of the gazebo, slowly, carefully, until she rested beneath him. Nuzzling her throat, he lifted her dress up to her hips and then linked his fingers inside the waistband of her panty hose and beige silk panties. After ripping the underwear down and off her body, he hurriedly unzipped his slacks and freed his sex from the confinement of his briefs. He told her in no uncertain terms what he was going to do to her, then thrust into her, possessing her completely.

He moaned a few more earthy, erotic phrases as he hammered into her, but he soon reached a point where he could no longer speak. Only the most primitive utterances rumbled from his throat. Bethany urged him on by her hot, sensual words and wild, undulating body.

They mated there in the tiny gazebo in the woods, under the stars. Mated with a raw, savage passion that possessed them both completely, to the very depths of their souls. And when fulfillment claimed them, first her and then him, their cries rent the soft sweet silence of the night, like a razor-sharp blade slicing through silk.

Chapter 15

Morgan hated crowds, especially when he was on an assignment and his client was the center of attention. He had tried to talk Bethany out of taking part in the fashion show at the mall, but she'd been adamant about not allowing outside forces to control her life. The pre-autumn fashion show was an annual event that she had participated in since opening her first boutique.

Even though he'd hired half a dozen security guards for crowd control—to keep out Jimmy Farraday fans—he would feel better if Hawk was here, too. But he thought it was important to keep Hawk on guard at the hospital. If Prescott's attacker could find a way to get inside the ICU, he'd kill Prescott before he had a chance to regain consciousness. And if WHNB's roving reporter came out of the coma, Morgan wanted Hawk on the scene when he started talking.

Linc Prescott had been swamped with visitors, most of whom weren't allowed to enter the intensive care unit. Morgan realized that just because all three suspects had stopped by to check on Prescott's condition, their actions neither confirmed nor disproved a damn thing. Hawk had told him that Vivian had cried and moaned and put on an Academy Award-winning performance of grief when she'd been allowed to see Prescott. And Tony had talked to his co-worker, assuring him that he'd pull through and the assailant would be caught and brought to justice. Seth Renfrew had not gone in to see Prescott, but had asked numerous questions about his condition.

The last model slunk down the runway, which had been set up in a central location, convenient for the five clothing stores that were participating in the event. The announcer finished her speech and invited the audience to attend the in-store parties, hosted by the five different establishments.

Gripping Bethany's elbow, Morgan cut a path through the swarm of reporters and curiosity seekers hovering around her. His formidable presence kept the vultures at bay, but it did not quiet the bombardment of questions.

He had breathed a sigh of relief when he'd noticed Tony Hayes hadn't put in an appearance today. But Seth had arrived with Eileen and James before the fashion show began two hours ago. And Vivian Crosby lurked about in the midst of the crowd. Several times, Morgan had caught her staring at Bethany. There was something about that woman, something strange in her eyes. Just at the thought of her, apprehension tightened inside his stomach.

Morgan ushered Bethany into the boutique where Eileen, Seth and James waited to congratulate Bethany on the success of the fashion show. Customers poured into the store, jabbering nonstop while they made a beeline to the refreshment tables.

Anne Marie hurried to her mother's side. "Great show, Mama. The clothes from Bethany's Boutique were by far the best of the bunch."

"Of course," Bethany said. "My fashions are always the hit of the show."

While mother and daughter chitchated, Morgan scanned the horde of women milling around inside Bethany's Boutique, sipping champagne and nibbling on fancy hors d'oeuvres. He tensed immediately when he saw Vivian Crosby enter the store.

He stayed at Bethany's side, like a huge, protective shadow, while she accepted congratulations, answered questions and welcomed everyone. Vivian lifted a glass of champagne from the waiter's silver tray and browsed casually through the boutique.

Seth escorted Eileen over to Bethany and the three discussed the fall fashions.

Keeping watch over the large assembly, Morgan frequently checked the entrance. Adrenaline soared through his body the minute he spotted Tony Hayes. Several ladies recognized him immediately and fluttered around him like moths around a flame.

Now, he had all three suspects inside Bethany's Boutique, each one a potential danger. But surely, no one in his right mind would chance an attack in public. Regardless, he didn't dare let his guard down for a minute.

Vivian approached Eileen. The two women exchanged a few words and a cordial hug, then Vivian glanced toward Bethany. Morgan's body tensed. He'd already seen this woman lose control. He suspected that Vivian Crosby was on the verge of a nervous breakdown.

Morgan took a mental picture of each suspect's whereabouts. Vivian and Seth were only a couple of feet away to the right, flanking Eileen. Tony Hayes was less than a foot away to the left, talking to James Farraday, Jr. Had Eileen told the boy that Hayes was his half brother? Or was Hayes filling him in on the news right now?

A young uniformed officer entered the boutique and searched through the crowd. He came straight to Morgan.

"Mr. Kane?" Officer Beldon asked.

"Yes."

"Lieutenant Varner instructed us to inform you that Linc Prescott has come out of the coma," the policeman said. "The lieutenant and your associate, Mr. Hawk, are waiting to see Mr. Prescott. The doctors are examining him and think he'll be able to make a statement within the hour."

Bethany squeezed Morgan's arm. "Oh, thank God, Linc is going to be all right. Now, if only he can identify his attacker, then maybe we'll find out who really killed Jimmy."

"Ms. Wyndham and I will leave shortly and go straight to the hospital," Morgan said.

"Yes, sir. Lieutenant Varner thought you'd want to be there when Mr. Prescott makes his statement. I've been sent to escort y'all straight to the hospital."

"I need just a few more minutes here," Bethany said.

"Then I'll wait outside—" the policeman nodded to the entrance of her shop "—until you and Mr. Kane are ready to leave."

When the young officer made his way through the crowd, Vivian left Eileen's side and walked over to Bethany, stopping directly in front of her. Holding out her hands in supplication, Vivian said, "Bethany, I—I want to apologize for the way I acted yesterday. My only excuse is that I haven't been myself since Jimmy was killed and then poor Linc was found...nearly dead."

"I understand you've been upset since Jimmy's death." Bethany's voice was calm and sweet, but Morgan felt her take a cautious half step backward. "You should be happy knowing that Linc has come out of his coma."

Vivian grabbed Bethany's hand. "Thank you for being so forgiving. And thank God that Linc is going to live. If he can identify his attacker, then perhaps the police will reopen Jimmy's murder case. There's a chance you might go free, after all, isn't there?"

Bethany jerked her hand out of Vivian's grasp, but Vivian immediately manacled Bethany's wrist, then slipped her other hand into her jacket pocket and pulled out a knife.

"I can't let you live! Not after what you did to Jimmy!"

Gasping, Bethany's eyes widened in surprise. "No, Vivian. No!"

Oblivious to her surroundings, to the shocked cries from onlookers and to Morgan's quick movements, Vivian raised the shiny blade into the air, preparing to strike. Shoving Bethany behind him, Morgan stepped in front of her and reached for Vivian's arm just as she lunged with the knife. The sharp edge ripped through Morgan's jacket and shirt, nicking the skin beneath. He tore the knife from Vivian's hand and subdued her with a minimum of force.

She fought him like a wildcat, screaming curses at Bethany. "You killed Jimmy! I know you did! I don't care what Linc tells the police. You can't go unpunished!"

The young officer rushed back inside the boutique from his post at the entrance. He called his partner, who was waiting outside in the patrol car. Two of the security guards followed close behind him. The crowd closed in around Morgan and the screeching Vivian. Officer Beldon fought his way through the throng, hurrying toward Morgan.

"Ms. Crosby just tried to attack Ms. Wyndham," Morgan said.

Officer Beldon helped Morgan shackle Vivian with handcuffs, and then Morgan turned her over to the policeman. The security guards parted the crowd, allowing the officer to drag her, kicking and screaming, through the horde of startled onlookers.

Morgan made a quick survey of the boutique. Seth hadn't left Eileen's side. But Tony Hayes had disappeared.

Bethany noticed the bloodstain on Morgan's jacket. "You're hurt. Vivian stabbed you before you got the knife away from her."

"It's just a scratch, honey," he said.

"I don't believe you." Bethany tugged his jacket off his shoulder.

He allowed her to remove his jacket, but wished he hadn't when she cried out in alarm. He glanced at his nicked arm. Bright red blood trickled from the wound, turning the sleeve of his white shirt to scarlet.

"We need to get you to an emergency room," she said.

"I'm all right. I've cut myself worse shaving."

"Don't be so damn macho," Bethany said. "I have a first aid kit in the office." She led Morgan over to a velvet Victorian sofa, glared at the two women sitting there until they moved. "Sit down. I'll be right back."

Lifting his injured arm, he reached for her, then winced slightly when a sharp pain shot through him. "Dammit, Beth, come back here."

But she didn't heed his command. He jumped up off the sofa. James and Seth and Eileen rushed toward him, along with a dozen nosy patrons eager for the sight of blood. They inadvertently blocked his path.

"Hey, man, are you all right?" James asked. "That bitch was crazy, wasn't she?"

"Thank God you were here to protect Bethany," Eileen said. "I had no idea Vivian was unbalanced. She's been so dear and kind since Jimmy's death."

Morgan shoved his way through the bevy of concerned and

curious. Scanning the room again, he couldn't find Anne Marie. And Tony Hayes was still missing.

"Where's Anne Marie?" Morgan asked, his voice one octave above a roar.

"She was here just a few minutes ago," Eileen said, then turned to Shelly Harris, who had taken over as manager of the Galleria boutique in Lisa Songer's absence. "You were talking to Anne Marie. Did you see where she went?"

"The last time I saw her, she was walking toward the office with Tony Hayes."

Morgan broke through the crowd, plowing a wide path as he ran toward Bethany's office.

She knew exactly where she kept the first aid kit. It would take only a minute to get it and return to clean and dress Morgan's wound. Bethany rushed into her office. She stopped so quickly that she reeled backward when she saw Tony Hayes holding a gun to Anne Marie's head.

"Come on in and close the door," Tony said.

"Mama!" Anne Marie's blue-gray eyes swam with tears.

"What are you doing? What do you want?" Bethany's instincts told her to rush forward, to attack, to remove her child from Tony's dangerous clutches. Common sense warned her to be careful.

"I want you and Anne Marie to come with me. Right now." Reaching behind him, Tony turned the doorknob, opening the door that led into the storage room. "We're going to go out the back way before anyone knows that we're gone."

"Morgan is right outside. If I don't return with the first aid kit, he's going to come rushing in here."

"That's why we're leaving. Now! Come on!" He backed out the door, dragging Anne Marie with him.

Bethany followed like an obedient puppy. She didn't dare take any chances with her child's life.

"Get that back door open," Tony told her. "Go on outside. We're right behind you. If you scream or try to alert anybody, I'll shoot her. And you don't want that, do you?"

"No, I don't want that." Bethany followed his instructions to the letter, fear gnawing away at her insides like a strong acid.

Once outside, Tony motioned for Bethany to move closer. When she did, he tightened his hold on Anne Marie, slipped his gun into his jacket pocket and stuck the hidden revolver in Anne Marie's ribs.

"Get my car keys out of my pocket and don't try anything," he warned Bethany. "When we get to my car, you're going to drive. Anne Marie and I will sit in the back seat."

Morgan Kane stormed into Bethany's office, calling her name. James followed closely behind him. Noticing the door leading to the storage area was open, Morgan drew his gun from the shoulder holster and dashed into the cluttered room. After quickly giving every inch of the place a visual examination, he closed his eyes momentarily and cursed himself. Why hadn't he gotten to Bethany's office quicker? Dammit, why hadn't she listened to him when he told her not to leave his side?

How long had it taken him to get away from Eileen and Seth and James and shove his way through the crowd? Three minutes? Four? But four minutes had obviously been enough time for someone to abduct Bethany.

Not Vivian Crosby. And not Seth Renfrew.

Tony Hayes! Had Tony panicked when he'd overheard Officer Beldon explaining that Linc Prescott had come out of the coma? Did Tony know that it was only a matter of time until Prescott identified him as his attacker?

Morgan jerked open the outside door. He spotted Bethany running alongside Tony Hayes, who held Anne Marie close to his side. Dear God in heaven, Hayes had them both. Bethany and her daughter!

"Get the police," Morgan yelled to James. "Tony Hayes has Bethany and Anne Marie!"

Aiming his Sig, Morgan pulled off a warning shot. Anne Marie screamed. Bethany stopped dead in her tracks. Tony Hayes jerked Anne Marie behind the nearest vehicle and motioned for Bethany to come to him.

Morgan ran out into the parking lot, his long stride rapidly spanning the distance between him and his objective. Tony Hayes pivoted quickly when Morgan was only a few yards away. Clutching Anne Marie in front of him, he jerked the gun out of his pocket and placed it against her temple.

"Don't come any closer, Kane, or I'll blow her head off!" Tony said. "Bethany is driving the three of us out of here, and if I see one cop following us, neither of them will come out of this alive. Do I make myself clear?"

"Perfectly," Morgan shouted.

Tony glanced at Bethany. "My car's right over there." He nodded to the left. "Go open the doors and get behind the wheel. Once Anne Marie and I get in the back seat, you take off, straight down 459."

Bethany looked at her child. All color had drained from Anne Marie's face. She trembled from head to toe.

"Don't hurt her," Bethany said. "If you do, I'll find a way to kill you."

"Go get in the damn car!"

Bethany did as she was instructed, praying that Morgan could save them. Right now, he was probably blaming himself for what had happened. But it wasn't his fault. No one could have foreseen the events that enabled Tony to abduct Anne Marie or instigate her own flight from Morgan's protection.

For every backward step Tony made, with Anne Marie in tow, Morgan moved forward slowly. He was close enough now to put a bullet in the man's head, but maybe not before Tony squeezed the trigger on his own gun and ended Anne Marie's life.

A young couple drove into the parking space behind Morgan. Damn, that's all he needed. Innocent bystanders.

Bethany unlocked Tony's classic GTO, got in and started the engine. Tony made his way to the car, hauling Anne Marie with him. He shoved her into the back seat, aiming the gun at her the whole time. Once he was settled, he reached out and snatched the long scarf from around Bethany's neck. She gasped.

"Get going! And don't slow down for anything. You and sweet little Anne Marie are my ticket to freedom."

Bethany glanced over her shoulder. "What are you going to do with my scarf?"

"I said start driving!"

Bethany shifted from Park to Drive and pulled out of the

parking space. Glancing in her rearview mirror, she saw Tony tying Anne Marie's hands behind her back.

The young couple who had parked behind Morgan got out of their Ford Mustang, both of them laughing and totally oblivious to the drama being enacted around them.

Morgan turned to them, brandishing the big Sig in his hand. The woman screamed and held up her hands in surrender.

"Look, I'm not going to hurt you," Morgan said. "I need to borrow your car. It's a matter of life and death."

The trembling young man rummaged in his pocket, pulled out his key chain and tossed it to Morgan. Morgan caught the keys in midair, then unlocked the Mustang, got in and started the engine. He drove off in a frenzy, tires screeching. The couple stood frozen to the spot, watching while the big man with the big gun zoomed out of the parking lot.

Bethany caught a glimpse of the blue Mustang behind her and recognized the driver immediately. But she didn't let on by word or action, hoping Tony wouldn't discover Morgan's presence.

"Where are we going?" Bethany asked.

"Just keep driving down 459," Tony said. "When we're far enough away from the mall, we'll ditch my car. We're going to make a little trip to the bank, and you're going to get me enough money so I can go into hiding in style."

"You'll never get away with this," she told him. "I'm sure Morgan has already alerted the police."

"Well, you'd better hope that the police don't show up. Because if they do, Anne Marie will die before they can take me alive."

Anne Marie cried out. Bethany nearly lost control of the Pontiac when she turned around to check on her child. Tony was running the edge of his revolver up and down the side of Anne Marie's face.

She had to find a way to help her daughter and herself, to save their lives. But if it came to saving herself or saving Anne Marie, there would be no choice to make. Anne Marie came first, always. She wouldn't want to live if anything happened to her child. Morgan's child.

"You don't have to do this, Tony," Bethany said. "You didn't kill Linc Prescott. He's going to be all right. And Jimmy was an evil man and I'm sure you had a good reason for killing him. Maybe it was self-defense. Whatever happened, I'll see to it that you have the best lawyer money can buy."

"Shut up! You and your damn money. Miss I'm-Too-Good-For-The-Likes-Of-You. You thought you were too good for Jimmy, too, didn't you? He really had a thing for you, you know? That's why I tried so hard to get in your pants. It would have killed him if I'd scored with you when he couldn't."

Keeping her vision focused on the highway, Bethany gripped the steering wheel tightly. "You framed me for Jimmy's murder. You deliberately set me up."

"It wasn't anything I planned," Tony said. "You just played right into my hands. You threatened to kill Jimmy one night and showed up at his office the next day and got into a fight with him. I saw you run out of his office, so I went in to see what had happened.

"Jimmy was wiping the blood off his face from where you'd scratched him. I saw your purse lying on the floor, so I picked it up. Jimmy was laughing about what a wild thing you were. I found the gun in your purse and pulled it out and shot him. He just stared at me as if he couldn't believe what I'd done. Then he called me son. That's when I filled the sorry bastard full of lead."

"Why, Tony? Why did you kill him? I thought you loved him?"

"Loved that good-for-nothing piece of trash? I hated his guts. Do you know the only reason he allowed me into his life, the only reason he made me his sidekick on Wake Up Birmingham? Do you? Huh? Huh?" Tony's voice grew louder and louder.

"No, why?"

"Because I was blackmailing the old son of a bitch! He didn't want his fans finding out that he'd deserted his pregnant teenage sweetheart and that he had an illegitimate son he'd never claimed. He didn't think his right-wing, conservative, redneck fans would understand if, as that son, I told them the truth about their beloved Jimmy Farraday. That he'd known all along where I was and never bothered to see me. Not once my entire life."

"He gave you everything you wanted," Bethany said. "Why kill him?"

"Because he promised me that if we could work it out so

that his fans believed we were a loving father and son reunited, he'd acknowledge me as his son and make me his legal heir along with James."

"What happened?"

"Whenever I asked him when he was going to claim me, when he was going to acknowledge me as his son, he kept putting me off. I finally realized that he had no intention of ever publicly claiming me. So I confronted him and you know what he did? He laughed in my face. Said I had it too good the way things were, that I'd be stupid to rock the boat."

"When—when did he say that to you?"

"The day before I killed him."

Bethany glanced into the rearview mirror. The blue Mustang was still following them.

Tony eased back in the seat, drawing Anne Marie back with him.

Morgan wondered how long it would take Tony to realize that he was right behind them. If Tony didn't look back or if Bethany didn't do anything to alert Tony of his presence, he would be able to follow them to their destination.

Suddenly Morgan noticed a highway patrol car behind him. His heart jumped up in his throat. Hell! How would Tony react if he saw the car? Would he panic? Hurt Anne Marie? Hurt Bethany?

The patrol car pulled out from behind Morgan and into the left lane, easing past him and up beside the black GTO Bethany was driving.

"What the hell?" Tony lowered the gun from Anne Marie's face to behind her back. "You'd better hope that guy doesn't cause any trouble."

Bethany held her breath, praying, pleading with God, offering Him anything, including her own life, if He kept her child safe.

The patrol car passed the GTO, heading northeast on Highway 459. Bethany let out a sigh of relief. Anne Marie gasped in deep gulps of air.

"Take the next exit," Tony said.

"Why?" Bethany asked.

"Just do as I say!"

Bethany kept watch in the rearview mirror as she exited 459. The blue Mustang exited right behind her. When they looped around the exit road and Bethany pulled the GTO up to a stop sign, Tony glanced out the back window.

Moisture coated Bethany's hands. Sweat trickled between her breasts. Her heartbeat accelerated as her heart frantically pumped blood through her tense body.

"It's Kane!" Tony shouted. "How long has he been behind us?" When Bethany made no reply, he kicked the back of her seat. "Answer me, dammit. How long has he been following us?"

"Since we left the mall."

"You're going to lose him, do you hear me? Turn right and put your foot down hard on the gas pedal."

"How can I speed through red lights and stop signs?"

"Go as fast as you can until we get through traffic, then you open her up and get away from Kane. If you don't get away from him, when we finally stop, he'll find your kid's brains all over the seat back here."

Bethany maneuvered the Pontiac through the traffic as quickly as she could, then following Tony's directions, headed the car away from the heavily populated area. The minute she reached an open stretch of road, she speeded up, going faster and faster.

Morgan pursued them, knowing for certain that Tony had spotted him. The idiot had undoubtedly told Bethany to lose him. Stopping Tony would be easy. Morgan knew a dozen ways to put an end to this chase. But he didn't know one way to end it without endangering the lives of the two people he loved most in the world.

Yes, he loved Bethany. And he loved her daughter. Being faced with the possibility that he might not be able to save either mother or daughter forced him to admit his feelings. Dear God, why had it taken something like this to make him realize it?

Morgan saw the big rig pulling out from a side road. What the hell was wrong with the driver? Didn't he see the black GTO headed his way, directly in his path?

Bethany saw the eighteen wheeler! Could she stop the car in time to keep from hitting the massive truck? Whipping the steering wheel around, she veered the car off the road to avoid hitting the truck. They bounced up and down as the old Pontiac skidded at high speed across a sloping grassy area. Bethany tried to slam on the brakes, but she lost control of the car as it flipped over and rolled down the hill. The GTO flipped over a second time before it came to a crashing halt against an enormous oak tree.

Morgan stopped, jumped out of the Mustang and ran down the side of the hill. The front end of the GTO was wrapped around a tree and steam poured out from under the hood.

For a split second Morgan's heart stopped beating. And he knew that if Bethany was dead, he didn't want to live.

Chapter 16

Tony Hayes crawled out of the back seat of his wrecked GTO. Unsteady on his feet, he staggered when he tried to stand. He clutched the revolver to his chest. Blood trickled from his smashed nose and oozed from his busted lip. He glared, bleary-eyed, at the woman and girl trapped inside the car.

Morgan Kane halted his descent from the road, watching as Tony moved away from the crumpled Pontiac. Sunshine reflected off the shiny metallic butt of Tony's gun. Morgan eased his Sig from the holster. He had to get close enough for a clean shot because one shot might be all he'd get.

"Stay right there!" Tony yelled, glaring at Morgan.

"Give it up, Tony. If you hurt Bethany or Anne Marie, you can't get out of this situation alive." Morgan eased closer and closer.

"I told you to stop, dammit!"

Pointing his revolver at the car, Tony fired twice in rapid succession. Anne Marie screamed. Morgan raced down the hill, stopping when he was within range, aimed his gun and fired. Tony Hayes dropped to the ground. Morgan ran toward the car, briefly glancing at Tony's lifeless body, at the bullet hole between his eyes, as he hurried past him.

"Bethany? Anne Marie?" Please, dear God, let them both be alive.

"Get Anne Marie out," Bethany pleaded, her voice a weak whisper.

"I'll get you both out!" Morgan smelled gasoline. Hell! Had one of the bullets from Tony's gun hit the fuel tank?

He tried opening the driver's side door so he could get to Bethany. It was stuck. He tried again and then again. Finally, he jerked open the crushed door. Bethany was trapped between the seat and the steering wheel, which had been forced against her chest on impact.

How much time did he have? he wondered. Was the fuel tank ruptured? Would the car catch on fire and explode?

He had to get Bethany out of the car. Had to save her. Without her, his life was meaningless.

Bethany looked at him. Tears gathered in the corners of her eyes. She couldn't move anything except her head. Her arms were trapped. And she couldn't even feel her legs.

"Not me," she pleaded. "Anne Marie. I don't know how badly she's hurt. She hasn't said a word since she screamed. Please, please, Morgan, save our little girl."

Every muscle in Morgan's body tensed, every nerve rioted. What did she mean, "our little girl?" She was probably delirious, probably didn't know what she was saying.

Morgan grabbed the steering wheel and shoved with all his strength. He managed to bend it forward, but not enough to release its grip on Bethany.

"Forget me," Bethany cried out, tears streaming down her face. Hadn't he understood what she'd said? Didn't he realize that Anne Marie might be dying? That nothing mattered except saving their child's life? "Morgan, you must save Anne Marie."

"I told you that I'll get you both out."

"There may not be time to save both of us," Bethany said. "I can smell the gasoline, too, you know."

"Just shut up." He ran his hand across her bruised and bloody face, wiping the blood that trickled from her mouth. "I love you, dammit! I can't let anything happen to you."

"You can't let anything happen to Anne Marie." Bethany gazed into his eyes, her heart pleading with his, begging him to understand what she wanted him to do, what he had to do.

"Anne Marie is your daughter. Do you hear me, Morgan? She's our little girl. Yours and mine."

The truth hit him like a sledgehammer in the gut. Anne Marie was his daughter! A part of him. A part of Bethany. The living, breathing proof of their love. They had created her together. She was their immortality. She *was* the two of them. By saving her, he saved Bethany. And he saved himself.

Kissing Bethany's bruised forehead, Morgan eased his shoulders back out the driver's side door and crawled inside the left back door that hung open. He found Anne Marie's unmoving body twisted into a heap against the back of the caved-in front seat.

When he eased his arms under her and lifted her, she groaned.

"It's all right, sweetheart. Daddy's here. I'll take care of you."

"Mama? Is Mama okay?" She lifted her bound hands and swung them over Morgan's head and around his neck.

He had no time to think, to consider things from every angle. He acted purely on instinct, on the dictation of his heart, the commands of his soul. His soul and Bethany's. Joined. United forever in the precious child he held in his arms.

Morgan eased backward, out of the car, and carried Anne Marie several yards away from the GTO. He laid her down on the ground and looked at her for one heart-stopping moment. His daughter. His and Bethany's child.

"I'll be right back, sweetheart," he told her. "I have to go get your mother."

When he started back toward the GTO, the smell of gasoline overwhelmed him. Don't let her die, Morgan prayed. Please, let me get her out of the car before it explodes. Ask any price from me and I'll pay it. Just don't let her die!

"I'm back, honey." He caressed Bethany's bruised and swollen cheek. "I got Anne Marie out safely. Now, we've got to get you out of here."

"Is she all right?" Bethany asked.

"She'll be all right, once she sees that you're safe."

Morgan worked frantically trying to free Bethany. His heart beat hard and fast. Sweat coated his face, trickling down his jaw and onto his throat.

Off in the distance sirens blared. The police? An ambulance? Maybe both. Hurry, he prayed. Hurry!

"I don't want you trapped here with me if the car explodes," Bethany said. "Don't die trying to save me."

"Shut up, will you, honey!" Moisture glazed Morgan's eyes. "Let's get this straight right here and now. Nobody's going to die."

The siren's wail grew nearer. A masculine voiced called out from the top of the hill.

"I phoned the police," the eighteen-wheeler's driver said. "I told them it was bad. I think that's an ambulance we hear."

Morgan heard the man but didn't take time to reply. If he ever got his hands around the truck driver's neck, he was liable to strangle the life out of him.

Finally the front seat moved a few inches. Morgan eased his hand under Bethany's hips and slid her sideways toward him. She cried out in pain. Sharing her suffering, feeling it in every fiber of his heart and body, Morgan froze instantly. Her agonized cry immobilized him momentarily.

"I'm sorry, Beth. I'm so very sorry." He was pleading for her forgiveness for the pain he would put her through in removing her from the car. But he was also asking her to forgive him for the past, for leaving her sixteen years ago. For leaving her pregnant with his child.

"It's all right!" She gasped for air. "Do what you have to do."

Morgan pulled her from the wrecked GTO. Bethany screamed when the pain became unbearable. She went limp against him. Lifting her into his arms, he ran with her, away from the car. He knelt on the ground, lowering Bethany down beside their daughter.

Anne Marie sat up and leaned over her mother. "Mama? Mama!"

"She fainted from the pain," Morgan said. He checked her pulse and found it weak.

"How bad is it?" A uniformed policeman called out as he ran down the hill. "An ambulance is on the way. Do we need to call the hospital and have them fly out a trauma team?"

"Yes," Morgan yelled. Yes. It was bad down here. And yes, they needed an emergency helicopter to med-flight Bethany to

Carraway. There was no way to know how serious her injuries were, but Morgan's training and instincts told him that she probably had severe internal injuries.

"How many are injured?" the policeman asked.

Before Morgan could reply, a loud explosion rocked the earth. Gasping, Anne Marie grabbed Morgan's arm with her bound hands. They stared at the fire-engulfed GTO. Flames shot high into the sky as dark smoke billowed around the burning vehicle.

Morgan paced the floor in the surgical waiting room. Wild with fear and regret, he was inconsolable. Once the emergency room doctor had assured him that, although Anne Marie had a slight concussion, she would be fine when her cuts and bruises healed and time repaired her sprained ankle and wrist, he demanded to speak to Bethany. He was told that she'd been rushed into emergency surgery and the prognosis wasn't good.

Eileen and Seth tried to talk to him. He snarled at them like a cornered animal ready to attack. James tried to reassure him, but he cursed the boy's youthful stupidity.

Guilt weighed heavily on Morgan's heart. This was all his fault. Everything was his fault. If he lost Bethany, he had no one to blame but himself. Was this his punishment for being a blind fool? For not appreciating the most precious gift a man can be given, the love of a woman like Bethany?

James wheeled Anne Marie into the waiting area. Her grandmother leaned over and kissed her. She maneuvered the wheelchair across the room to where Morgan stood in the corner, his back to the room.

"Morgan?"

He tensed, but he didn't turn around.

"Don't be angry with her for lying to us," Anne Marie said. "I don't know why she kept the truth from us, but I know my mother, and she had to have had a very good reason."

Oh, God in heaven, he wasn't angry with Bethany. He was angry with himself. It all made sense now, a crazy, painful sense. Bethany had allowed her mother and his parents to force her into marriage with Amery because she'd been pregnant and she'd had no idea where on earth her baby's father was.

His poor, sweet Beth blamed herself for being weak and insecure. She blamed herself for Amery's death. And all along she should have put the blame where it belonged. Squarely on his shoulders.

"Morgan?" Anne Marie called out to him again. "I—I suppose we should have figured it out, huh? I mean we should have guessed that you were my father. It's funny, but when Nana used to tell me her Morgan stories, I'd pretend that you were my father and not Amery."

Morgan cleared his throat. "I didn't know anything about you. If I'd known..."

Eileen clasped her fingers over Anne Marie's shoulders. "Your mother didn't realize she was pregnant until after Morgan left town sixteen years ago. No one knew how to get in touch with him. You were three years old before anyone knew that he was in the Navy."

"She married Amery because she was pregnant with me?"

"Yes," Eileen said. "We...that is Henderson and Claudia and I thought it was best. We were wrong, and we've all lived to regret it."

Morgan's broad shoulders trembled as he tried to keep the tears at bay. They ate away at his insides. They clawed at his throat. They flooded his eyes.

Anne Marie laid her hand on her father's back. "Daddy?"

He turned slowly, looked at his daughter—his and Bethany's little girl—then reached out, grabbed her and pulled her into his arms. He held her with fierce, protective possessiveness.

"Oh, Daddy, she's going to live. God wouldn't take her away from us now. Not now." Sobbing, tears streaming down her face, Anne Marie clung to her father.

"I love her." He swallowed his tears. "And I love you." Tears cascaded down his cheeks, over his nose, into his mouth and off his chin.

Father and daughter held each other, sharing a grief too great to be borne alone.

Morgan waited outside the intensive care unit, waited to be told when he could see Bethany. Anne Marie and Eileen were with her now. They'd been the first people the doctor had allowed to see her after the surgery.

The doctors had said that, barring any unexpected complications, Bethany would pull through. Her recuperation would take months of slow, often painful rehabilitation. Morgan didn't care how long it took her to recover, he was going to be at her side, taking care of her, loving her, making sure everything in her life was as perfect as he could make it.

Eileen wiped the tears away with her lace handkerchief as she exited the ICU. Seth waited for her with open arms. Anne Marie paused at Morgan's side when she walked out into the waiting room.

"How is she?" he asked. "Will she see me?"

"She looks like hell, but she's still beautiful. And she says she's not in any pain, but I don't believe her." Anne Marie glared at her father. "Will she see you? What do you think?"

"I want to make it up to her," he said. "And to you. I want to be a real father to you."

"You're going to have to work things out with Mama before you and I can straighten out our relationship."

"You're right." He caressed her cheek. "How'd you get so smart so young?"

"I had a good teacher," Anne Marie said. "Mama made sure I learned from all her mistakes."

"Wish me luck with your mother."

"She loves you. What more luck do you need than that?"

Morgan entered the intensive care unit cubicle. His heart lurched to his throat when he saw Bethany, battered and bruised and connected to an endless assortment of tubes and wires.

She looked right at him, and he knew she was waiting for him. He had to choose his words carefully. Everything—his future, Bethany's future and Anne Marie's—depended on how he handled this situation.

"Hello, honey." He stopped at the foot of her bed.

"You look awful," she said. "When's the last time you shaved? Or slept? Or ate?"

Rubbing the stubble on his jaw, he grinned. "Shaving and eating and sleeping didn't seem very important. Not when I didn't know if you were going to live or die."

"They say I'm going to live."

Morgan eased away from the foot of the bed and walked

slowly toward her. She held up her hand, lifting the tubes connected to it.

He grasped her hand, clutching her fingers, avoiding putting any pressure on the tubes.

"Anne Marie doesn't hate me," Bethany said. "I was so afraid that—"

"If she should hate anyone, it should be me. I'm the one who deserted you and left you pregnant."

"She doesn't hate you, either."

"You've raised a remarkable child," he said. "Mature beyond her years. I'm not sure I deserve to be her father, but I want to be. If she'll give me the chance. If...if you'll give me the chance."

"What are you saying, Morgan? Are you telling me that you forgive me for keeping you and Anne Marie apart all these years?"

"There's nothing to forgive. As far as I'm concerned, I'm the one who made all the mistakes, and you and Anne Marie are the ones who paid for them."

Bethany squeezed Morgan's hand. "I want you to be a part of our daughter's life. I know it'll take time for both of you to adjust, but if you'll give it a chance..."

"What about us, Beth? What about you and me?"

"What about us?"

"Are you willing to give us a second chance?" he asked.

"For Anne Marie's sake?"

"No, not for Anne Marie's sake. For my sake. Because I don't think I can live without you, honey." He leaned over and brushed her lips with a featherlight kiss. "Marry me, Beth, and I'll spend the rest of my life trying to make you happy."

"Oh, Morgan, there you go making promises again." She smiled weakly.

"Promises that I intend to keep," he vowed. "I love you, Beth. I never knew how much I loved you until I thought I might lose you forever." Tears glistened in Morgan's warm, blue-gray eyes.

"You know that I love you," she said. "I always have and I always will."

"Then marry me as soon as the doctors say you're well enough."

"Yes. Yes, I'll marry you."

Careful not to place any weight on her, he lowered his lips to hers again, his big body hovering, and kissed her tenderly.

Thank You, God, Morgan said silently, his words of appreciation a heartfelt prayer. *Thank You for giving us all a second chance. This time I'll cherish the wonderful gift You've given me. I'm man enough now to know the value of love.*

Epilogue

Dogs barked and children squealed. The sound of galloping paws and running feet echoed through the old Cullman farmhouse. Bethany wiped her hands off on her big, gingham apron and rushed out the kitchen and into the wide hallway.

Pausing by the open door to the study, she looked at her husband, who was bent over the stone fireplace adding another log to the fire. During the ten years of their marriage, she had never once looked at him and not been filled with love. Warm, giving, contented love. Hot, passionate, sexual love.

"Morgan, I think that Anne Marie and James are here," she told him.

Brushing his hands together, he stood up straight and smiled at her. "You think they've come home this weekend to make an announcement, don't you?"

"Let's just say that I know our daughter, and she's been giving me subtle little hints the last few times she called."

"Well, it's about time they made it legal," Morgan said. "They've been living together for the past year."

"Oh, aren't you the old-fashioned father?" Smiling, Bethany motioned for him to hurry up and come on. She knew Morgan hadn't had an easy time letting his daughter grow up into an independent woman. "I think they wanted to wait until James finished law school and went into practice with Maxine, and Anne Marie got her MBA."

Morgan walked out into the hall, clasped Bethany's hand in his, and together they joined their younger children and the two springer spaniels on the front porch.

Given life by the chilly afternoon wind, colorful autumn leaves fluttered from the trees and danced across the yard. The cloudless sky spread out above them like a bright blue canopy. Sunshine warmed the rows of colorful mums and marigolds that lined the walkway.

A sleek, black Ferrari pulled up in the driveway. Morgan squeezed Bethany's hand. She laid her head against the side of his arm. She remembered the day Morgan had given his treasured Ferrari, the car no one else was allowed to drive, to Anne Marie. On her twenty-first birthday.

With the dogs and their baby sister at their heels, eight-year-old twins, Richard and Robert, raced out into the yard, hurrying to Anne Marie's side the moment she emerged from the car. James stepped out from the passenger side and waved at Bethany and Morgan, who waited on the porch. James reached down and swooped up six-year-old Claudia into his arms. She giggled when he tossed her into the air.

Robert tugged on his older sister's hand. "Come on, Anne Marie. Let's go down to the stables. I want to show you Lady Marian's new colt."

"Yeah, you've got to see him," Richard said.

"A trip to the stables can wait until after lunch," Bethany told her sons.

With a brother on each side of her, Anne Marie rushed up the sidewalk and into her mother's open arms. Bethany shoved Anne Marie away and grabbed her left hand. There on her third finger shimmered a diamond solitaire.

"You knew, didn't you, Mama?"

"I guessed," Bethany admitted.

With little Claudia perched on his hip, James stepped up on the porch, gave Bethany a kiss on the cheek and shook hands with Morgan.

"So, you're finally making an honest woman out of my daughter?" Morgan said, only half joking.

"Yeah, yeah." Anne Marie leaned over and kissed her father. "People in glass houses, Daddy, shouldn't—"

"So have you set a date?" Bethany quickly changed the subject.

"Next June," Anne Marie said. "I know that since you and Daddy disappointed her and had a small private wedding, Grandmother will want to put on a major production. A big church wedding with a dozen bridesmaids and a country club reception. Something to equal her wedding to Seth."

"Is that what y'all want?" Bethany asked.

"Funny thing is, yes, it's exactly what we want." Anne Marie glanced at James and he at her, and her parents saw the love in their eyes. The same love Bethany and Morgan had shared since the first moment they met over twenty-five years ago. "I wish Nana could be at my wedding. I miss her so much." I can't believe she's been gone five years now."

"She'll be there," Bethany said. "In spirit."

"Mother would be pleased with you," Morgan said. "You're living in her home and carrying on the Morgan traditions."

Anne Marie smiled, then threw her arms around her parents, hugging them fiercely. With tears swimming in her eyes, she said, "I'm so happy."

Morgan enveloped his wife and eldest child in his arms and held them close. As long as he lived, he would never take their lives or their love for granted. He'd come so close to not having them in his life, to losing them forever. Each day with Bethany was a blessing. Each smile on Anne Marie's face a joy to behold.

If any man on the face of the earth knew the true meaning of happiness, Morgan Kane did.

* * * * *